EXISTENT:
IN THE
CLASSROOM

DEAD

dead
dot
pink

THE MIRROR, 2025.

I'm staring at a blank page on my laptop. Words are coming at me, but it no coherent order. What do you say about something that happened in the past?

... somebody... I used to... know.

Gotye, Making Mirrors is playing on my CD player whilst I stare. It's one of the best albums I've ever listened to. It feels like it goes places emotionally.

EXISTENTIALISM IN THE CLASSROOM went publicly available a year ago this month. It's not been the year I expected.

... walk the plank... eyes... open.

My sister was one of the first people to read it. I was excited and nervous to hear what she thought and, on 18 March 2024, she messaged me to say she had finished it. Among the many things she said, there was one thing that stood out to me.

```
[04:36] Sister: …I'm afraid I can't positively review (I just
won't do one, I'd never do a negative), and I can't recommend
it to others.
```

Because of some things I had written that concerned her, she took the book personally. She found it offensive. She didn't understand the point of EXISTENTIALISM IN THE CLASSROOM at all. And for clarity, this sister actually only gets mentioned once in the entire book, on DAY 92.

... are you... trying to... please them?

I replied within the hour, thanking her for reading it and reminding her that the contents of this book reflect the thoughts and actions of someone who is mentally unstable. That EXISTENTIALISM IN THE CLASSROOM is about being open and honest with feelings, regardless of how fucked up they might be. But her reaction had caught me off guard and it unhinged me. If that was the reaction of my own family member, what were other people going to think? The book is fucking stupid, I thought. I gave up on it. I gave up on a lot of things. I spiralled again, like I have done so many times.

...didn't know... what to do... stumbling around.

Several months later, enjoying a new straightedge vegan lifestyle and no longer in the spiral, I realised this book is likely to offend people regardless of what I do. That's what happens in art, it's about evoking emotions. And if it does happen to you, I can only apologise and say once again that this book is about someone who is mentally unstable and it reflects a person I am no longer. With that in mind, I decided to update the manuscript.

… in your light… nothing… brings… me down.

There are various sections I had left out, such as about the Teachers' Standards and my NQT year, so they got added back in. I updated the names of all characters to something I found more enjoyable. I also made various other small changes, such as adding back the messages on DAY 13 and the quote on the LAST, LAST DAY. The font has also been made smaller to better reflect the type of book it is. The bits that offended my sister, however, have not been changed.

… I know… I let you… down.

On making the updates I found it interesting to look back at the sentiments written in NOTES OF WHEN I TOOK ACID. As much as I still agree with them, they didn't become the answers to my mental health problems that I thought they would at the time. Little did I know that my life had only just begun to unravel. The aftermath of the events of this book were, to put lightly, pretty shit. I've been someone I didn't want to be.

… I could not… love… myself.

The words all echo.

But I say with confidence, you and your life can change. Albeit slowly.

All my love,
DEAD x

For everyone that gets forgotten…

EXISTENTIALISM IN THE CLASSROOM

DEAD

PART ZERO

NINE MONTHS BEFORE.

DAY UNKNOWN.

HELP.

The information feels very overwhelming. And it seems ironic that I'm trying to read about helping my anxiety. As every word in front of me buzzes with irrelevance, my heart beats and pulses erratically in a time signature completely different to my breathing. It's like they're listening to different songs at a silent disco, whilst on way too much coke.

Breathe. Breathe. Breathe. It's OK.

When I clicked onto the Education Support website, I'd liked to have seen some kind words like:

It's OK that you're here. Remember to breath and take a look at which links you think will help you the most. Well done for looking for help, it's going to be OK.

Instead there's rows and rows of words of different colours and sizes of font, over lapping text and images and statistics. There's so many links I don't know which to click on. And there's red text. *Red text!?*

Breathe. Breathe. Breathe. It's OK.

Two days ago I decided to be honest to one of the SLT and wrote a short email explaining that I'd been, well, here's the email.

```
From: DEAD
To: Alice

Hi Alice,

In all honesty I have been struggling at the moment in a sense
of personal well-being. But I have put in a lot of work to
remedy that recently, which is why I've been a little aloof in
the past few weeks.

Wanted to let you know,
DEAD
```

I was quite proud of being honest, it felt so long since I last had been about my mental health. The email wasn't asking for anything, it was more of an FYI, acknowledging the importance for openness. In return I got sent a URL with this little bit of wording.

```
From: Alice
To: DEAD
```

Thanks for being honest. I am sorry that your well-being has been affected. This pandemic is a challenge.

Take a look at the Education Support website, link attached.

Alice

Blah blah blah. Mother fucker, fuck you.

1. I didn't want their opinion.

2. I didn't want their magic potion website.

3. It's nothing to do with the pandemic, I've had these problems for years.

Never-the-less, today I decided to look at the link and wasn't best pleased with what I saw. Because I couldn't read it! There was just too much. *What, do they just think that because I'm an adult, no, because I'm a teacher I enjoy reading?* There's an alarming hypocrisy in teaching.

PART ONE

SPRING TERM (LOCKDOWN).

DAY 0 (SUNDAY).

THE FINAL DAY.

I feel sick. In some sense the feeling is as if I have one day to live. I had to get out and enjoy this last piece of freedom and so I've ventured out to find somewhere new. Exploring a place I have been many times but never really explored. It feels like what could be true freedom, given different circumstances.

Down in Robin Hood's Bay I walk along a stretch of the Cinder Track and into the jungle of seaside cottages. Paths and alleyways web through the buildings, giving a sense of complete disorientation as to where I am. Eventually I find myself walking along a concrete sea barrier and onto the beach, looking out at the North Sea. It's nice. It's nature. There's no one here.

Tomorrow we go back to normal, whatever that is. For me it's different to the other teachers. Two weeks into this lockdown I had finally broken. Snapped, after all these years, it finally fucking happened. Every day I'd been going upstairs to my desk at 8:30am, but instead of teaching online, I would spend the next eight hours just sitting and staring at the wall, scribbling on my desk "why do I exist?" It sounds ridiculous but it's true.

I had been ignoring all meetings, messages and emails until I got this one short email from a student.

```
From: Lucky
To: DEAD

Don't we have lessons?
```

At first I ignored it like the rest and went back to my staring and my scribbling. It was an hour later that it all dawned on me and I frantically emailed my boss, the Director of Maths.

```
From: DEAD
To: Margie

Margie, I'm in the middle of a nervous breakdown and really
losing my shit. Can I take a few days off please?
```

Those few days turned into months, which takes us to now. Tomorrow goes back to normal, back to being in school, teaching as though everything is OK. I'm afraid.

I could have walked the Cinder Track home to Whitby, out of Robin Hood's Bay, through Hawsker and Stainsacre, then passing over Larpool Viaduct and the River Esk to home. But I was in my van and it would've taken hours. It was late and I realised that, since I'm back teaching tomorrow, I wouldn't want to have sex anymore. I drove back with a singular purpose and that night I fucked Fuchsia on the sofa. She came multiple times. I came on her chest. We showered together, had a cup of tea and watched 2001: A Space Odyssey until we fell asleep. In a dream-like state, all illuminated in red, I could hear breathing and the slow voice of the computer, HAL 9000.

... I'm afraid... my mind is... going... I can feel... it... I'm afraid.

The words echo.

I found the relevance disturbing, turned the TV off and fell asleep.

SPRING TERM (MID-MARCH RETURN).

DAY 1 (MONDAY).

THE DELUSION RETURNS.

I had a feeling I would be there before anyone else and I was. It was 7am and I was stood in the rain outside the school front door, waiting for the Principal to arrive. I concerned myself with the thought that the Principal would turn up and ask if I was feeling better and I was ready to freak out in response. Instead, Bertha arrived and was waiting at the door for about a minute with me and, god, she was doing my head in. It took her about ten seconds to start talking about when she lived in Cyprus, gobbing off about how she isn't used to needing a coat and so doesn't wear one. I wanted to ask if the truth was either that she was so fat she didn't need a coat, or she couldn't find one big enough.

Anyway, Leopold was OK. It surprised me. He just said hello.

The students in my Form were doing belated Christmas presents and I was delighted to find a 75cl bottle of Jack Daniel's with my name on it. Then... I'm not sure. The next thing I remember was the IT technician sat at his desk looking up at me. My memory played itself back to me like a worn out VHS on fast-forward and it didn't make much sense. I mumbled some noises at him but I had no idea what they were or why I was in his office. And judging by his facial expression, neither did he.

At that moment I realised that the school day had finished and all throughout it I had been in a daze, unaware of what was happening around me. If it wasn't for the IT technician, I might never have known. It was as if I had just woken up stood in his office and I wanted to run home.

At the bus stop I nearly cried because I thought I missed the one bus per hour. Thankfully I hadn't and I calmed myself on the hour long ride along the coast road, looking at the trees and moors.

In the evening I live streamed some exam answers to Twitch. No one was watching, it was more for the sake of trying to get my head into it.

Later on I woke up startled and confused, running an internal dialogue.

"What am I doing?" *You were asleep.*

"Where am I?" *On the sofa.*

"What day is it?" *Friday.*

"Where's Fu... Hold on. No. No. No. Fuck me, it's Monday. It's Monday."

Fuchsia was sat next to me and confirmed that my mind had tried to delude me. I lifted my groggy body to sit upright and comprehend I had four days of work left this week.

I tried to reassure myself. *Soon.* It's the same shit tomorrow, though.

DAY 2 (TUESDAY).

BEING HUMAN.

This morning the door was already locked, but it was the usual situation where I am in so early that there are only a few people in the whole building. It stays like that for the first hour. In the quiet of no one else being in the maths office, the Jack Daniel's found its way into my coffee. About five minutes later the rough toilet paper was giving me a sore bum hole after I shit the JD straight back out. Think I put too much in the coffee. I kept drinking it afterwards though.

First two lessons were rather scatter brained. It's hard teaching fucktards. They had forgotten how to do a histogram, which is a basic GCSE skill. I feel bad because they have had a rough deal with education last year, what with COVID and the lockdowns. We managed to scrape through the lesson by working on some mundane examples and questions that I made up on the spot. Rudy chatted to me for a while at the end and I thanked him for his email that he sent a month ago, checking up on me. It's nice to have a human relationship with the students. Some people can't understand this being possible. He asked me if I got up to much in lockdown and I said the best thing I did was buy a tattoo machine. We spoke for a while about tattoos and he says the first one he wants is in memory of his grandparents, placed on his chest. A few months ago Rudy would stay behind on evenings to do extra work with me because he wanted to put off the time until he went home. It wasn't anything in the area of safeguarding concerns, just the usual situation of being a teenager living at home. When you are developing so much as a person, it's really easy to fall into a trap of thinking your parents are dicks, and your parents thinking you're a dick in return. I did it as a teenager and I hear students talk to me about being in the same situation all the time.

Last year I had a heart-to-heart with one student about how he essentially had no where to live. The whole problem was because he liked to stack the dishes in a certain way and his mother didn't like that. She liked it her way. Fuck me, I never even did the dishes at his age. I think his mum was being a bellend, she needed to chill. That student once walked out of my class and called me a dickhead as he went, his year group were really strung out. After about ten minutes I went to find him and asked him to come back into class. We didn't even mention what had happened, we just got on with some maths. Last thing I said to him was over the phone, after an end-of-Form meal in a restaurant. I called him a dickhead and hung up. I know he knows I didn't mean it. He might still think I'm a dickhead, but that's OK. I encouraged him into a less destructive direction by being human. I felt that was the right thing to do.

Back to Rudy, we're chatting about tattoos and I suddenly realise I'm meant to be teaching another lesson in a different room. I grab my laptop and coffee and run down stairs.

My students were sat outside the class waiting for me patiently when I turned up.

"Sorry, my previous lesson over ran."

They laugh, knowing me to be like that. It means I'm on the back foot for starting the lesson and my scatter brain can't recall what we were meant to be doing. I wonder what it looks like from the student's perspective. I stand wondering what the fuck we're doing this lesson and in an instant it collapses into a void of asking what the fuck am I doing here altogether. *Do they know I'm having another existential moment right here in front of them?* Inside my head I stare at the white board whilst a sensation of falling backwards and decaying away hollows my eyes. They feel sunken in my skull. Somewhere, something makes me aware that I'm in front of people and I stir some kind of mumbling noises to stall. I don't even know what the noise was, it might have been words, it might not. The students all have masks on and I try to read their eyes to understand if I said something. In this groggy state I start to wake up. I definitely say something, although I'm unsure what it is. But my hand is moving and it's writing on the whiteboard. The lesson has begun.

This is a quintessential lesson for me. My lessons are freestyle. In fact, my entire teaching career is freestyled. I am an unplanned teacher, I walk into a classroom with zero preparation and improvise. I actually love it. I love the freedom. I love the challenge. I love that I'm fucking with the system, as the fact is that you are never allowed to do this. If I was found out, I'd have to be subject to an extensive intervention programme. Fortunately, you get a little bit of prior warning of when you are going to be observed so you can make a fake lesson and tell the kids to not rat you out. Because I'm human to the students, I can ask them to do that and they will. My last observation was in autumn term where my observation, god, I fucking hate this one, was given by one of the Vice-Principals, Alice. She said my lesson "Requires Improvement", and out of the four grades, it's nearly the worst.

Grade One: Outstanding.

Grade Two: Good.

Grade Three: Requires Improvement.

Grade Four: Inadequate.

R. E. Q. U. I... ah, fuck it. These were her three reasons:

1. When asked, a student didn't know their score from the last assessment they did and hence cannot reflect on learning.

2. No students were sat on the front row of the classroom, so not utilising full learning environment.

3. Teacher not wearing socks, not demonstrating professionalism.

It was as if they were listed in increasing order of pissing me off. Fucking stupid. There wasn't anything to do with my actual teaching in this feedback. I gave her reasoning for each, but it didn't change the outcome, well, except for the last one.

1. The student did know their score but they were too embarrassed to say, knowing full well that they did terrible and had a lot of work to do catching up. This was the only student who did bad in the assessment.

2. We are in the middle of a pandemic. There is a line of green tape across the front of all the classrooms as a marker of the two metres distance we are meant to keep from the students at all times. Having no one on the front row makes it easier and safer to maintain this distance.

3. If you look at any female member of staff, it is likely that they are not wearing socks. Therefore if this issue is raised, it is an issue of my gender and we are entering grounds of gender inequality.

I took that last one to Quinn. The situation is that I don't even identify as a man anyway, I'm just a human, but I have to be fucking called Mr and Sir. I just want to be gender neutral. I wear a shirt, tie and suit trousers, but they have this one issue with the fact that I roll my trousers up to my shins and wear Toms with "no" socks. I only wear Toms because I get foot cramp, a result of running the London Marathon a few years back. SLT deleted the third point from the official feedback of my observation. I was a little gutted I couldn't cause a ruckus from it.

Anyway, in this quintessential lesson today, my freestyle whim has led me to showing these year 11 students the concept of a three-dimensional Pascal's triangle. I explained that it can be used for expanding trinomials, so like $(a + b + c)^n$. The students tilted their heads to a side, I had confused them, so I started to explain further. Marcel interrupted me, pointing out I must have written it wrong. I stood back and looked at it for a moment. I had. It was nice to see they understood it and could spot an error already, but it was also annoying that I was wrong.

* * *

Bitter sweet thing about free periods is that I get to do no work. Even though we are supposed to do work, my freestyle teaching means I don't need to. But with that free time I end up listening to my thoughts, which can go rather cyclic and be kind of detrimental. The other maths teacher, Doc, walked in and disrupted my fuck all. At first I'm annoyed but we ended up having a conversation about central heating boilers and Bill Hicks.

Later on I was stood outside smoking with some of the students and realised my head was vibing. It was the afternoon and all I had drunk so far was the coffee laced with way too much Jack Daniel's. Even after that realisation, I still didn't drink anything else and my head still aches as I write this on the bus home.

My gut feeling now is that I'm not a good teacher. In period five we had a discussion about being super-straight. It's a sexual identity I'd not heard of before and we continued to talk about it and designer vaginas. Drake said it would be "OK, if you got a good design brief" and that he thinks he could "knock one up in CAD". It was an interesting conversation and they mentioned how they like being able to talk to me about things like this. I said it's always been my ideology that education isn't just about exams. And if they don't get to talk about these things with me, who are they going to talk to instead? Themselves? But I also thought it would be funny if someone walked passed the open door and overheard our conversations.

I forgot to write earlier that I gave Drake his Secret Santa present in Form and he was genuinely appreciative and even said it was a thoughtful gift. It was Zen and the Art of Motorcycle Maintenance by Robert Pirsig.

I still have a headache this evening. Today I wish I took the blue pill.

DAY 3 (WEDNESDAY).

JUICE WRLD.

I feel sick. Like I need to be violently sick. I'm not sure what it will achieve. I just need it. I wish this bus wouldn't stop. Only 15 minutes left.

A student I used to teach has just got on the bus. God, he was an idiot. I would explain how to do something, he would do it, then he would forget about ten seconds later. "Billy, you just did it. Take a look at the work you just did." I would point through his work, "see, you already know how". "Oh, yeh" he would always agree. "So how about this one now?" "Hmm" he would reply as if he was even thinking, "I don't know". *Kill me. I must be a shite teacher.* I pull my hood up and stick some Juice WRLD on. I think he clocked me, but he'll get the message.

Listening to Juice WRLD sing about taking prescription drugs in Wishing Well is strange. He says about how much he depends on them, acknowledging he needs them but also acknowledging that they are having other affects on him. He died in late 2019 from a drug overdose. Reading about his death, it seems he just swallowed a load of pills to hide them from the law. Whether I believe that or not, I don't know. I watched his live performance with Charlie Sloth on YouTube a couple of weeks ago. There is a part where Juice WRLD toots on a vape machine and Charlie Sloth assumes it's weed, but Juice says it's just nicotine and Charlie Sloth has a taste of it. It's such contrasting personalities. Everything Juice says seems to be something philosophical, even if it's as mundane as talking about a vape. His songs make my eyes start to squeeze. Whilst wondering about prescription drugs, I roll a cigarette and drain it in the rain on the walk from the bus stop. Once inside I leave my hood up and I'm still listening to Juice WRLD. I still don't want to talk to anyone. The first person I see in the building is myself on an A0 size poster, teaching some sixth form students a few years ago. Two of the same posters hang in the atrium, each with the heading "Teamwork and Kindness". I silently point at myself in an accusing and apologetic manner, first at one and then the other. "Where did he go?" The bottle of JD can stay in the drawer today.

This school is new. It was set up in this purpose built building four years ago. It's a specialist school that focuses on teaching life skills and getting jobs. When I went into teaching I wanted to teach in one of these schools, so I wangled my PGCE to get me a job in this one near where I grew up, so I could move out of London and come back home. It worked. I didn't even apply for my job, I was just offered it after taking six months out after graduating from my PGCE. They wanted me to join straight away but I turned them down as my would-be-boss, Margie, was going on maternity leave and I didn't want to work here without someone I trusted at the helm. When she came back she emailed me and simply asked if I wanted to exclusively teach sixth form. Easy as that, but I have taken on some GCSE teaching. What I don't get, though, is that in a brand new building with electric taps, electric soap dispensers and electric hand dryers, why do only half of them work? Especially now in a pandemic? Even in the first floor disabled toilets the soap dispenser doesn't work and hasn't done for two years. I know it's been two years because I was the one that broke it whilst in a rage one day, kicking it to bits. Those particular disabled toilets are rather unusual. They are right next to the maths office and I often see five students walk out of them at once. It's just a small square room with a toilet and sink. When we had a phase of needing to lock all the toilets because of vandalism, staff would just unlock these disabled toilets from the outside with a coin. It caught me out once when I was pissing and a cleaner walked in on me. For some reason I turned around in shock to see what was happening. It shocked the cleaner more though, as the next morning Margie had to "talk to me" to remind me to lock the door. I see the cleaner at fault here, why would you just barge into a toilet? At my age, my dad cleaned toilets at a military base nearby and he put my mind to rest by saying how you would always knock. Amusingly he got fired from that job for picking up some military official and hanging them on a coat hook. It was only my dick she saw though, I don't understand the need to complain.

Anyway, I'm not the only person this has happened to. We once had a PGCE trainee teacher working with us who had been told to open the toilet door with a coin. Mid-lesson, a student of mine walked back into class looking like a rabbit in the headlights; "I was just taking a shit and that trainee teacher walked in." Apparently some trainee teacher we had at the time had just walked straight in and stared at the student on the toilet, taking some time to realise that he, the trainee teacher, shouldn't be in there at the same time. That student was Kevin and I do believe every word he said. He was a good student but made constant daft mistakes in exams, they really stressed him out. He once had to give a presentation in assembly and was being violently sick in the minutes before doing it. He had the same attitude with exams. When it came to submitting TAGs last year, because exams were cancelled due to the pandemic, I was getting nervous of what evidence would be needed. If evidence was needed, I had nothing to confidently say he could get anything higher than a grade U, so I suggested we move him and another student to an AS-Level qualification which I could evidence him a good grade for. The AS-Level is seen as half an A-Level and can normally be done in one year, unlike the two years needed for a full A-Level. Turns out this change of qualification wasn't communicated with Kevin and wasn't even done for the other student. Rightly so Kevin was angry and let down about this. My standing at the time was giving honest grades based upon my evidence of what the students could get. I know this was the right thing to do, even if other teachers inflated their grades just because they could. Morally, I can't lie like that. I need to be honest. But thinking about Kevin opening his results and seeing an AS-Level when expecting an A-Level and the other students all getting an A-Level, well, that stings me a little. I let Kevin down here, and I learnt a lot from him. Then it turned out that no evidence was needed that year and I could have given him whatever grade I wanted. It won't happen again, no matter what.

I'm actually in those disabled toilets now, sorting my hair and my tie, taking a break away from everyone. Sometimes I feel like I'm the person from the mirror. I get sensations that everything that was on my left is now on my right. And everything that was on my right is now on my left. I am the person in the mirror. What if that was true? What if that was an alternative reality which, when you look into it, happens to have the other version of you looking back? Sounds like an episode of Sabrina. I don't like this mirror.

In the office I check my emails. At the weekend just gone I got a COVID testing kit in the post from school. Despite being back at school for three days now, I still haven't done it. Even though I've done them before, I've not done it because there was no message from school saying to do it. There was an email referring to a message somewhere else about it though.

As written in [some different fucking place every fucking week]
you have your home testing kit now.

That's what always happens here. Information isn't given to you, it's just referred to. Even as I write this I've gotten an email saying:

As per the bulletin, the science trip is happening today.

What trip? The bulletin is just a bullshit OneNote document they email about. I don't even know how to access it so I've never read it. Why don't they just say the information in the email and not have to reference it? It's so passive aggressive. I might reply and put a bibliography in my email. God, I work with some cunts.

I sat and watched Bill Hicks instead. He spoke about legalising drugs and giving a bifta to an angry driver. They'd smoke it and say "Oh, sorry, I was taking life seriously". I should be doing that with the cunts I work with. Either that or to myself.

*   *   *

This day ended without anything interesting. Drake was reading ZAMM in Maths and I had to tell him to put it away. I had to teach two lessons in one because the person who made the timetable is an incompetent fuck and it's impossible to change now. I wanted to tell Margie that I intend to quit, but I am making myself save that until after the Easter break. In my last job I quit earlier than I intended to and it felt good. Here, however, I have to give a three month notice and I also really want to stay until my year 13 Form group leave. I want to see them to the end. That kind of thought of losing students is sad. I like them kids.

DAY 4 (THURSDAY).

T. I. P.

A bird shit on me this morning. Thankfully not enough to be noticeable.

That was the most important thought in my mind until Julia, the Director of English, waltzed into my lesson and asked my students why they didn't have masks on. I almost told her to get the fuck out. Instead I held my tongue and said "ooh, I'm not sure". She walked to the front table where Marty and Pudge were sitting, and demanded they put their masks on. The rest of the class were quiet, as was I, all feeling the same tension that if we stay quiet she won't pay anyone else any attention, won't ask any other students to put masks on, and won't question me for letting this happen. None of us had masks on. So I sat patiently, watching Pudge and Marty play the sacrificial goats, begrudgingly putting their masks on. Julia stared at them, furiously daring them to do anything else right now. As soon as their bodies slumped on the desk and the first drip of blood touched the floor, she left. Martyred, the sacrifice was complete and the rest of us silently watched it happen.

Lessons are sacred. They belong to the students and the teacher. What happens inside that room is like a pirate ship, I am the captain and they are my crew. Learning the content is our plundering. Julia had done the equivalent of a kraken attack and me and the students were ready to spear the bitch in the eye. I have a skull and cross bones tattoo, so it's just as fucking well.

It's undermining me as a teacher.

Later on I found out Julia had also done it to Doc and he was seething. I was still seething myself but making a conscious effort to not reveal the full shit storm going on inside. Secretly I was imagining that I had crushed her skull in the fire door as she came in, whilst me and the students continued our lesson like nothing happened. Nowhere in the school's risk assessment does it say students have to wear masks in class. It is apparently a government decision and the school, however, didn't pass that onto the teachers, leaving some of us blissfully unaware. I spoke to Monty, Doc and Margie about this in the first floor break-out-area during break time. Julia didn't do it to Monty, no one even knows what he fucking teaches anyway. Once it was settled in the sense of "it's happened now", Monty asked why I wasn't wearing a tie today. He said I looked dumb, whereas he has a tie on and so looks smart. He's a cheeky little shit, though he doesn't mean any harm. I asked him to tell me what the purpose of a tie is and then I lamented about how it's actually a hazard but no one seems to care about that. Monty then had the audacity to be an actual dick.

"Does your dad have a beard?" He says to me.

"Yeh."

"Thought so. I saw him near the tip when I was cycling."

"What do you mean?" All I really heard was one word, the phonetic harshness of each letter ringing in my ear. *T. I. P.*

"In Hawsker?" I further questioned him.

"Yeh, on the corner. Where the tip is." *There was that word again.*

"You know that's where I grew up, it's not a tip, it's someone's house."

"Well, I call it a tip."

"We can't choose our parents, Monty."

What a fucking arsehole, calling my parent's house a tip. Granted it's not a palace by a long stretch, but I wouldn't refer to someone else's parents' house as a tip to their face. He turned to walk off and I crushed his skull in the fire door. His limp body slumped on top of Julia's leaving a streak of crimson blood down the white door frame. The private schooled fuck.

Next two lessons came and went. And, man, I'm sick of teaching shit lessons because I don't care. I left school early, after lunch, to go to a physiotherapy appointment and I imagined throwing a brick through Monty's car window as I crossed the car park. Julia doesn't drive, so she was let off.

In the evening I felt like shit. I hated my work. I hated my friends. I hated my life. I wanted to be dead. I smoked myself high to forget it. It did more for my back pain than physiotherapy did. They didn't know what to suggest, it was a waste of time, I'll not be going back.

Today was an expensive day. Not in the sense of money but in the sense of emotions. If you look at negative emotions as outgoings and positive emotions as income, it can be an interesting insight into your mental health. Naturally I'm a bit of a book keeper and I love to look at numbers, money and keep receipts. So this viewpoint makes me able to look at my emotions of the day with similar level of interest and see how my emotional bank balance is doing. I've been in the red for some time. I can see what's happening, but I can't magic more income even if it is just metaphorical.

DAY 5 (FRIDAY).

THE POEM.

I woke up at my 5:30am alarm with the same feeling that I went to bed with, including the back pain. Checking the weather forecast I saw the chance of rain is slim, which means I don't have to wear black today. Because of the pain, it took me 20 minutes to get dressed, during which time I distracted myself with thoughts about my outfit.

My grey suit trousers are from Topshop, they have the hemming kicked out because they felt too short and I liked the look. These are held up with a green leather belt I got from Spitalfields Market a few years before I went vegan. On top is a straight point black shirt and the matching suit jacket to the trousers. Underneath is a pair of black Adidas sport boxers and some orange Naruto socks that Fuchsia got me. I wanted to wear a white shirt today but they all need ironing and I only have 30 minutes to get ready on a morning.

Every suit I've ever owned has come from Topshop. I think they are great suits. The cut and the sizing sit well on my tall skinny frame, and the trousers are in the skinny style that I like. A few years ago whilst working at the Royal Society, I was going to an event and sort of had a date for it. We both clearly had feelings for each other, but neither of us seemed prepared to make any moves. It ended that way and she's married now. I was happy when she told me, but definitely sad that it meant she was off the market, even though I'm not looking. Strange feeling that one. Anyway, I wanted to impress her at the event with an amazing suit, so I went to Oxford street and checked in Topshop for the baseline, then went mooching about. In every suit shop there was something I didn't like. They didn't fit on the waist, they didn't fit on the leg, they were too short, too long, felt too cheap, felt too expensive, were too expensive, made me look like a polygon and so on and so on. I even went into Moss Bros, but the guy told me off for wearing a vest. He said it was unhygienic for me to be trying on suit jackets whilst wearing only a vest on top. I still don't understand that. Did he think my underarms were dripping with sweat? I'm quite a clean person, I even shave my underarms for cleanliness, but maybe I was dripping. Maybe my sweat was cascading down my sides, trickling into streams that became rivers flowing across the store, attracting wildebeest and zebra and other creatures from the distant Serengeti. African safari animals pounding about the shop flicking shit and piss in the excitement at the fresh, albeit salty, watering hole. To be fair that would be unhygienic. And maybe that was happening and I had no idea, I do tend to become hyper focused. I actually bumped into someone I knew in that shop. I can't remember his name, he was another Leader I met back when I was a Scout Leader in London. "Wow, look at these elephants!" he said.

I ended up buying a really nice dark blue-grey suit with black lining. The outer material was a bumpy kind of one and looked almost fancy. It was different and I liked that. The colour of it looked blue in some lights, grey in others. I knew I could rely on Topshop, even after searching every other suit shop on Oxford Street. I was sad when it was bought by ASOS, it's not the same. Even the Topshop staff were great, we were talking about the sizing as I was saying I wanted to hit the gym and get a bit of muscle. I'm still skinny but I did hulk out of that 38R jacket last year. I'm now 40R.

Anyway, I took a detour from the bus stop this morning for the sake of doing a different routine. I walked down the main street and along towards the Grand Hotel. Here I lit up my cigarette and put my headphones on full volume. I had my "Vibing" Spotify playlist on, which features JPEGMAFIA and an Eiffel 65 remix by Flume. A girl walked past, maybe about 20, with a skateboard under her arm and a skid lid tied to her backpack. She had blonde hair and rosy cheeks from the end-of-winter chill. We look at each other for a moment. It's 7:30am and I suspect she's off to the skatepark to use it before the knobheads get there. I used to do the same trick in Brighton where posers and general dickheads would loiter at the skatepark most of the day, making it difficult for people like me who just wanted to get better at skating. I continue to walk towards school and then abruptly stop. I have a decision to make. Do I take the steps down to the Rotunda Museum and onto Weaponess Road, or cross Valley Bridge and take the grassy path down onto the other side of Weaponess Road? Both routes take me to the road I need to be on and it doesn't matter which side I end up on. The thought of crossing a high bridge at this moment, however, is not to my taste and so I opt for the Rotunda route. I've never been in this Rotunda and I don't really know what it is, but I have been in the one in Copenhagen.

*   *   *

I wanted to read a poem that Fuchsia had sent me this morning, to my classes.

> [08:45] Fuchsia: Roses are red. Violets are blue. Existence is pain. I wish I was dead.

But I decided to not read it aloud, as I don't want them to feel my nihilism at their age.

I wanted to confront Monty today about what he said yesterday. But I also didn't want to make it happen. If I went looking for him I know it would have ended with swearing and a high chance of punching. Julia came into my enrichment at the end of the day as she saw us all playing chess though the open door. The last two hours of every Friday is enrichment, where students sign up to do something that isn't a lesson, depending on what teachers are putting on. I like chess, so I put on chess club. We talk civilly and she says she is going to buy chessboards.

"What for?" *Is she being serious?*

"My book club."

"But do you know this is chess club?" *We are all playing chess.*

"Is it?"

"Yes." *We are all fucking playing chess!*

"Why don't I know that?"

Ding ding ding. And once again we have the zero-fucking-communication in school alarm. The exasperation quickly flooded my face, I'm sure of it, then it came out of my mouth.

"I have no idea, Monty is in charge of letting everyone know. And I don't even have chessboards, we're using a website. I asked Frank for money from the budget to get chessboards and he said to put it in an email. Which he ignored."

What a stupid fucking situation. Chess club can't buy chessboards but book club can. What a stupid fucking situation. Whilst talking to Julia, Stitches has been entertaining himself by drawing a map of Spain on the whiteboard, including all the provinces and their names from memory. But he can't remember the names of the other two students in the room, Pudge and Marty. Funny situation.

By the way, I forgot to mention that in lesson Rudy told me someone jumped from Valley Bridge this afternoon. A former student who lives near the bridge had messaged him. I caught sight of the message and saw the word "dead". We could hear sirens all afternoon.

In the evening at home my mood was resting on a knife edge, trying to not let myself fall. I realised I hadn't updated my Twitch livestream schedule to reflect being back at work, so I forced myself to go stream. It was quite hard trying to talk about maths whilst playing Animal Crossing, it seemed like a clever idea when I planned it. Only two people were viewing, but I didn't mind. At the 36 minute mark, Apple Notes decided to update so my livestream flicked onto my Notes app, showing all my writing from yesterday's diary entry. Abruptly I ended the stream and deleted the video from my channel. What a cock-up. That's how I write this diary, using Apple Notes on either my MacBook or iPhone. It seems to work well but I worry about sync issues.

It wasn't long until me and Fuchsia were watching our friend Hopper livestreaming himself DJing house music on Twitch. Personality-wise, he's a lot like Charlie Sloth and is really fun to watch. He DJs using a VR headset whilst about ten of us watch and listen along, talking about random shit in the chat. This time Hopper also included a Countdown style game in the middle of his set for us to take part in. Fuchsia called me lairy whilst we did it. It upset me. I went and hid in my office room, making a bed out of clothes on the floor. I think this is the first time in my life I don't enjoy anything. There is nothing I am excited about.

I want to self harm but don't know where my knife is. And I don't have the energy to find it.

DAY 6 (SATURDAY).

MUSHROOMS.

It's the weekend, it's what I've been waiting all week for and I have no interest in being awake today. Me and Fuchsia didn't talk much last night and I woke up at some point on the floor and shamefully skulked back into the living room to find her an hour into a Disney film. I sat down and spoke to her for a moment, I don't know what I said, and then I fell back asleep. At 8am I woke again, finding Fuchsia asleep and the film off. I got up and showered then checked the news. The human remains are confirmed as Sarah Everard, a man did jump from Valley Bridge and did die, and Hamilton was having reliability issues at testing in Bahrain. I don't know what to do today.

It took me and Fuchsia until midday to get out of our shit mood and be talking to each other pleasantly. She suggested we should plant our mushrooms today. That was her referring to a mushroom-growing kit we got a few days ago, which I've not actually seen yet. It was Fuchsia's idea and I must admit I'm a little hesitant to do it because I don't want to fuck it up. But the sooner we do it, the sooner we get to eat them.

We didn't plant the mushrooms in the end. What we did do, I'm not sure. The day just ended. This was a day off. What a piece of shit, tomorrow better be better.

DAY 7 (SUNDAY).

RENDERING.

I didn't want to write today, but since my MacBook is taking forever to render this video, I thought I may as well.

It's Mothering Sunday and I went to see Mother this morning. I didn't get her a card, I don't like cards as I think they are just landfill material. Should have got one, though, to go with the children's sunflower planting kit I got her. She seemed happy never-the-less. She was asking about my work but I don't like to tell her the truth. She knows that I plan to leave, I've been seeding that one for a while, but I'm not telling her that I'm planning to make comedy and write a book. She would never understand, so I just said that I have a plan but can't say. She did ask why don't I go part-time, but I explained that I have to commit to my plan.

One thing that I wanted to achieve today was to record more of my lessons and upload them to my YouTube channel. This is something that I've been doing on-and-off for almost two years as a personal goal. I do it because there are never any maths videos that mix a personality with syllabus-linked material. Hegarty Maths, Dr Frost Maths, Kahn Academy... none of them do it, so I try to. As I say it's been an on-and-off goal for two years because I easily lose interest in it and it feels completely pointless sometimes. Barely anyone watches my videos anyway. Right now I have a little bit of renewed interest in them as I decided to make them all black and white. It goes with my feeling of emptiness and I like that. It also gives me the feeling of being slightly creative and I like that too. The videos are just me explaining topics on my chalkboard in my little office room.

At first I did it all secretly, but then last year I ate a space cake at school. It was the last day of term before the Christmas break and one piece of the cake didn't seem to do anything so I scoffed the lot. Childish error, I know, and for the next hour my classroom became a den of chaos with my Form group. Amidst the screaming music and wheeled whiteboard races, I showed them my YouTube channel. I can't remember what they thought, I was in fact completely blazed but, funnily enough, I still hadn't peaked yet.

When the students had gone, we did the staff Secret Santa. It was a lucky dip styled one so I had no idea who was going to get the present I contributed, which I had beautifully wrapped in pink paper with a black ribbon, no sticky tape. It caught the eye of the brand new English teacher, Gladys. She's young and attractive, and she delicately unwrapped and unboxed the present to reveal a mug with my face printed on it. It looked pretty damn fucking good in my opinion, it was well printed and I looked great. In an awkward new-starter fashion, she tried to swap it and the room erupted in laughter. Hidden in that eruption was me completely losing my shit unable to stop laughing. I was peaking. When it came to my turn to choose a present, laughing uncontrollably I selected a big long dick shaped one. I think it was meant to be a Christmas cracker but gone horribly wrong. I was so stoned I couldn't open it. The minutes passed in slow motion as I stood laughing like a maniac, peeling tiny bits of paper from my Christmas dick with all the staff silently staring at me. Eventually, Frank had to help me. I'll reiterate that, a Vice-Principal had to help a stoned maths teacher open a Christmas dick. My present wasn't a dick after all, it was three cans of Jack Daniel's and coke. Two of which went onto the table and the third got popped and swigged into my still laughing face. Best day ever. I was still stoned three hours later when I got home.

A few days after, I remembered that I told my students about my YouTube channel and I panicked. I told myself to embrace it and make it work, in the hope of not letting it put me off making videos. As for the mug, it got put in the staff kitchen and would occasionally resurface with someone's coffee in it. Recently, however, it has gone missing and I think I know who stole it (Diana, before she quit). The whiteboard, sadly, is still broken from those races we had. It wobbles when I write on it.

Back to right now, the black and white effect on my video is making the rendering take ages, even on this brand-new MacBook. But the thing is, I want the videos to look old-fashioned kind of like the Feynman Lectures, so I'm keeping the effect on. It's nice to pretend that maybe one day they will be as impressive as the Feynman Lectures. I doubt they will be. I know they won't be.

Currently exporting from Final Cut Pro is the edited version of a video I made weeks and weeks ago, before I had the breakdown and took time off work. It's been rendering for an hour already and will maybe take another 30 minutes. I took some of this spare time as an opportunity to learn Wishing Well on guitar. It felt good to sing it too, it's how I feel right now.

... I'm fine... I'm lying... don't want you... to worry.

The words echo.

Come the evening, the video had finished rendering and I uploaded it to my channel. I smoked a bit of weed out the front door with Fuchsia and we watched a documentary about The Notorious B.I.G. Well, we watched half of it. I was too stoned to concentrate. *Maybe I will quit tomorrow.*

DAY 8 (MONDAY).

CHARITY AND THE GROUP CHAT.

OK, so let's get started with this morning. It was all going fine, listening to Juicy, until I checked my emails. Interestingly, it's not what I imagine you would think. I had zero new emails. And in their place I had a feeling of relief and, unfortunately, disappointment. I used to get quite a lot of emails in my last job. Most of them were ridiculously daft and interesting, about inventions and interviews and all sorts of stuff in between. I used to keep an email folder called "LOLz" and I once did a stand-up set all about its contents. I had printed a load out, travelled to the Boiler Room in Guildford, stood on stage, read some out, made some comments and got some OK laughs. I probably breached several confidentiality rules, but I don't think anyone believed they were real emails. Actually, now I remember, I didn't stand on stage because the comedian that performed after me used a wheelchair and there wasn't wheelchair access to the stage. Before the gig, the organiser asked her to perform from in front of the stage and she didn't like the idea. So I offered to also perform in front of the stage, to put her at ease. Seemed to work, she was happy. I recorded my set with a Go Pro stuck to a beam. It was a bit of a cringe to watch back as I clearly put very little planning into the set. I wanted to be really good, but I had just delivered a massive event at work which had 300 students come to the Royal Society for a conference. It was a good event and pretty high brow considering it was for 14 to 18-year-olds and had talks from Nobel Prize winners. After I gave my end-of-event speech, one of the students told me she thought I was really funny. I replied by saying "it's a good job because I'm doing stand-up tonight" and we laughed. It's an unusual one to remember for that reason. After the event was over and everyone had left, I ran upstairs, printed out the emails and got the train straight from Waterloo to Guildford. I re-read a few of the emails but didn't plan anything coherent.

When it finally came to being "on stage" I did get some OK laughs, as I said, but I did a lot of fumbling through the sheets of paper and giggling to myself. It's a shame because the MC that night was a little wee-wee that I'd met before and I wanted to be amazing just because she pissed me off so much. I mean, she didn't even remember me. And not to sound like a dick, but I was the only dreadlocked white northern boy in the science communication scene. She had a PhD in physics, but what a fucking imbecile, she must have saved up a lot of crisp packets for that. We had actually met only six months earlier at the Institute of Physics when she took part in a science communication competition. I was on the panel that judged her and, at the time, I judged her properly and made no opinion of her personality. That day, however, I took a dislike to her for being mousey and annoying, and for being the MC when I could do a better job. I thought she might not be mousey and annoying on stage, but she fucking was, I didn't understand how she got the role. She never won the competition that I judged, the winner was someone who I ended up finding really fucking annoying too. The winner was OK to talk to and I got on with her fine, but when it came to working with her she became really fucking annoying. Now I wonder if it was because I was jealous of the work she was doing. Maybe. But she was really fucking annoying. And looked weird.

Anyway, I digress. Today I am not important, nor working at an interesting organisation. No emails for me.

And then one came in. It was from Alice, it was the Monday Form-time presentation. It's been about three months since I used these and, god, I hate them. I completely forgot about them. Let me describe them a little.

Alice makes them and all Form tutors have to present them in their Form on a Monday. Here is the first thing about the presentations, they always start with some dumb theme of the week, and it seems to repeat over and over. I'm sure we have LGBT week several times a year. This week is Comic Relief and I'm supposed to encourage students to buy a red nose.

1. I don't believe in charity as it clearly isn't solving the problem, since the problem never goes away, and instead it only delays it. This isn't my own original opinion, it's one that I took from the philosopher Slavoj Žižek and I completely agree with it. I will never give to charity and I never give to the homeless. The latter of those two is actually done out of my indecision of which homeless person to give to. You can't give to all of them so I figured I'll give to none. Sure, I've bought food and coffee for homeless people many times, but I feel that's different.

2.   It's plastic tat. Landfill waste.

The second thing about the slides is their awful design. Here are some things that stand out this morning.

- Offensive colour scheme, not even matching school colours.

- Poorly written text with long sentences that don't make sense.

- Blue background with blue hyperlinks.

- Slides with images and no explanation.

- Stretched images that no longer have their original aspect ratio.

- Poor resolution images.

- Clipart.

- Comic Sans.

An email then comes in from Julia, announcing the word of the week. The email says to log onto her Google Classroom to check it. *Why not just say in the email what the word is? It's one word! It's less effort!*

Alice then walks into the maths office to ask me about the Further Maths timetable for a prospective student. The parent wanted to know if we did it like other schools, where the full A-Level course in Further Maths is finished by the end of the first year of sixth form. I pointed out how that is impossible, as you need normal A-Level Maths knowledge to be able to study Further Maths. We just teach it as two subjects, but I have designed the scheme of learning so they complement each other in their timing. There are a few instances where we get a slight hiccup if the normal class has been delayed, but that's it. Alice then said she really likes my videos on the website. I didn't know what she was talking about so asked her to clarify. Apparently some of my maths videos, my YouTube ones I mentioned yesterday, are on the school website to advertise A-Level Maths. *Wow.* This kind of puts the pressure on. What if kids come here especially because of me and then I quit? Well, I guess the same could be said if I killed myself rather than quitting. Honestly, I have thought about jumping from the top floor balcony several times.

It seems I am still annoyed at Monty today. Margie had replaced Alice in the maths office and was expressing concern about her outfit, saying that someone might say it's not professional enough because it shows a bit of cleavage. I said "Monty might comment on your outfit because he's a misogynistic bellend, but otherwise it's fine". I recall when he once said he was going to email me because someone's tits looked huge and he thought I'd want to come and see. I didn't know what to say to him, but was glad he didn't email. Perhaps it was just a joke and I didn't pick up on it. If it was a joke, it wasn't funny. I still wonder if I should have said something to a senior member of staff at the time, but I had no proof. You see, the someone was a student. He did get into problems once, and he explained it all to me when he gave me a lift last year.

The allegation was that Monty said something inappropriate to a female student, who then got offended and complained. However, no other student in the full classroom heard it happen. And Monty isn't even really liked by the students, so they wouldn't have been trying to defend him. He seemed very genuine when he explained it to me and I do believe that he didn't say it, even though I could easily believe he did. His story reminded me of when I was 14, doing work experience at a local secondary school in the science department. One afternoon I had nothing to do so a member of staff asked me to shred some documents. Naturally, I read them beforehand. One of the documents was a letter to some parents about their daughter, a student at the school, who had been overheard talking to her friends saying she was going to pretend a male teacher inappropriately touched her. I shredded it and forgot about it until now. For different reasons, I got fired from that work experience yet here I am working in a school. But here I don't have access to a chemical store, so I guess that's OK. Anyway, the student who had all the allegations with Monty, she's now in my Form group.

* * *

Whilst stood leaning on the door, waiting for my class to turn up for period three, Lucky walked towards me and continued past to his locker.

"Don't we have a lesson now?" I asked him.

"It's break," he says whilst taking out his coat.

"Oh, thanks."

I walked back into the classroom to get my jacket.

The rest of the teaching day came and went without much to say. I was on duty at lunch and teaching periods four and five, so got no lunch of my own.

In period five, Drake says he didn't get chance to do much of the assignment I set, as he was working in a chip shop at the weekend. He says he doesn't work for the money and goes for the free lunch. He can get anything he wants so long as it's fried, but that's all he would want anyway. He says he can't wait until he is in a job where he doesn't have to deal with customers. One where he sits in a nice comfy chair and designs things on CAD. I said he'll get fat, he said he's OK with that.

Since Margie reminded me of the rota this morning, I did both break and lunch duties today, meaning I actually didn't get a break to eat. The incompetent fuck that made the timetables also made the duty rota. Now it's period six, I've finally got chance to eat but I should use this little bit of time to catch up on marking in the maths office. I never really mark since I don't enjoy it and it feels like a complete waste of time. Students get feedback whilst in class anyway, but SLT like to do book inspections twice a term and so I'm in the office fake-marking a selection of the 100 or so books I have to do. We don't even get feedback on our marking, it's an entirely pointless procedure. I get up and leave the room to go to the toilet for the first time since before I checked my emails this morning. When I come back, Graham is stood in the empty room. Just stood there. He says he needs to use a phone so he can ring his students' parents tonight. Personally, I use my mobile phone, dialling 141 before the number but he clearly doesn't want to do that and so I offer to go do my marking in the classroom where the books are, so he can have some privacy. I like Graham and he's been through a lot at home recently. Finding a brother who's been missing for a year dead in some woods would be difficult for many people. I tidy my folder and paperwork away for him whilst we chat and catch-up a little. We used to carpool together before SLT said we couldn't for fear of infection, however, they're fine with me travelling on a bus full of random people. I do miss that hour of idle bitching we used to do on the way home, it felt needed as if it was a daily work therapy session we had, but I also really enjoy my solitary bus journey.

Marking wasn't so bad after all. The fear is more in the amount, rather than the process. Monty came in whilst I was marking, asking me what I was doing. He started being a bit of a dick, saying things like "you're fucking brilliant you are" and "without you, this place would go to shit". He asks if he's annoying me and I reply with a disinterested "no" as I continue to mark. I know he wants a rise out of me for his own entertainment and I don't give him one. Soon enough he left the room. You wouldn't think he's

20 years older than me. It's also made me realise I got through the day without quitting yet. *Nice, keep to the plan.*

On the bus home I have a moment to decide if I need to listen to music or not. I opt for giving my ears a rest from earphones and it's rather fortunate. The old fella sat in front of me keeps doing an impression of the bus stop announcements. Over and over he mumbles "the next stop is", never completing it by saying the stop name. He got off halfway towards Whitby in the middle of nowhere. What a strange man.

With the window open, it's getting cold on the bus, I can feel my fingers losing blood. Visibly they are going ghostly white. This kind of thing happens to my fingers a lot, it's probably going to take an hour for the blood and feeling to go back to normal now. It might even be longer since it's going to be cold for the rest of the journey.

I should make a plan for when to do the rest of the marking this week. The quick session I did made me realise the sheer volume that I need to be doing. It's rather daft that I've been neglecting it, the feedback loop is a vital part of learning after all. Fuchsia needs to do some marking for the course she's lecturing, so I'll bring my books home and we can do it together this week. A marking party! It'll have to be this week as I'm doing copious amounts of cocaine this weekend.

You know, this will be a new experience for me. Fuchsia has only just started lecturing and so we've become a teaching couple. I can see the merits, with similar holidays and similar workloads. We can even empathise with each other now. She trained as a VFX artist and worked for a big company in London, quitting to go freelance just when we started dating. She described it to me and it sounded like a crazy career she had. Recently, the university she studied at contacted her and asked her to lecture three courses online. Having never taught before and being used to working short-term freelance jobs, she's taken to it really well. It's bitten into her lifestyle quite a lot, however, and I worry that it's beginning to grate on her. I'm probably being paranoid because teaching grates on me. Fuchsia has messaged me a link to a video of a snake eating a mouse. Well, it's trying to eat it but keeps attempting a strike but misses. It made me laugh so I scroll through some more of the r/unexpected subreddit. When I finally look up from my phone, I take a short moment to notice I'm at the bus stop after mine, so I grab my bag, press the bell and run to the door.

On the seat behind the stairs to the top deck, I notice someone slumped over, almost on the floor, exposing about ten centimetres of crack. It was a little unnecessary, I didn't need to see it. At the door I turn to the driver and say:

"I think some guy is passed out."

He checks in the mirror. "It's a girl," he says.

Right, this driver isn't getting the main point here. I stare at him and say nothing.

"I'll take a look when I get to the next stop," he says.

The next stop is Whitby Bus Station and so I accept his answer. I hop off and notice the person must have heard our conversation as they started moving. I caught a glimpse of their face, they looked a little dishevelled.

* * *

We started to watch Casino, but the film was some reason really small on the TV screen and wouldn't go bigger. We gave up and decided to play some games. Fuchsia was desperate to mong out tonight and she clicks at her laptop to play Assassins Creed, the original. For some reason, it was really small on her screen and wouldn't go bigger. When her controller wasn't working, she had had enough and decided the evening was a disaster. I was sat playing Animal Crossing, catching fish and bugs, but turned it off after a short while as I was falling asleep anyway.

Some messages started coming through on the Group Chat. No cocaine this weekend. Would I "like to take salvia?" I don't know what that is but a quick Google search decided I would like to take salvia. I doubt it will happen though.

In bed I ended up getting a blowjob. I don't know how it started and I didn't realise how much I fucking needed it. Grunting and groaning, I would have liked to have had sex but was so tired. I really did need that. I know it wasn't sexsomnia, I've not done that for a while and it freaks the hell out of me afterwards when I do. So all good.

DAY 9 (TUESDAY).

STILL SEARCHING.

I notice I'm at the stop where Billy the previous student gets on. Frantically I'm searching in my bag for my headphones. I can't find them. The bus pulls over and I feel the cold air rush in as the doors open. I'm still searching. I hear someone get on and buy a ticket. I'm still searching. I panic and pull my jacket on, wrenching the hood up and over my head. I resume the search, burying my hooded head into my bag. I can hear them walk to a seat near the back where I'm sat. I can smell them, a pungent aroma of washing detergent. He sits down, facing the other way and I give up on the headphones. He lives with his grandparents, which could explain why he smells so strongly of washing detergent. It honks.

Walking from the bus I realise these moments to and from the bus stop are the only time I get outside during the week. It's quiet at this time of day. It's overcast and there's no blue in the sky. It's not raining but it must have done not long ago, everything is wet. A little pile of vomit that was there yesterday has started to collect receipts and dead leaves in it. I look around to take in more of the scenery. Pigeons peck at the damp grass next to the pavement. Above them the trees have started to go lighter shades of brown, signifying the new growth and the start of spring coming. It's actually quite nice out, but I can't enjoy it too much as the cold is stinging my toes in my left foot, which was already starting to hurt on the bus, and I'm rushing to go warm up inside. It surprised me to see the new shoots on the trees, I feel like I didn't experience winter very much. I suppose that's because I didn't experience winter very much. I wasted it like I do most seasons. Even the summer is wasted because I'm so exhausted from work.

In my first half term in this job I wasn't exhausted and managed to move house and go on holiday in Gran Canaria with Fuchsia. It was great. We hired a car and toured around the beaches and mountains in glorious sunshine. On evenings we would still be out, in bars and restaurants. There was this one night I got so drunk that I slept in the shower, vomiting. God, that was funny. I blamed the blunt I scored off some random local for the amount of sick I did. The next day I was hanging out my arse and we had the best game of mini-golf in the entire universe. The course was nothing special, but the feeling of being in the sunshine with Fuchsia near the beach, whilst huge butterflies flapped around our heads as we played mini-golf, well, that was one for the memory book. If I stayed in this job I would have enough money to go away every half term. But would I want that? It really would be something, but would I really be living between those school holidays?

Murphy comes to mind at this thought. It's a name I've not recalled for a long time, he's a head teacher at a primary school in Cumbria now. I met him several years ago whilst working at the Royal Society, and the last time I saw him we were chatting just before he gave an interview for a promotional video for a book competition. Being interviewed before him was Lucy Hawking, Stephen Hawking's daughter, as she had written a children's science book or something, I can't recall. But whilst waiting, Murphy looked well nervous so I figured I best take his mind off the interview by chatting his ear off.

One of the things Murphy said was that as a teacher you work your socks off during term time but then you get rewarded with the holidays. I liked that honesty. I don't like working my socks off for something I feel I don't enjoy though. Sometimes I like to wonder how dedicated to my work I would be if I was single. If I was, then I'd sit alone on an evening and I imagine I would work. But would I enjoy that work? It's a tough one to know about since we're talking of an alternative reality. I think I'd be hell-bent on making comedy videos like I used to; that feeling has never left me, and it's been there since I left university. Murphy and I chatted about some more mundane things like going solo camping, which he smiled at and he confessed that he never gets to tell people about it as no one he knows is into it. Both smiling, our conversation went back to comedy and teaching. He said some of the best lessons he teaches feel like a stand-up gig because the entire class are enjoying it. I liked this idea of making a class laugh and learn, and a year later I told it to someone at the Institute of Physics when I was being interviewed for a teacher training scholarship. The look the interviewer gave me was like I'd just shit on his shoes. It almost put me entirely off teaching before I even started. Needless to say, I didn't get the scholarship.

I didn't quit yesterday.

* * *

My first lesson was not what I expected. Literally, it was not. I thought I was teaching year 13 Maths and then I watched them walk into another class. I quickly ran to the maths office and checked my timetable and saw I was teaching year 12 Further Maths. *Shit*. Last lesson I had told them they are doing a test. I ran back to the classroom and got them started on revising whilst I print the test. Unfortunately I hadn't checked the test and what I wanted to test them on was scattered across three different official AQA topic tests. I clicked to print half of the first one and decided to just set that. Time was running out. I ran down the two flights of stairs and logged onto the printer. The test wasn't in the queue. Fuck, it didn't send to the printer. Julia came over to print her work, hopefully she'll be done when I come back down. Back up the stairs, click print, back down the stairs, log into the printer. There's now two tests to print. Typically the first one came through somehow, I don't understand how this printer works. Julia has gone but her documents are still printing and piling up. I don't like looking like a disorganised fuck in front of other teachers, but it happens a lot. Once hers are printed, mine print and I run back upstairs. I explain which questions to do and set them to exam conditions. This means I have 20 minutes to mark some of the year 13s' work and be disappointed. Really this test should take ten minutes but, looking around the room, they all are still writing and I leave them to it. After 20 minutes they stop and I ask Marty if he finished, as I'm surprised he was still writing so close to the wire. He was in fact practicing drawing curly brackets and finished five minutes earlier. I don't think I'm stretching his mind much, but I tell him that he better have got 100% otherwise he wasted his checking time. We go through the mark scheme, students marking their own work. Lucky and Marty were the only ones who got 100%, I was disappointed to not say I told you so. He's a good lad is Marty, he wants to do particle physics, which I like since that's what my PhD was in.

I do like particle physics but unfortunately I found it morally wrong when studying for a PhD, which is why I quit. The fact Marty wants to do it makes me feel a little conflicted. I'm pleased that he might pursue something I quit and thereby I live my life through him, but I also regret that I found it immoral and quit. Saying that, I don't know if I still find it immoral. How can I find a career like that immoral when I doubt my entire existence now? It was actually a particle physics frame of mind that made me really doubt my existence, with the Schrödinger's cat revelation I had on the bus about a year ago.

Schrödinger's cat is a thought experiment (I dislike that phrase, but it works) where you put a cat in a box with some poison and the cat has an even chance of either dying or surviving. When the box is closed you can't see the cat so you say the cat is both dead and alive. Once you open the box you determine whether the cat is in fact either dead or alive. Mundane shit, we've heard it all before.

But my bus time revelation was why say the cat is dead and/or alive, when we should really say the cat is and/or is not in existence. Surely by quantum probability there is some chance that the cat can disappear? In fact, there is a finite chance that the cat can quantum tunnel into a distant black hole and cease to exist. Or maybe it just did not exist and never did. It's kind of like Big Brother in 1984, the Ministry of Truth rectifying history. It's doublethink. It's newspeak. It's true, if we say it's true. Consensus reality. I shouldn't get into this here, it's only a thought. But society can understand the concept of something being dead or alive, but it can't understand something being in existence or not in existence. Society chooses to be dead or alive. Society cannot comprehend in or not in existence.

* * *

I went to do my break duty again, which for me means standing in the same spot in the canteen, near the nerd table. I hear one of them talk about the primary school I went to, saying it has the word "cum-stain" in it. Hawsker-cum-Stainsacre. *How have I never noticed that?* I like the nerd table as they sit and play mobile games, amusing me as they chat incomprehensible shit. One kid ate four doughnuts and then a slice of pizza. Another took out a frozen cheesecake to de-frost and handed out knock-off Oreos. Nearby I can see the kid who scored full marks on an IQ test. He's sitting at a table on his own, watching something on his phone. I wonder what he's watching. He seems to lack personality a little, but they all do in year 10. Stitches is also sat on his own. He got up, walked to a bin and opened and drained a smoothie drink whilst stood there. He placed the empty bottle in the bin and returned to his seat. Alice walks down the stairs next to the bin. That makes it seven members of staff for 60 students. Maybe Alice will say I don't have to be here. That would be good as I just had a cigarette before duty and I'm starting to need the shit that I couldn't do this morning. The need is starting to bug me, actually. Alice comes over and says I can go take my break. Success, I certainly will take a break.

As I walked up the stairs I took in the scene. The dinner lady straightening the pop bottles for sale. Frank and Leopold talking to each other. The new pastoral manager standing and observing everyone. Bertha talking to the man that I don't know what he does or what his name is. The building manager walking through the students with a bucket of paint, wearing decorator's overalls that are unpleasantly too small. The little fat kid that just finished an entire family packet of Doritos. The amount of junk these students eat is disturbing, all coming with more plastic packaging than food. And it's tough shit if you get school meals and you're a vegan or have some other dietary requirement. It wasn't long ago that it was the staff Christmas meal and I asked what options there were for me, as a vegan. The answer was boiled vegetables. Thankfully they ordered something especially for me. I don't mean to be a hassle, hassle just follows me around. God, the year 10s are all so short. Come year 11 and they will all have magically grown, just like I did.

* * *

I checked the duty rota and it turns out I wasn't supposed to be on this morning anyway.

Last night I came to the realisation that this diary, this that you're reading, will document the end of my teaching career. I don't think I'll ever be able to go back to teaching because of what I'm writing.

I've broken every single one of the Teachers' Standards, both in part one and two, in many varying ways. DfE love that document and by extension so do schools. You can't actually become a qualified teacher unless you can present a substantial portfolio evidencing that you have met every standard whilst training. I've argued with myself whether to put them here in full or not, but they're kind of amusing.

Part one is about teaching. It contains eight generic standards:

1. Set high expectations which inspire, motivate and challenge pupils.

2. Promote good progress and outcomes by pupils.

3. Demonstrate good subject and curriculum knowledge.

4. Plan and teach well structured lessons.

5. Adapt teaching to respond to the strengths and needs of all pupils.

6. Make accurate and productive use of assessment.

7. Manage behaviour effectively to ensure a good and safe learning environment.

8. Fulfil wider professional responsibilities.

Part two is about personal and professional conduct. It doesn't have separate standards, instead it has three broad statements:

Teachers uphold public trust in the profession and maintain high standards of ethics and behaviour, within and outside school, by: [five further broad, boring statements].

Teachers must have proper and professional regard for the ethos, policies and practices of the school in which they teach, and maintain high standards in their own attendance and punctuality.

Teachers must have an understanding of, and always act within, the statutory frameworks which set out their professional duties and responsibilities.

Part two is my favourite part. I'm not sure anyone does it.

This diary could be written anonymously but it would still be too easy for someone to realise who's written it. I could subtly change names and places, but then it either would still be easy to figure out it's me or it wouldn't be true at all. I want to write it real, as it is. What has brought this to mind is what I wrote yesterday about Monty. But the point I need to remind myself is that there is no point to my existence, nor anyone else's that I write about, and so I may as well make an accurate description of what it is to exist. At least from my perspective, that is. The things that I write about other people aren't secrets, they are just how I experience them. No one has ever told me to not tell anyone. And besides, I'm laying my life bare here too. I don't want my mum and dad to read about me taking drugs, contemplating suicide and having, can you imagine, sex. But the point still remains, although I'm OK with doing this, any future employer or funder will not be interested in me. Graham did mention today that the Brewery are advertising for staff. We joked about getting a job there, but I honestly wouldn't mind. Sometimes I ask myself if I would want to go back into teaching one day. Maybe if I live to 50. But really I should focus on the goal of working in comedy and fuck any consequences, it is something I need to be prepared to die for. Students keep walking past my door. It reminds me I should be working instead of thinking about all this.

In period five, Tammy, a year 12 student said she's thinking of doing maths at university. I don't know why but I felt like crying. I've never taught to subscribe students to university, let alone maths at university, but this would be my first student to do it. I felt a sense of achievement, but also a sense of loss at knowing I won't be here to see her through her last year of

A-Level and off to study a maths degree. But if I leave, it's likely she will get a better teacher and better grades. It's better that way.

In the next lesson I get that sense of failure amplified as the year 13s struggled to complete their work. I know they learnt it last year, but if they can't do it now when they need to, what was the point? I keep thinking I'm a bad teacher, it's an intrusive thought. We spoke about hallucinogenics in the lesson. *It wasn't anything interesting so why did I let it happen?* They should have been working on their maths. *Maybe I should've taken that ADHD test at Imperial.* Pretty sure I've not got it, though, and I act like this to hide my emotions underneath. I'm distracting myself from the pointlessness of life by metaphorically jangling some shiny keys in front of myself. The sound, the motion, the obscured reflections of something that I don't need to care about, made beautiful by the metallic surface of each key. At the end of the lesson I sit. I sit and feel pain. I walk from school and feel pain. I sit on the bus and feel pain. I'm not physically in pain, but my eyes scrunch and my brow furrows as if I am. Something hurts inside. *What am I doing?*

I want to quit now but tell myself I just have to get through these two weeks and then we are OK. Then I can quit. I think about the keys that live in my mind, they don't match where they come from. They look like small modern cylinder keys but they belong to a medieval jailer, taken from their stoop in a damp and dingy dungeon. What exactly are the keys for, I don't know. I feel like I should want to find out, but I don't. They're just a visual construct my brain made without me asking for them.

Oh, apparently the coke is back on the menu this weekend. This time last year I had never actually done cocaine. Then one night in the summer someone asked me if I wanted to do some drugs. I didn't even ask what drugs, I just said yes. Two minutes later I was shovelling it up my nose with the handle end of some dirty tweezers. I'd been offered it before, but turned it down. I was even offered it in Gran Canaria by the locals I got the blunt off. Without having it before, that summer night last year was the first time I had even seen it and so I thought that a bag the size of a ping pong ball was ordinary. We refer to that night as the Pablo Escobar night.

DAY 10 (WEDNESDAY).

NOMAD CLASSES.

I woke up with my book dropping to the floor on the bus. I only have a couple of stops left so roll a cigarette to try and stay awake. It seems that I'm back into my perpetually tired cycle. Last night I was happy to be back at home with Fuchsia and after forcing myself to cycle on my turbo trainer, I fell asleep mid-conversation. I was asking about Rosario Dawson, as I had recently seen her in Death Proof and Clerks II, and woke up with Fuchsia staring at me. I hadn't really seen many films until recently. Fuchsia's job and passion is in film so I asked her to educate me last year and have seen a lot since. I don't know what I was asking about Rosario Dawson, but she's becoming one of my favourite actors.

The remainder of my morning routine went off without a hitch. I walked the long way from the bus stop, getting to walk through a little park where I stood and took photos of some ducks and geese. It really is the end of winter. Monty waved at me as he drove past but I didn't respond, I was too cold. The bus had had all its windows open for ventilation but there was only me on it. I closed half of them but it was still cold. Walking through the building, lights sense me approaching and darkness comes to light. I ditch my bags in the maths office and go to the year 11 boys' toilets adjacent. No one else uses those at this time of day, meaning I can peacefully poop, put on my tie and do my hair. Back in the office I eat a cheap and cheerful croissant and drink my coffee. I'll be honest, financially they aren't cheap since they are vegan ones, but the quality is pretty cheap. Better than none, though.

I'm listening to a playlist Fuchsia made for me at the weekend as Frank walks into the maths office to put something on Margie's desk. I quickly mute Shake That. Good song, I like Eminem, but not for Frank at 8am. He leaves. Two songs later, R. Kelly comes on and, whilst I remember, I message Fuchsia and ask her to remove it. I don't like his music anyway and then I found out about the multitude of sexual controversies and allegations made against him. He's never been convicted but there is some strong evidence against him, including video. When Fuchsia told me that last year, I asked why are we listening to him. The natural response of "it's still good music" and "it won't make a difference". I don't agree with listening to music by such a person. I don't want to knowingly support someone like that. It's why I haven't listened to Lost Prophets for over ten years, and they used to be one of my favourite bands. I'm actually a little bit disgusted that R. Kelly was on the playlist. I know disgusted is a strong word, but I am.

Doc and Margie arrive, then Monty comes into the office to ask Doc something. He mentions how he saw me earlier, saying I looked like a homeless man, and that he thought about giving me a sandwich. Then it was brought up about me being vegan. Once again he's wanting a rise, like some dog dropping a ball at your feet. I didn't want to encourage it, but I did reply.

"You private schooled boys always think you're doing the world a favour." *The middle-class fuck.*

Was pretty fucking funny and got a good laugh all around. The sense of achievement and failure was thankfully short-lived.

My first lesson wasn't on my timetable. I teach five smart kids some maths that they actually don't know. If I left them in their normal classes they may as well be taking a shit, it would be as inspiring and developing for them. With it not being timetabled properly, it meant we did the usual routine of wandering around the building looking for an empty room. I call these my Nomad classes. I have two Nomad classes, a year 10 one and a year 11 one, and they are students that I teach GCSE Further Maths to as ordinary higher GCSE Maths is way too simple for them.

The one room I was told was free today in fact had a lesson in it, so I resorted to the engineering workshop room without windows. At least it has a whiteboard, albeit ridiculously wobbly and fragile. As per normal, someone has cleaned it with disinfectant and the dry wipe ink doesn't want to wipe off. It takes me several minutes to remove enough of the engineering babble to use it. If people used whiteboards more then they'd realise that you shouldn't spray disinfectant on them as they need a layer of grease to be able to wipe the ink off. But of course, I'm the only teacher that doesn't use PowerPoint. Ancient civilisations didn't use PowerPoint and they had some pretty fucking smart people. I think people only use it because it's quicker to have everything prepared rather than write it out and easier for behaviour management. But I say that the students should learn some patience and self-reliance to use any spare time constructively.

That feeling crept in today of not wanting to leave. Not wanting to quit. Sometimes it happens when I think "maybe it's not that bad". Today was a good day, I taught some good lessons and felt like the students really learnt, based upon their interactions and hard work. I set independent study and I ran an extra study session with two students who were struggling. Margie and Doc were talking about what Form group I might have next year (another sixth form one). I think about the year 11 students that I would like to teach and the ones that say they would like to be taught by me. But then I recall those feelings I felt yesterday, all the existential bullshit and doubt. *These days don't match together, is it just because the sun shone today?*

The truth is that I want to be a comedian and I cannot commit to that whilst being a teacher at the same time. On the bus home I imagine all the things I want to do. I have plans. Grand ideas for sets, for gigs, for entertaining. And I need to do them all. It all feels so clear those plans like it's all been pointing towards this. *What about my degree and qualifications?* Well I can still side hustle, but they are mainly what makes me and my comedy unique. It's all part of my USP.

It was St Patrick's Day today and I wore green nail paint.

DAY 11 (THURSDAY).

SO, WHAT'S THE POINT OF MY LESSONS?

This morning was slightly different. I woke up with an erection and immediately knew this was going to make me late. This is a little like in There's Something About Mary, I don't think it's a good idea to go out with a loaded gun, especially in a job like teaching. So my shower takes a little bit longer than usual. Running out for the bus, I'm pleased with myself for being on time. And then I realise I've not got my rings on. That's going to annoy me all day. Also this shirt isn't exactly clean, I should've ironed the clean ones last night.

Walking from the bus I felt that gorgeous feeling of just wanting to walk. Like to be free, walking where I want until when I want. Maybe like a big hike, with my backpack on. That feeling doesn't last long as I'm now looking at the main entrance, stubbing my cigarette out on the fence. Bertha is walking from her car and it looks as though we are going to get to the door at the same time. I don't want to listen to her talk about herself this morning, I want to listen to the rest of this Depeche Mode song, Policy of Truth, so I speed up and pass her. I don't know if she said anything to me, my headphones were pretty loud.

The morning routine ensues, with the lights flicking on as I cross the building. One thing that was different, I had to wet-wipe some dry crusty substance from the hairs on my inner thigh. I laughed, I don't know how I missed that in the shower.

We talk about existentialism in year 13 Maths. This was a fairly deep conversation and I touched on the idea of absurdism. It all started by asking Drake if he was OK with the apprenticeship he has been offered, and if it aligns with his goal of working in Formula One. I don't want him to give up on his goal already. We spoke about a few things like my nephew taking a "gap year" and about emotions changing like the weather. Drake said he thinks true happiness cannot exist otherwise we would have had peace by now and religion is used as a distraction and a comfort. This is why my students like me. We have discussions.

I feel like I enjoyed today. And that makes me feel conflicted again. I don't want to enjoy it because I want to leave, but there was something about today that made me feel like I'm in a position to change education. I feel like our education system is wrong. In the maths office we were talking about our research projects and I said to Margie that I want to do it on something I actually care about. (SLT insists on all teachers doing research projects every term as part of our CPD.) Margie suggested researching about the misconceptions (one of the many education buzzwords) work that I set today, where I gave students wrong answers and they had to figure out why it was wrong. (Margie had seen me with the work in the maths office this morning.) I wasn't a fan of the idea as it's just doing the research for the sake of ticking a box, whereas I want to actually care about what I'm doing otherwise I won't do a proper job. I suggested about using PowerPoint and trying to dispel the idea of every teacher needing to use PowerPoint, but then we started talking about what the PowerPoint presentations are for and what information they convey. Their essence is not just for work, it's mainly to convey the message of where the students are and why they are learning what they are learning. I've always struggled with this because I feel like students learn what they are learning because it's what the government decided should be in the A-Level Maths syllabus. In other words, we teach it because someone decided that this is the content that represents a well-rounded knowledge of maths at the 16 to 18-year-old age bracket. For me, that doesn't work. Some person said "learn this" and we say "OK"? No, not me, I say "why?" *Why do we teach this? Why should they learn that?*

I sat and thought about why students study maths, until eventually realising that the entire A-Level Maths syllabus can be swept into one single goal: to gain a basic understanding of calculus and its application. Sure there are some aspects of geometry that are irrelevant to calculus, but they can be used in examples of the application of calculus to geometry and vice versa. So, *what's the point of my lessons?* (That sounds like an essay title and I like it.) One answer is to make it really clear in every lesson why what they are learning is on the syllabus. But I still don't like the idea of using slides and making those bullshit lesson objectives based on Bloom's taxonomy. They are just more educational buzzwords. "Success criteria", how will they know they have achieved the goal of the lesson? By being able to do the work? It's an interesting question and I'd like to not spoon-feed my students too much, I know it can have a detrimental effect, but I'd like them to learn how to figure this stuff out for themselves. Learning to learn is the key we are after here, it's not the content.

*   *   *

At home, Fuchsia was on a cliff edge. She said she had been on the verge of a panic attack all day and was beginning to think she should just let it happen. She tried meditation, getting on with work, and going out for a walk and seeing my sister. She was sat in my arms on her office chair and the panic attack seemed to start to come in. I was still in my shirt and tie. I stank of sweat and I wanted her to defeat this panic attack and not have one. We also need to go to the supermarket and grocery shopping, which with anxiety is definitely not fun. I get an epiphany. *We go to my parents' for dinner.*

So we do that and watch Michael Portillo doing his train series on TV. It's nice and seems to put us both in a good mood.

Mum told me that Spike has applied for a job at the Brewery. Later I told Fuchsia that I'm happy for him to move job as he doesn't seem to like his current one, but I also felt as though the Brewery was a different group of friends for me and I would prefer that those two worlds didn't collide like this. My mum, sister and brother-in-law, who works at the Brewery, are all such gossips. Mum has never even met Spike.

Back at home, I change my nose piercing and I'm up past midnight. It was hard to change the piercing as it's swollen and looks to have a keloid for some reason. Also, I'm squeamish as fuck, despite having pierced myself several times. I almost vomited. What a fucking achievement and experience to get through, it felt.

DAY 12 (FRIDAY).

AND SATURDAY MORNING.

I want to make chess club better. I want to maybe even make a Whitby chess league, I don't think there is anything like that. I haven't felt this motivated for a while, I'm even researching chess on the bus. God, it pisses me off that Julia is getting chess boards, but only because I don't want her to steal the crown of chess club. When I first got on the bus my feet were painfully cold but with the excitement of chess I completely forgot about them until I got off the bus.

I find myself doing the walking dance on the way from the bus stop. Oingo Boingo and 80s music in general does that to me.

The building is closed when I get there but it's not long until Leopold turns up, smiling and saying the weather is a bit grim. I laugh and agree. Grim. What an exceptional word, it really does fit this weather. It's cold, damp and misty. It was like this last night and was making street lights glow like terrestrial nebulae, flickering between the silhouetted galactic black hole trees. Grim, but I like it. Bertha and Monty turn up. Before I forget, I ask Monty to change the name of my enrichment to chess club. For some reason he decided to call mine "maths club" at the beginning of the year, despite the form I completed clearly saying "chess club". He's wearing his cadet uniform for his CCF enrichment and says he will change the name, but he acts too nonchalant for me to believe him. I explain the conversation with Julia about chessboards. I'm trying to be pleasant here and so I also ask about CCF.

"You're a lieutenant, right?"

"A what?"

"A lieutenant."

"A what?"

"A lieutenant." He looks at me like he's hard of hearing. "What CCF rank are you, Monty?" I emphasise rank heavily.

"Lieutenant. Lieutenant is an Americanism."

I'm not sure this is coming across in this writing, since they are spelled the same, but he was ignoring me for pronouncing lieutenant the American way, without the F sound.

"I don't really care, Monty. Military is ridiculous anyway."

We are silent for a moment. It has bothered me.

"Do you know why I say lieutenant? Star Trek."

I didn't wait for an answer to the question. I don't care about his opinion right now. We both keep walking silently and he goes into his office as I go upstairs, but I still have time to say one last thing.

"It's not even got an F in it," I shout it out into the atrium.

Walking up the rest of the stairs I compensate for the lack of an F by swearing to myself. That's how it works, right?

I forget the toilets are locked this morning and walk into the door, bouncing off of it. SLT decided yesterday to lock the doors to the students' toilets because students keep making a mess in them, pissing on the floor and throwing tissue paper at the walls. So if you need the toilet, you need to get a key from reception. It doesn't really matter though, I decided to not smoke this morning and it's disrupted my routine.

It's Comic Relief today. Yesterday I was supposed to remind my Form to bring money and buy a red nose. Instead, I said I don't believe in charity and don't believe in the manufacture of pollutant-tat like the red noses. Keeping it honest. Amusingly I did do a fundraiser for charity last year, completing a marathon on a rowing machine in the hall at school. I had never rowed like that before and did it as a personal challenge, but I also thought I may as well do it for charity whilst I was at it. £10 per kilometre was my goal, so a total of £420. I ended up donating £50 myself to make it to the goal. Drake donated £10 himself, which I thought was really nice. Out of the staff at school, only Doc donated even though he has the same belief about charity as me. When I made my last donation, taking the total to my goal, I closed the online fundraising page and contacted the charity to check if they got the funds. They said yes, they did, and then didn't even say thank you. That fucked me off.

In Form we had assembly. It was being done online through Google Classroom, even though students and staff are all in classrooms next to each other. Because of social distancing, SLT have decided to not do assemblies in the hall, the biggest room in the school, even though all these students sit together and on top of each other in their common room and lessons. I don't know what the theme of assembly is today.

Whilst the assembly was being adequately ignored on the big screen, Bianca was watching TikTok live with music on and wouldn't turn it off when I asked. What a fucking cunt. Eventually I raised my voice and she did turn it off. Really I shouldn't have needed to, kids can be so dumb and arrogant. We chatted about it at the end, so we could put it behind us. She knew it annoyed me but she wasn't bothered.

I have first period free and me, Doc and Margie are sat chatting in the maths office. I decide that since I'm here with the other two, I may as well get them to show me how to use a teaching website better. I'm not writing the name of it, I don't like using teaching websites. I don't really like using technology in teaching at all, but this website is essentially a never ending resource of questions and that's gold dust in maths teaching. Rudy comes to the door and Doc talks to him whilst Margie is explaining to me. He probably wants to do an extra study session with me, but what he says is not what I expected.

"You know we have a lesson right now?"

Obviously fucking not. I've been looking at the wrong week of the two-week timetable. It must be week 2, or B, or whatever they call it. I grab my laptop and run up to the classroom. I'm 20 minutes late but all the students are quietly working from the textbooks. It stuns me and I contemplate leaving again. I don't and we had a pretty fucking good lesson. The fact that they all decided to do work is something really fucking touching. At the end of the lesson, we decide we'll play Mario Kart in lesson next week for Tammy's birthday and the last day of term. This is the effect I have on a class.

Next two lessons are both in this high spirit. I skip lunch and in the afternoon it's enrichment and we play chess, doing three minute games and analysing our openings. We also gained a new member to the club. I leave immediately at 4pm because I want to try and catch the earlier bus so I can do a cycle before going to Audie's for booze and drugs. I actually run to the bus stop, I'm cutting it so close. My chest feels like it's exploding, the cold is making it sting. Nate tried to stop me in the car park to ask if he can join chess club, I said "yeh, sure, I've got to go", and then I sprinted so hard that three-quarters of the way there I was struggling to move my legs. I kept going, determined. Traffic was stopped when I got there and I wasn't sure if I was in time. Ten minutes later I realised I had missed the bus. I walked into town to pass the time, the next bus is in an hour and I'm cold and need a piss.

I talk to Fuchsia on the phone. She's done some exercise today and planted her mushrooms. This leaves mine still to do, they're called Golden Teacher. She's done well to power through today, she messaged earlier and said she still felt like she was on the verge of a panic attack. I tried to not let it worry me through the day, there wasn't much I could do. My hands are so cold, I tell Fuchsia I'll let her know when I'm on the bus, hang up and sink my hands into my pocket. It's kind of gross in Scarborough. I take a photo of the main street. It's more busy than I thought it would be, yet it still feels like a desolate nuclear winter town. Most shops are shut and there are no cars since it's pedestrian only. To me everyone looks either special needs, a chav or an OAP. It affects how I walk and I scrunch my hands into fists in my pockets without realising. At the junction to the road I was at the other morning, the one that goes to the Grand Hotel, I stand and wonder what to do. It feels like I'm there for minutes. Maybe I was. I'm hungry and cold and need a piss. Fuchsia suggested I get a coffee but I want to save that money for when I don't have a job. I genuinely think £3 will make a difference when push comes to shove. Priority number one is piss, so I turn and go into the empty shopping centre. It's only me and a cleaner in there, all the shops are closed. Leaving the centre I thrust my arms into the air in an actual celebration. It was like a horse piss, I didn't realise I needed it so much. Priority number two is food so I pop to Gregg's for a vegan steak bake. There aren't any so I opt for a vegan roll. It's cold and stale and I wish I had kept that pound for when I'm unemployed. But I still eat the roll within a minute. I still have 20 minutes to waste so go to look at alcohol for tonight in the Aldi near the police station. It turned out to be the most stressful supermarket ever. It was really busy and all the aisles were thin and the shelves felt like they were collapsing in on me. It was claustrophobic. I grab four energy drinks and scoot through the checkout, sad that I didn't get ID'ed just because I wanted to be a cunt. My back starts to hurt, maybe from the sprinting almost an hour ago, and I wait the remaining ten minutes now fully aware that my chest is also still stinging from the run. Maybe I should cut back on smoking. On the bus, I pop some ibuprofen and zone out to Oingo Boingo again.

I don't want to go tonight. I want to stay at home and play chess, but I have no one to play against and I don't enjoy playing online. I should just make a Whitby chess club, hope I do that this weekend. I really don't want to go tonight, though. I don't like planning to get fucked up. Fuchsia is with me on this one, but our friends aren't. We could just not go but then we don't see our friends and we haven't seen them for three months and so we are making the effort. If anyone talks about sex or being naked tonight I'm going to be so pissed off. But who am I kidding, that's all they talk about, they are desperate for an orgy. I don't help these things though, I was naked at the last party. It's also likely that everyone will be fucked up by the time we arrive since I get home from work later than them. Also it's a "drinking receptacle" party, which was my own stupid idea anyway. We have to take something novel to drink out of the entire night. Fuchsia's taking a saucepan. I'm taking my ukulele.

*   *   *

Fuck me. It's five in the morning and we are all still awake. Half of the party are naked but I've had a proper fucking moment. I cried. The coke hasn't done anything but keep me awake. Audie and me have some chemistry going on, it feels pretty strong. We sit and talk about it and it immediately converts into me wondering what I want in life. This group is obsessed with sex. I like sex, but I don't see it in the same way as them and they can't accept that about me. I don't lust. And Audie is struggling to accept that, I think. My opinion is that she lusts after me and wants me to reciprocate. It doesn't happen though and I don't know what my feelings are for her. I feel like I shouldn't question it as it adds more to the shitstorm inside my head. She asks what I want. I think she means between us, but I say I want to know I exist. We had several shots each of some clear liquid from a hollowed-out dolls foot.

My throat is sore from cigarettes and, mainly, karaoke. I don't think it's the drugs or alcohol, but I spoke very honestly tonight about my feelings. I think it's more because of the excitement of being around people that I can be honest with. But at the same time, I feel like I wish I wasn't honest. I don't want to tell people that I think of hanging myself in my van. All these emotions came out like diarrhoea. Speaking of which, the drugs are making me shit so much, it's disgusting.

At six in the morning, I realise I've been alone in the living room for perhaps an hour. My ukulele is on the floor next to me, the neck and body connected only by the strings and some splintered wood. A couple of people have gone to bed, but the rest are in the bathroom. They don't seem to mind or even be aware that I am alone downstairs. As I start to fall asleep I realise I may as well be at home. I get my coat on, pack my bag and think about just leaving without saying anything. Knowing I'll get calls wondering where I am, I go to the bathroom to let them know I'm going. They are sad and don't want me to go. They are actually trying to convince me to stay but I point out that they have ditched me for the last hour. They are being such hypocrites. I wonder if they are genuinely sad I'm leaving or just doing it for the show. Audie hugged me for a very long time.

I'm walking back over the big bridge now, along the main road, fiddling with a dolls foot in my free hand. The dawn sky looks nice, it makes me smile.

DAY 13 (SATURDAY).

BLEEDING.

I think I am perpetually bored.

    [06:55] Audie: Remember what I said tonight.

    [06:56] DEAD: Which bit?

    [06:56] Audie: I'm always going to be here for you.

    [06:56] DEAD: Thank you.

    [06:56] Audie: I think the world of you.

I finally fell asleep at about 8am watching an episode of the Grand Tour. When I awoke I was about half an hour into a completely different episode, I can't be sure how many episodes I slept through.

I got up, cleaned and ate. The sun outside is shining, it's warm, and I don't want to waste it, so I put on some shorts and decide to go get my van. It's parked at Audie's house. Walking along the viaduct, down the hill and along the back lanes I bump into a student, he's also making the most of the sun but I don't tell him what I've been up to. My plan is to go see if any of the others want to go out for a walk. If they are still taking drugs and staying awake, they may as well be seeing the outdoors whilst they can.

They are pleased to see me when I turn up, and they are clearly still taking drugs. Al has had a sleep, however, and looks like he's in a similar place to me. Stella is still in bed. I suggested the walk and no one is interested other than Al. Not quite the reaction I was expecting. They seem to not be a fan of being around other people. If that's what drugs do to you, then what's the fucking point? So me and Al go out in my van, get a coffee and walk on the beach. It was nice, we chatted in a vague sort of way, trying to get to know each other more. We don't really know each other very well at all but do feel comfortable around each other. Saying that, I don't know what Al is even short for, if anything at all. The tide was out and the sun was pleasant. I wore just a vest and jean shorts. There was quite a lot of people around but it didn't feel busy. After a couple of hours we head on back to the others and I suggest we make it into a two-day session. The thought was good, but kind of dumb in hindsight. At the time I thought I'd be sat at home doing fuck all, so I may as well be sat here with friends doing fuck all. Stella and Spike had already left when me and Al returned so the four of us ate food, drank and I smoked some weed. Fuchsia and Audie were keen to take more cocaine and I tried to encourage them to try to go without. Eventually, at 7pm they went to the bathroom. Me and Al sat on the sofa bed watching Ace Ventura, eating crisps. After an hour they are still in the bathroom and I'm beginning to feel tired and like I may as well not be there. The decision is made in an instant that I should go home. It's like this morning all over again, I've been ditched. Granted, I'm with Al and their little cat, watching a film, but I really feel like I'm ditched. I hop upstairs to tell Fuchsia and she must have heard me coming as they left the bathroom once I got to the top step. They both try to convince me to not leave, Fuchsia also asks if I'm mad. The conversation circles and I maintain I just want to go to bed. The truth is that I am mad. Mad that I have been ditched again when earlier in the day she said she was really pleased I came back and that she felt really bad for ditching me. Well, here she is ditching me again. But it's OK, she has the option to come with me. But of course, she doesn't want to and I'm not going to tell her to, or even ask her to. I want her to make up her own decisions even if I think they are wrong for her. I ask when I will see her. Maybe in a few hours? Probably tomorrow? She's drunk. I'm a little drunk too but I've not taken coke since I left the party this morning. It was an awkward goodbye. She looks sad, but I don't know why. Even Audie tried to convince me to stay but they are both fucking hypocrites.

"Stay. You sit downstairs whilst we are in the bathroom taking drugs for hours on end, powdered in the ignorance of you sitting and waiting for our return." She doesn't actually say this, but she may as well.

It seems time moves differently on drugs. I jump into my van and go home. I'm sad. I wish Fuchsia was with me. But I'm angry at her. I feel like she has let me down. At least I'm home and the drive went fine. But I'm really fucking sad. I don't know what to do. I message Fuchsia. I'm alone and I don't want to be. Fuchsia hasn't replied to my messages. Did I mention I'm sad? And that I'm alone? I always feel alone. And sad.

Today I walked along two high bridges, it was fucking hard. You see, that feeling has been stirring up again for days and now the words have finally formed again in my head. I wish I was dead.

This isn't good. I need to not be alone right now. No one is answering their phones. I'm starting to shake. Maybe self-harm will relieve some of this feeling? I need to do something.

It felt good for a moment. I think it has helped but I can't stop shaking. I keep trying to ring people and they don't answer. I feel the blood is hot, running down my thigh, sticking to my jean shorts. I can't stop shaking. I'm going to have a bath. I should have stayed.

Minutes pass as I sit and silently stare at the stain on my shorts.

Fuchsia rings and I say I need a bath. I keep repeating that I need a bath, starting to get worked up that I cut myself and so tell her. We talk for 16 minutes, she says how much people like me, although that means nothing to me in the mind I'm in. Hearing that she is OK makes me feel better, though. She asks what it is on my mind and I say how I feel alone. Part of me felt let down that no one is there with me, but I have calmed down a bit. I doubt Fuchsia will be home tonight.

*   *   *

In the bath the tap keeps dripping cold onto my foot. I soak my thigh to remove the blood from my leg hairs without irritating the skin. I picked up a book just in case I wanted to read, it's on a towel on the bathroom floor next to the bath. On Anarchism was the only book I could stomach reading, even though I know I won't. My speaker is also on the floor playing Caspian. Under the water I am warm whereas the parts of flesh above it is cold, as is the air in the bathroom. What will I do when I get out of the bath, I'm not sure. But I have calmed down a bit more. These cold drips are really annoying me.

DAY 14 (SUNDAY).

JUDGED.

Fuchsia came home at about 2pm on Sunday. We spoke on the phone as she walked back. Once she was home I don't really recall too much of what happened. She couldn't sleep and so I stayed up with her. We watched Hamilton, I played Animal Crossing, she had a bath, we walked on the beach, we watched Cool Runnings, I made toast, we fell asleep. In the midst of all of this, she said Audie wondered if I cut myself as a cry out for help. So the one time I tried to talk to someone instead of cutting myself, I'm judged as crying out for help. That is the thought that ruled and ruined my Sunday.

DAY 15 (MONDAY).

NUMBERS.

For a brief moment I saw a reflection in the glass near the stairs to the upper deck, showing the queues of cars behind us. The sun is shining to the left, over the North Sea. The pine forest is brown and green to the right. This bus is a metaphor and I'll happily sit on it, taking a slow ride to nowhere whilst I watch the world outside move past. *But what are the cars behind me?* Are they a version of me wanting to get past and move on in new exciting directions, not held back by this careless version? *I'm thinking about this too much.*

I'll be honest, I'm thinking about the party a lot, particularly one person from it. I wonder if I could be the kind of person to be able to have two functioning relationships at once. But I don't really like the idea of those kind of things, it just means that you are not happy with the one you are in. *Doesn't it?*

Fuchsia has a three-hour lecture to give today. I hope she slept enough for it, but she hasn't had time to prepare. I've got a full day of teaching, but I wing everything I do and so feel nothing about today other than it's another day in the way of nothing.

Getting the classroom ready for my students, I got annoyed at the state the CCF group left it in on Friday and I threw the board eraser in anger. When Derwin came in he picked it up and gave it to me, trying to help tidy the room. I explained that I threw it. A slightly sobering moment.

Margie sent me an email and it just said "numbers". It cracked me up and it made sense, based on a random conversation we had in the morning. This is one of the reasons I like Margie as a boss, no fucking about.

DAY 16 (TUESDAY).

TERRIBLE TEACHER.

I heard a sneeze but there was no one else on the bus. It must have been the driver. I heard him sneeze again. He kept good control of the bus whilst he sneezed, but maybe he wouldn't next time and we would crash. That would be exciting, I wouldn't have to go to work. A crash where the bus flips and is on the news. I don't die but have some miraculous survival. Unfortunately the driver didn't sneeze again.

Off the bus I nip to Sainsbury's to get some snacks for the week. Inside I see this old fella I've seen some other mornings. He looks like Bernie Sanders and is running about the shop with his trolley. He freaks me out a little. I've actually only ever seen him running with his trolley. Not like sprinting, just jogging in normal clothes.

Today I was so tired, probably a fallout from the weekend. Regardless it wasn't good to be so tired with a full day today. Doc came in through the front doors whilst I was running down the stairs to the printer. It's a worksheet day. I noticed he had wet hair, he must have been out surfing this morning. When I catch up with him upstairs, he says he didn't have breakfast and asks if he can steal a banana. I say it's not stealing if he asks as I hand him one. He scoffs it in a second and I wave some croissants at him. He's delighted and takes one. I leave the packet on the side, even though I desperately want to stow them away out of sight. My precious pastries.

In Form, Chai and Bianca asked me if I'll get a new Form when they leave, then Chai said:

"Didn't you want to leave when we leave?"

I was shocked and deny this, even though it is 100 percent true. I must have let it slip once. It was a little awkward because not much earlier Margie was asking me if I'd like a big interactive whiteboard in my class next year. *Sure, but I won't be here to use it.*

Drake seemed sad today because he scored badly on a Maths test. It makes me feel bad.

It's been said that Tammy is now thinking about what universities to study maths at.

I think I was a terrible teacher today. I think I vocalised it a couple of times too, to my classes. Not much I can do about that.

In the afternoon I found an article about someone who has recently been fired from their teaching job for an anonymous blog they wrote called the Provoked Pedagogue. The news article quoted bits from it, where they had said things like how the prom meant more to students than GCSE results, that students can't read instructions on fake tan bottles, and that when students should be studying for exams they are instead on ASOS spending money they don't have.

I thought it was hilarious and right-on that this person should be OK to write this stuff down, so long as no private information is breached. Which it wasn't. They got fired for "breaching professional conduct". It annoyed me and so I reached out to them on Twitter and they followed me back. They are my third follower on my maths teaching account. I tweeted that I'm in a similar position.

On the bus home I was messaging for the entire duration. I described my feelings as obstructions to my goal in life. I don't need to dwell on them when I could be committing to becoming a comedian. But then again, what do I talk about if I don't acknowledge my feelings? We agree to see what we think of all this when we next speak and are both sober. I was messaging Audie.

DAY 17 (WEDNESDAY).

CLOSE. REOPEN.

I keep getting this feeling of anxiety that I'm a bad teacher. Sometimes I don't think students are learning and I don't know what to do about it. *What even is learning?* It's the process of acquiring knowledge, which is to say finding some truth. If you have successfully learnt, then you can both recall the knowledge and apply it. Did students learn today? I really fucking doubt it.

At home in the kitchen, I'm in my underwear as Fuchsia is cooking. She's the regular cook in our relationship. I'm good at cooking and enjoy it, but I also really enjoy basic food. A bowl of porridge for tea is OK with me. Fuchsia on the other hand is much better at cooking, enjoys it and tries new exciting things, but is also a lot fussier than me. Even though I'm a vegan, I'm not a fussy eater. Anyway, the main part of what happened was that I stood behind Fuchsia and hugged her tight. Then a little tighter. Then my hands reacted to her neck pushing back against me, resting the back of her head on my shoulder. I never know how these things really progress, it's almost like a performance where the curtains close and when they reopen you are in the next scene. But instead of curtains, it's your eyes. Close. Reopen. My hands were on each side of the galley kitchen, Fuchsia was knelt on the floor with my dick in her mouth. Close. Reopen. We are eating some noodle curry thing, sat on the sofa, talking and watching Teenage Mutant Ninja Turtles II. We didn't get chance to finish what we started in the kitchen, but we're both pretty happy about it. Sometimes a journey stops but it isn't finished. It's just stopped for now. It will resume again next time, sometime.

DAY 18 (THURSDAY).

MEETINGS ONLINE.

For some reason I got an urge to look up quotes from the Bible. I think my original plan was to send one ironically to the Group Chat, to change the subject from the party. But then I found one I actually liked and set it as my wallpaper on my phone. It says:

```
Fear not for I am with you.
Isaiah 41:10
```

I'm struggling to concentrate this morning because I am thinking about when I leave. I really don't want to leave because I do enjoy it here, but it's not what I want to do. It's that odd little feeling when you are fully aware that something is not bad in the slightest, but your feelings warp it perfectly. There are things in this life I want to achieve, and being a teacher here and now is going to get in the way.

We had the staff meeting on Microsoft Teams and they were talking about eating meat and Cleo said she doesn't eat lamb because they're cute. I messaged in the meeting chat and said if you eat meat then you should eat all types of meat. *The fucking hypocrites*. If you eat a cow then eat a calf, a horse and a foal. Eat a dog, eat a cat, eat a fucking human. I'm not a hypocrite. I've got no problem with these animals being killed, I'd kill all of these myself if I needed to. I just have a problem with my life depending on them when we are living in this modern 21st century. All the technology and societal progress yet we still eat meat.

I must have been feeling a little manic, I kept messaging in the meeting chat to wind people up. Julia was presenting about key terms she uses in class to speed up the lesson. For example, rather than wasting time asking someone to sit up properly, she has trained her class to respond to the phrase "professional posture". There was another I liked, "track" for students to look at her. I messaged and said "I use heel instead of track". Margie asked me to remove it as she will get it in the neck for my messages this morning. I obliged and deleted it after ten minutes.

In the afternoon she confirmed that Cleo, who's part of SLT, mentioned it to her.

In the evening me and Fuchsia went to the supermarket.

DAY 19 (FRIDAY).

WAKE AND BAKE.

The bus driver crossed the lines and the entire bus shuddered over the cat's eyes. We snapped back onto the correct side of the road. I think he just fell asleep. He's going incredibly slow. We were going up Harwood Dale hill at the time, which is a blind summit to drivers from the other direction. Imagine if a lorry was coming and ploughed into us. I might be OK and could rush to the front of the bus to check on the driver. I'd have to call 999 and describe him as strawberry jam so they wouldn't expect me to resuscitate a man that looks like a condiment. The lorry driver would be OK as they are sat higher up. There's no one else on the bus and so that would be it. The three of us waiting for emergency services. I have my Nintendo Switch in my bag so could get on Animal Crossing. Smoke a bifta too.

The driver goes slow and steady, eradicating any hope of drama this morning. He must have been aware he's sleepy, I would go talk to him if it were a normal situation in the world. The woman who usually gets on in the village doesn't today and so I take this moment to roll that bifta I thought of. I'm not a fan of wake and bake but since this is my last day without anyone knowing I'm leaving, I'd like to do something different. I struggled to roll on the bus, almost as if the slower speed makes me feel every bump in the road. For some reason I go to the effort of a roach and not a filter. This means that I'm still skinning-up as Billy gets on and I wonder if he knows what weed smells like. I'm going to get off in town and enjoy the walk in this morning.

Last night was fun. I fell asleep on the sofa. Fuchsia woke me and I brushed my teeth and went to bed properly. Not long after Fuchsia walked in wearing the black silk Victoria's Secret night gown that I got her for her birthday last year. I fell back asleep but woke up a few minutes later, desperate for sex. Close. Reopen. Fuchsia is lying on her front on the bed with one leg pulled up exposing what I need. Close. Reopen. Fuchsia is facing away from me, bouncing up and down on my lap as I'm on my knees arching my back like some yoga position. I pull on her hair, slap her ass and she vocally confirms. The solitary street light illuminated Fuchsia's pale and delicate skin through the thin curtains. She expressed herself loudly, making it difficult for me to concentrate on not cumming immediately inside her. Eventually she finished what she started the evening before.

I walked the long way around to school through the little park with the pond and light-up whilst there. It's a windy overcast day, but really pleasant. I'm cold but can feel my underarms starting to sweat. Three swans are on the pond and I watch a duck take its time to carefully gauge and prepare for jumping into flight. His little tail gives a vigorous shake and he takes the jump, gracefully gliding down the hill to the pond. The three swans watch the duck, tracking his movement. At this point I realise the swans are geese. I rolled this bifta fairly well. I'm noticing a lot more things as I take this regular walk and one thing that caught my eye was an anchor placed in a garden of a bed and breakfast. It's about two metres across and the top straight bar is warped in some artistic bend towards the sky. This must have happened when in use at sea, scraping along the seabed. Was it rough water or a captain trying to force their boat to move when it was anchored? I guess anchors are meant to take a lot of stress, so perhaps this one was just a lesser-quality metal. Maybe they warp quite frequently. Maybe it was overused and it wasn't just one snag that caught it. Whatever happened to it, it's dead now. At this rate I'm going to stink of weed and so I look at a man walking his dogs to see if he reacted to my smell. He didn't. Maybe I'm OK, but I'll go buy some gum just in case. The final stretch up to school has a headwind that lifts my jacket and I hope it can cool my underarms. The rest of my body remains chilly but not cold. I doubt I'll smell of weed. Sniffing, I smell manure in the air, reminding me of hiking in the countryside.

Inside, Monty is using the printer as I fumble with my ID card at the turnstiles. He says something to me. I'm making stoned babbling noises in return, but my mind is working perfectly and I find it amusing. The silly dickhead is wasting his time trying to make conversation with me right now. He says something about the vaccine and I want to say that I don't believe in vaccines, just as I don't believe in painkillers. I say "believe", but that's not really the correct word. What I really think is that I personally want to try and live my life naturally without them. We all lead a very synthetic life anyway, but when given a barefaced decision like this I try to avoid it. The lights flick on as I walk through my part of the building and into the maths office. Bertha walks in not much later and says she is the bearer of bad news, I've got cover first period. I say I'll have to check if I'm teaching and explain that my timetable on the system isn't up to date. *Is up to date not one word? Am I still stoned?*

In Form we have an assembly given by Alice about Easter and it feels very religious. Her voice plays through the TV speakers and it has a tinny pitch to it. Her slides are playing on the display to no one. She is sat in her office a few classrooms away. The assembly feels really religious, it's like when I used to teach in that catholic school and I'd just mentally check out. I don't blame my Form for doing the same here. Some are playing games on their phones, others have a deck of cards and are playing 21. They are doing it quietly and I appreciate that they are respecting the situation. We had a few quiet conversations and then I heard Alice mention that the cross Jesus was executed on is like a bridge. We didn't understand that and then she started to talk about the bridge over the river Kwai, which prompted us to talk about Top Gear. Egbert said the assembly was depressing and I replied "it's great!" clearly trying to feign enthusiasm. Drake clocked that I was playing naughts and crosses against myself and I admitted the assembly was depressing me. Bianca offers to play against me and, since I'm not a fan of one-to-one interactions like that, I decline. Egbert does however offer to deal me into the next game to cheer me up and I agree, prompting a few more students to take part. We play quietly in case any other teachers walk past and look in through the window from the break-out area. Alice can still be heard babbling away in the background. They are a mature Form group in this sense, although they weren't always. I didn't win anything in our games but it was good never-the-less.

In the first lesson I am covering, I arrive late because I had to walk from the other classroom. Bertha is here mothering, asking if she needs to take the register for me. The TAs are also here asking if I need help. I say no and get rid of them. On her way out, Bertha says one student is already on his final warning and so I say to all students "let's not get to the class removal stage". I explain to the students that they need to be quietly working as I need to work too. After a few moments they are silent and at work using Chromebooks. I show them no emotion and so they respond by being calm themselves. It's a simple trick, even the student who looks and acts like Angry Kid was calm. I check they are working every once in a while and they are. After half an hour, Angry Kid needs to get a different laptop and does a weird walk across the class. It's his attempt at acting out, trying for attention.

"That's a funny walk, it's a little bit annoying," I say, not looking up from my work. Zero emotion. Monotonic and deep like a Gallagher.

He sits down and continues his work, no one else reacts. Works a fucking treat. *Has this lesson gone so well because I'm stoned?* What an interesting thought.

Mario Kart was fun in the afternoon.

EASTER BREAK (TWO WEEKS OFF).
DAY UNKNOWN.
SOMETHING OUT OF NOTHING?

What have I been doing these last seven days? I tried to force myself to not fall into that hole of nothingness, somehow driven by my decision that the next day I'm at work will be the day I hand in my notice.

- Picked litter.
- Had a lot of sex.
- Went walking near the white horse near Kilburn.
- Had sex outside.
- Drove a forklift truck.
- Applied for a job in Antarctica.
- Painted the gate.
- Went running and did my fastest mile ever.
- Wrote half a song.
- Learnt a Deftones song on guitar.
- Went walking in York.
- Watched Formula One.
- Made a skirt.
- Got some money back from the University of Manchester.
- Got fined by HMRC.

That money back from the University of Manchester was from an online part-time MA I started last year in Digital Education. It was so shite that I left after a couple of months and demanded my money back. I didn't understand how they were so shite at teaching online on a course about digital education. What a farce.

That job application was an odd one. I've kept an eye out for years looking for a job with the British Antarctic Survey that I could do, both in terms of skills and position in my career and life. Although it's do-or-die-trying with the stand-up, this is a once-in-a-lifetime chance if I get to go work in Antarctica for nine months. Gut feeling is that I don't want to do it, but I also like to live to the philosophy of apply now and then decide later, if I am offered anything. Truth is that I'd be an idiot if I said no.

Anyway, it's been a week of doing random shit to distract my mind, and now I've run out of steam and have to listen to it again. There is still another week of holiday left and so I decide to start making some sort of mental plan of what I'm doing when I walk out of school for the last day. I know what I want to do, but the idea is so skitty in my mind that I feel as though I'm going to lose focus really easily. I need to employ the idea of an organised mind, which is not something I am great at.

Just before I sat down in my little office room to sketch some plans, I messaged Spike to start the conversation of saying how he is becoming creepy and making people feel uncomfortable around him. He just talks about sex so much. The first part of this conversation is quite clear as it is based on the fact that he demonstrated to Audie how he likes to sexually choke someone. This was whilst they were alone, having a cigarette together last weekend. She said she just put up with the situation at the time and waited for it to end, leaving her neck bruised. She hasn't said anything to Spike. Her partner, Al, hasn't said anything to Spike. Fuchsia hasn't said anything to Spike. I'll be fucking damned if I don't say anything to Spike, what a fucked up society it is where everyone is for equality but when it comes to being active, no one fucking wants to do anything.

Spike's response is rather weak, he only asked who told me this. Well, it was Audie, which I tell him through a representative gif of some guy drifting down a wet hill in a little children's car, smashing it into a curb and going flying. It came up when I searched "Audi" and I thought it would help ease the tension. I thought that it would let him know that I'm not angry with him, I'm just making the communication that he did something he shouldn't have and therefore should be more aware of himself and his actions. He didn't seem to like it and said the gif wasn't the correct response. *What a fucking dick.* I just hope he doesn't start messaging Audie and making things worse. He should just apologise that he can't read a room and can only read the small writing on his dick.

Earlier on I walked to town to get some materials to finish my skirt. I really want to make more options for male clothing. If you go to the shops, all there really is for men is trousers and shirts. If you want to wear something like a skirt, you have to resort to something feminine, even if that isn't what you're wanting, it's all there is. So I decided to not whinge about it and to instead learn to make the items of clothing I want for myself. I needed some buttons and on the way to the shop I had a pre-rolled smoke that I found in my tin. Turned out to be a small bifta and I was tweaked out of my little mind whilst staring at hundreds of different types of buttons.

At home, I sit. Later, at the supermarket, I walk. On the way back, I drive. I visit my mum, and I sit. I listen. I listen to all the same stories she always tells. I drive again. At home, I sit again. I sit in the bath. I have that feeling again. *Why am I alive? I wish I was dead.*

The issue with Spike got somewhat resolved by the end of the night, but I was left with the taste of being the one in the wrong. I stand up for what is right and I am the one who gets pointed at for making "something out of nothing". Other people fear change, fear confrontation, fear fear itself and so do nothing. They are pathetic. As am I for letting this get to me.

PART TWO

SUMMER TERM (FIRST HALF).

DAY 36 (MONDAY).

NOTICE.

Well, I'm on the bus again and feel like absolute shite for being here. The past ten days since the last entry have been crazy. They started with another cocaine weekend, and we kept drinking through the next day; Me, Audie and Fuchsia. At the time I really enjoyed it and I'm quite convinced I feel a lot for Audie. But the days that came after it were dark. I managed to pull myself out of it near the end and treated myself to piercing my right lobe and changing the jewellery in my nose piercing again. So since I was last at school, I'm plus two on the shiny scale. It feels nice when you look in the mirror, it makes you feel different.

I spoke to Margie in the morning and set the seed for what was to come. It's a teacher training day today, I'll tell her when we are alone.

*   *   *

Once meetings were all over, I sat down and opened a Word document ready to write my resignation letter. Alice came in with Margie, I had only gotten as far as my address and "Dear". She says she has heard the news from Margie and that I'm a good teacher and that the students really like me, I'm a member of the school. It's very nice to hear and I really appreciate it but at this moment my mind is set and I don't want to get emotional. I feel my face get a little damp, although it's hidden under my glasses. She is really trying to convince me and, no matter how wrong it feels to leave this place, it feels more wrong not to leave. My phone rang, it was my sister and I rejected the call but it set the time for Margie and Alice to leave me. I finished my document, printed and signed it and went upstairs to the third floor.

I had written the letter to Quinn because I figured it would be hard to get hold of Leopold. I'm not sure what Quinn's job is, but she seems to be in charge of everything that isn't teaching. She wasn't in and Leopold saw me looking through her office door and asked if he could help. I handed him the letter and he said he had heard about this from Alice. It seems she had gone straight to tell him whilst I was printing the letter downstairs. He asked if we could have a chat and I agreed out of politeness; I'd actually not been in his office since getting the job.

I should've written what we spoke of at the time, as my memory of this has become a little fuzzy. The main thing Leopold wanted to know was why. But I couldn't help feeling that I'm doing him a favour as I've always been the teacher who speaks out and goes against the grain. The teacher that causes him and the school hassle.

*   *   *

In the evening my body ached. I don't know why it ached so much and I ask myself is it from working out, from hiking, from putting up those plaster boards at my sister's in half term? Or am I infected with something, maybe the flu or just from piercing my ear? I lie there on the sofa unable to move. All I can achieve is looking on the internet for new underwear. And then I wake up because I can feel my phone being tugged from my hand. It was Fuchsia. I didn't realise I had fallen asleep, but there I was with my phone still in my hand like a body frozen in place on the way to the summit of Everest. Except, I wasn't wearing green boots.

DAY 37 (TUESDAY).

ROADS DIVERGE.

I told Doc and he thought I was joking. He said I can't leave him and that he'll get stuck with some "boring teacher, A-Level maths teachers are like rocking horse shit". I genuinely felt bad and I struggled to put into words why I wanted to leave. He understood to some extent when I mentioned doing stand-up. God, it felt hard to tell him.

He left and I listened to a reading of a poem on YouTube. It helps. It's about not knowing which of two identical paths to take in a yellow wood. Ultimately neither matter, but we wish we could do both.

Later on, Doc said that he wasn't talking to me anymore.

DAY 38 (WEDNESDAY).

LUCKY.

I noticed that Lucky has some new piercings on his face, he didn't have any before the half term. Today I asked if he got them all done on the same day and he said he did them himself. Helix, lobe and nose. I was impressed and almost felt responsible as I had mentioned I did all my ear ones myself, but for him to do his own nose is brave. He said he had to do it three times too, as the first time he didn't go all the way through and the second time it fell back out. I didn't really understand but his helix looked bloody sore and I said that one would hurt for a while. He smiled and said he knows. My helix piercing hurt for about six months, but I did do mine with a safety pin which I left in. My dreadlocks at the time constantly irritated it, knocking the safety pin and attaching to it. I showed Lucky my fresh lobe piercing, which is still sore to the touch. It's interesting to see students like Lucky, arguably the best at mathematics in the entire school, coming out of his shell. It feels like every term something is new; wearing rings, an alternative hairstyle, darker clothing, and now piercings. It is interesting.

What else happened? Marcel told me about how he used to rent out comics when at a summer camp.

In the evening me and Fuchsia went to the Brewery. It's Wednesday after all, and I have just handed in my notice. We stayed drinking way late after it closed, talking to Benjamin, the owner. I told him I'd quit. We went to school together, all three of us and his partner. Even back then Benjamin used to brew his own beer in a shack he built in his parents' garden. Fuchsia was one of the few people brave enough to drink it.

DAY 39 (THURSDAY).

"I DON'T KNOW".

I was so tired I turned my alarm off without snoozing and rolled over. It was stupid really, if I missed my bus I would have to drive and I would definitely be still under the influence. Thankfully I heard a cat meowing at the front door. He was my alarm this morning. I got up, unlocked the door and held it open whilst he slowly walked out, unsure if he wanted to go out into the cold. I realised this meant I was standing bollock naked at the open door and so I quickly shut it, squashing him in it. He wasn't bothered though. He's weird. And he's not even our cat, he must have snuck in last night. I didn't smell, so decided to not shower until I remembered the sex and Fuchsia being sat on my face.

* * *

I got an email saying that Derwin was "concerning" in a mock interview. He wants to work for GCHQ, so needs to be pretty good at interviews for that. Sadly his mock interview feedback said he couldn't answer many questions, including "why do you want to work here?" and even "tell me about yourself". I laughed so much about this because he is very bland. That's not to say he's not a nice kid, he's just got very little character. Whenever I ask him a question, in Maths or in Form, he usually replies with "I don't know". It's infuriating. That's what made me laugh as I could just imagine him in the interview.

"Why do you want to work here?"

"I don't know."

"Tell me about yourself."

"I don't know."

"Are you taking the piss?"

"I don't know."

He reminds me very much of my nephew, but maybe that's just because they are both ginger. He's going to have to sort himself out if he wants this job, to try and get more passion than a glass of water.

I decided it was time to tell my students I've quit. Every lesson was as if someone had died. The year 12s had a double too. It was difficult.

DAY 40 (FRIDAY).

STUDENTS THAT DON'T GET IT.

I think I have these days numbered wrong. Surely I can't be at 40 already?

A car drove past and it sounded like it was from a French cartoon. This was whilst me and Fuchsia walked down to the supermarket to get vegan scampi to go with some chips from whichever chip shop wasn't full of tourists. It was about 6pm and it felt much earlier. There was a lot of people walking about town and it was still bright and fairly warm for an April evening.

School was something that I just wanted to get through today. This morning we had our first assembly back in the hall and one student talked through the entirety of it. He pissed me off for being so rude. He was wearing a face mask, I knew it was him, but I didn't want to ask him to be quiet mid-assembly as I knew it would achieve nothing, so I waited to speak to him at the end. By that point, I had gotten really pissed off with him and I asked if there was a reason why he was talking throughout the entire assembly. He began to reply and immediately I recognised from his body language that he was about to say "it was boring" and that twigged me. I abruptly interrupted him and said:

"No, I don't give a shit. That was embarrassing, don't fucking do it again."

I was angry and we both walked off, both knowing it was the only way to end it. What a fucking dickhead. The Principal was in the room whilst I swore at the student and I wondered if he heard or cared. I've resigned now, what's he going to do? The student was actually meant to be in my first lesson and I fully expected him to not attend it now. If he did, I had the scene ready to play in my head. I will say "you can piss off" and stand there looking at him until he leaves. I realised it's probably for the best that he doesn't turn up.

I don't even know why he does A-Level Maths, he's a fucking idiot. He's one of those students who can occasionally answer a question, but all the working out has been done subconsciously. So you ask them to explain what they did and they start drawing little diagrams, connecting random numbers with arrows and circles, and none of it makes sense because they don't even know what they did. Unfortunately, if they can't explain it, it means that they haven't actually learnt it, especially if they can't do it again, which they never can. I give this student some of the simplest maths questions and they just guess answers, even when you have explained how to do it. It's not just a case of me explaining and expecting a student to get it, we work together and develop a foundation from which the student is able to figure it out. That's what a good teacher is meant to do. I'm just not good enough to know what to do when that still doesn't work. The classic example is writing $\sqrt{x}$ as $x^{1/2}$, it's a simple rule of indices. You show how it makes sense and how it's obvious and, my god, do some students struggle with this. It's like it's an alien language to them, but these students aren't stupid. They just shouldn't be doing A-Level Maths if they don't grasp things like that. Just like you wouldn't expect a mute to become the next Pavarotti. If this is that, and that is this, connect the fucking dots and make a fucking picture. Geez, it's a good job I've quit. Patience is a virtue and I have none.

He didn't come to my lesson.

DAY 41 (SATURDAY).

KIMONO CLUB.

I woke up in a bad mood, or at least I ended up in one very quickly. Fuchsia stroked my face twice in bed and both times she jabbed me in my fresh ear piercing. I said "ow" and she got annoyed that I was hurt. Or at least, that's what it seemed like. Later on in the day, she said she thought I was angry at her. I don't know if I was at the time, but I decided to get up and sort a bit of personal hygiene in the bathroom.

My electric razor was full of someone else's hair. Fuchsia used it to give my sister a trim not long ago. I vacuumed out the black and noticed the guard was snapped. I went to use my other razor but the guard for that one was missing. So I use the one with the broken guard to cautiously trim my pubic hair and then I do a clean shave of my underarms. I wash my hair but for some reason the water pressure from the shower is just a dribble. What a disappointing morning so far.

In the evening we went to watch a film with Al. I thought Tropics of Thunder was going to be an actual war film, I was a little disappointed. Audie came home and joined us before it ended. Me and Al had kimonos on, we called it kimono club, although her and Fuchsia were dressed normally. We smoked some weed and Al, not being very used to it, ate 12 packets of Quavers and kept giggling to himself. At some point before the weed, me and Al posed for some photos in our kimonos. I felt a little uncomfortable because Al for some reason wanted to pretend I was sucking his dick and I didn't want to. So I didn't. But we did this one daft pose where his hand was on the back of my head, near his waist, and he pushed me towards his crotch. It surprised me the strength he was pushing as I resisted. I didn't get the vibe he was doing it malevolently, it was more like he was going into autopilot or, perhaps, doing a lad-ish joke. Either way, it was disturbing and I didn't like it.

DAY 42 (SUNDAY).

RESPECT AND RESENTMENT.

Woke up and watched Formula One qualifying from the day before. Norris put in a crazy fast lap and would have been second on the grid if he didn't go slightly off track and get his time deleted. Was exciting.

Today felt good for some reason. I didn't feel hungover so walked along the Cinder Track to get my van. Wanting to enjoy the slight bit of heat and sunshine, I wore my custom black skirt, a black vest with my white Mercedes cap and my white Adidas Pro-Models. To top it off I had my shades on and a black chain around my neck. Sometimes I think an outfit looks so good that I feel like a dickhead for wearing it in this little town. Like I'm some sort of urban celeb going out to the sticks. On the walk I wondered if people were looking at me for my outfit and judging me, but I soon got over it. I think too much about this kind of thing.

It was a pleasant and uneventful walk, however I did overhear some older people talking and I nearly pitched in. It was a couple from Bradford, I heard them say, talking to a similarly aged man, who I assumed was local. Well, it was more that the local man was having a rant to the couple, saying how kids have no respect and it's to be expected if you can't clip them around the ear. I wanted to say how my father used to get regular lashings but it didn't stop him from taking a rail vehicle for a joyride along the lines as a child. He used to get up to all sorts my dad did, as a child, he even blew up a portion of the cliff with a home-made bomb. But he wasn't a bad child, you can tell from how he acts now that he is very morally grounded and wouldn't do something to the detriment of another human. This man here seems to think that physically abusing a child is meant to make them miraculously respect you. What I wanted to say was that, as a teacher, you get respect by giving respect. It's so fucking obvious, I don't understand why people don't get this. I can get students to do anything I want because I spend time treating them like humans, building up relationships. My problem there, though, is that I have to want a student to do something to be able to get them to do the something, such as study and homework. No one believes someone who doesn't believe themselves, and in teaching I don't see the point anymore. Existentially, I don't see the point. As for the clip around the ear, it will fuel resentment and make people either act out or become internally fucked up. I don't see the point of that either.

When I got home I saw Audie had sent me a video of me getting in my van and driving off. It was taken from her bedroom window just a moment earlier. The dirty pervert.

DAY 43 (MONDAY).

I CHOOSE AZIZ.

School was locked when I turned up so I rolled a cigarette and smoked it to pass the time. Audie had sent another video to the Group Chat last night, showing that one of her kids had put a prank ant in the bathtub. It made me think of The Offspring song Original Prankster so I stood listening to the Conspiracy of One album for a moment until I decided to take the plunge and listen to I Choose from the Ixnay on the Hombre album. I Choose is a song that means a lot to me because, not only do I think it's a great song, my school band did a cover of it and there is a section in the song with crazy mad lyrics. Crazy mad because of the reference to someone not living to age 21 and that life's a fucked up thing if we choose.

... they didn't make it... fucked up... nightmare... playground... I choose.

The words echo.

The two guitarists in my band were brothers and the younger didn't make it to 21. When he died I wasn't in the country and I didn't find out for a while. I'd actually lost touch with all my school friends due to a break-up at the time and, this makes it worse, from getting into an argument with his brother. I never understood what the argument was about, but they had been having problems at home with their mother. I was messaging Aziz one evening on MSN and suddenly his brother had taken over their computer and started to message back. He said I'd changed and was being mean to Aziz. It was the first time I'd felt hurt by a friend, so I binned my friend group and made new ones. What a fucked up thing we do.

Anyway, because of an unclear message when I found out he died, I thought he drowned surfing and it wasn't for another seven years until I found out the truth. It hit me like a sack of shit that did. A few of us were celebrating my 29th birthday on the beach near where they held the first memorial service. My brother-in-law lived with Aziz whilst at university and he said to me "it's sad that he did it". I asked what he meant.

The sack of shit fell from the sky.

He hanged himself in the garage at their childhood home.

*   *   *

First lesson was with my year 10 Nomad class. Because these lessons weren't timetabled, I don't actually get to see these students for all of their Maths lessons because I'm teaching other classes. So half of their lessons are with the ordinary higher GCSE Maths class. In those lessons, my students either do the mundane dumb-dumb stuff or try to be independent learners and do my assignments whilst sat among the dumb-dumbs (comparatively, they really are dumb-dumbs). Either way, it's a shit situation. Because of this, it's quite difficult to know what the students in my year 10 Nomad class already know. The year 11s are fine, I got them into a routine last year. For the year 10s, today I was planning on going onto the cosine rule, after doing the sine rule last lesson (whenever that was). But I had a feeling that some students were actually a little sketchy on basic trigonometry like SOHCAHTOA. So we ended up doing a mixed bag of trigonometry.

The rest of the day is just another drag. None of the students care because of lockdown fucking up their education, motivation and perspective on life. Being their age is delicate enough.

At lunch I decided to ring HMRC to sort out my Self Assessment tax return that I missed the deadline for. People keep asking about this and why I need to do it myself, but the reason is I did freelance work two years ago on the side because I was fat broke. My Self Assessment says I owe £246 in tax and I can't help but think that's wrong, I didn't earn much more than that. So I rang HMRC and was in the queue for 50 minutes. My lunch is only 30 minutes so I was still in the queue whilst teaching my year 12 Further Maths class. I left them to get on with work whilst I was yapping at the front of the class about how much I earned. The end of the phone call was to ring back in 72 hours so the Self Assessment form can enter their system and we can discuss it properly. Not really the outcome I wanted, I'm trying to save every penny with quitting, but it is what it is.

Fuchsia messaged and asked what I ate for lunch. Despite having recently eaten, I couldn't remember. I guessed and said it was the chickpea thing out of the fridge. She did meal prep for us both on Sunday so my meals this week are all sorted.

It's now final lesson and I'm trying to get the students to be better independent learners, so it's like guided self-study. It's for two reasons:

1) I've given up; and

2) there is no guarantee that they will get a good teacher to replace me.

They may not even get one, SLT are having ideas of saving money themselves.

*   *   *

Fuchsia pointed out that I ate the lentil chilli, so we ate the chickpea thing for tea.

DAY 44 (TUESDAY).

INTERNET BANKING.

School was locked when I turned up again, but this time Leopold's car was in the car park meaning he had gone in and not opened the door properly. Problem was that I really needed a shit. I wrote an Instagram post about The Wombats to distract myself. The plan was to not think about needing to go shit and wait until Monty turns up and sorts it.

The Wombats post was because I had been listening to their song Kill the Director. It has a nice line "if this is a rom-com, kill the director". Quite a nice song about romance and how love fucks with your head. Or at least that was my interpretation. When I was moving into student halls in Liverpool in my first year of university, my parents were in the city and met The Wombats. They had given my dad a promo CD when they were very unknown. It was just a blank CD with "The Wombats" written on it in marker pen. My dad said we should keep the CD in case they become famous one day. Being in a band myself I didn't expect them to make it. I threw the CD out.

Monty turned up and slid along the side of the building to shout up to Leopold's third-floor window. I wasn't sure if this would work but left him to it. Bertha turned up and said the doors could be forced but it can damage them. I had thought this earlier but had put the idea out of my mind. Now she's said this, I'm suddenly a little more desperate for the shit and I force the doors open and saunter in. Monty must have managed to get Leopold's attention because I hear Leopold shout something from the balcony on the floor above. He's on his way down the final staircase as I beeline through the barriers and he asks how I got in.

"I forced it open."

"You shouldn't do that as it can break the door."

"Sorry, but I really need a shit."

Beeline uninterrupted. I think I'll get some follow-up about this later but I don't care. What would they prefer, me forcing my way in or no maths teacher today, he's had to go home because he shit his pants?

Given this morning's situation, I decide I need to be clear to everyone that I'm leaving. First person on this list, despite him pissing me off recently, is Monty. I do like and respect that man. He's sad but understands my simple explanation, perhaps because he's an outdoors person too. He says he became a teacher because that was the only thing he could do, whereas I'm young enough to go on and do something else. I tell him I know what I want to do, but I don't tell him what. Just that it's "not for certain and there is no clear pathway".

At break I told Graham. I could see he was sad, but also completely understood and we both agree that we'd be happy being a joiner or a roofer or anything where you could do a bit of manual labour and be outside. He said he was going to tell me we could start carpooling together again. Like with Doc, we spoke about how this isn't a bad school to work in, but if you don't enjoy it then you don't enjoy it. Graham left teaching himself a few years ago, triggered by mental health issues. He didn't expect to come back, but here he is now. I think he understand what I am feeling as he is one of the few people who know I took time off earlier in the year due to having an existential crisis. I don't recall how we got onto it, Graham was talking about how in this school it's nice to see a member of SLT saying thank you to the staff. In the school near where we both live, which he used to teach in, he said the hierarchy was: Principal, SLT, students, all other staff.

* * *

I don't know what was wrong with my year 12 class. They kept talking. Not in a bad, dicking about way, but in an oh-my-god-you-are-being-so-loud kind of way. Nate annoyed me because he had his Pokemon cards out. He's 17 and playing with Pokemon cards in lesson. Then I catch him picking his nose and eating it. I repeat, he is 17 and I'm facing the class getting a full view of this vomit-inciting act. Four of the class are working at a different pace and I have set them a past paper to complete as I don't want them to go onto the next topic.

At the end of my last lesson I get a message from Fuchsia. It's a worrying one, saying HSBC rang to say her account has been hacked and all her money has gone. Thankfully though the person on the phone said the money will be sent back to her within 25 minutes. Alarm bells are going off in my head and I message to ask her to ring me. She says she will once she has rung HSBC, as the money has not gone back in yet.

Since it was the 20th of April, I had a bifta on the way to the bus at 4:20pm. I had to roll it in the disabled toilets, squatting on the floor as Doc and Margie were in the maths office and there is no toilet seat anymore. It was hard work. Doc was having to fill out a form because a GCSE student had whipped out a can of Desperados at the end of his lesson to drink on the bus on the way home. It was Bob, the one I bumped into on the back lanes a few weeks back. Given that he's 15, Doc confiscated the can and had to fill out a safeguarding form.

It wasn't until I was on the bus that I finally spoke to Fuchsia on the phone. The penny had dropped and she was crying. The phone call wasn't HSBC it was a very convincing scam, they knew everything about her and coaxed her into a trap. She lost everything and her overdraft. £11,000 gone in an instant. This is our wedding fund. I felt sick and managed to calm her a little and tell her to get back on the phone to HSBC. It was when she was on hold that the penny dropped for her and she immediately hung up and rang me.

DAY 45 (WEDNESDAY).

MAD DOG.

Today I need to put on a smile and forget about what happened with Fuchsia and the bank. We just have to wait. Saying that, I still told my Form about it and we ended up talking about wedding things since they all want to come to our wedding. I don't know if it's a good idea that they come, but I'd like them to be there. It would be funny, as long as they didn't invite all their mates along too. That would be something I'd do at their age. They point out that with me quitting, it would mean it's less awkward and ask if it is possible to stay in touch with teachers. They are right about it being less awkward, although they would fast realise I can be a bit of a wreck-head.

But currently no one is invited as we have no idea when it is going to be. As for staying in touch, I'd like to, I want to know what they end up doing with their lives.

I also caught-up with Chai in Form, asking about her interview she had with McLaren as an Engine Apprentice. Well, the job title was something like that. She said that the interview bombed, as they were asking questions that she had no idea about.

"What do you know about four-stroke engines?"

"Not much, I've never seen one."

"What would you do if you dropped a battery in the workshop?"

"Clean it up."

It's at least better than Derwin. I think that this apprenticeship was aimed at someone with a little more experience than just A-Levels, anyway.

With talking to Chai, we leave Form a few minutes late and I can hear a bit of a commotion downstairs. I run down to see what's going on. Monty has a student pinned against the wall, the student's arms are flailing and he's swearing madly. His lip is swollen and there is blood on his collar. I quickly put my laptop down in Monty's office nearby, as I might need to get involved here. Frank turns up as I do it. Monty is talking to the student, trying to get him to calm down. At the other end of the building I can see Doc calmly stood next to a student who I recall was involved in a punch-up last year. The situation quickly becomes apparent that the kid with Doc has punched this one and now this one has gone wild. He's in Monty's arms going mad, shouting incoherent swear words at the other student. Monty is doing his best to hold onto him, to stop him from harming himself or anyone else. I stand by for support, not wanting to add to the stress of this kid by being another adult in his face. He's like a mad dog and I'm very alert and ready to react. It looks like Monty could get punched and if that happens I wouldn't mind sneaking one in too.

Monty manages to usher the kid into his office. *Fuck, that's where my laptop is.* I make sure my laptop is safely out of the way whilst Monty and Frank repeatedly ask him to calm down. Frank offers him to take a seat a have a coffee, but the kid fucks that comment away. Surprisingly Frank asks me to contact the police. That fucking caught me off guard, aren't they meant to be calming this kid down? I'm not leaving them alone with this kid so I dash to reception, pass on the request and then I'm back in seconds. Amusingly the kid says he just wants to go home and have a spliff. He's upset and angry, it's a dangerous combination. It's like Scrappy Doo shouting "let me at him" but actually concerning. Frank decided to let him go outside the building as it was not looking to improve. Essentially he's letting the kid have the chance to have that smoke, without saying that's what he's doing. On the way out the kid kicked a plastic chair, snapping it in half, and ripped his blazer off, throwing it on the floor. It was odd to see him wait patiently for the barrier to open at reception, however. As I watched him leave, something on the floor caught my eye. It was a tooth.

And now I'm late for my next lesson too.

*   *   *

I think I've lost the plot to teach. It's giving me bad anxiety. I just don't know what I'm doing anymore. I don't know what to do when kids don't understand. It's not that hard, even I learnt it once. But Nate thinks he is struggling. I know he is struggling and he says he is thinking about dropping the course. This is hard because I think he should, but he needs it to get into university to study Computer Science. The problem is that he is another one of those students who doesn't think, and I don't know how to get them to think. My mind turns to my brother who taught in the Royal Navy for a while after he slipped in the shower, breaking his collar bone and making it impossible for him to do his normal duty on ship. He once said how he can teach some of his students things that no one managed to at school because he can explain it in the basic way needed. I think he's deluded. What people fail to appreciate is that people, students, mature. A GCSE kid thinks GCSE is hard, but when they come back after summer they have matured and can understand maths more. I'm not explaining this very well, but the mind is always learning. Learning new skills or learning about itself and you perpetually get a little smarter. Not necessarily in the sense of IQ tests, but in the sense of capabilities. What this means is that sometimes a person can come back to something years later and understand it suddenly. My friend Velma comes to mind here. I met her at the Summer Science Exhibition at the Royal Society and she once told me she failed A-Level Maths, bummed about with her life for four years, matured a bit, then went back to education and smashed it. Last year she completed her PhD in cosmology and now she's a lecturer. The downside of this maturing idea is that for some people it doesn't happen when it needs to. And maybe it never even happens at all, it's not guaranteed. For me it happened twice; once from GCSE to A-Level, and then again when I started teacher training. Right now there are kids I'm trying to teach a skill but when it goes into the part of their brain where the maths lives, it's like throwing a ball into a big bucket of slop. When they need to use the ball again, either they can't find it or they find it covered in slop and incomprehensible, unusable. I don't think there's anything wrong with that, but it is wrong to try and force this to work.

I'm planning the assessment for the year 13 students. These are for the TAGs that we submit to government since national exams aren't happening again. The great thing is that, since I'm setting this assessment, I can do targeted revision. Don't get me wrong, if I think a student is shit I will give them a shit grade. I said before, morally I can't lie like that. But I also said I won't let a student down again. I will help them achieve a good grade no matter what.

Doc emailed me a link to a newspaper article from last year with the headline "Teenage boy released on police bail after girl dies having taken drug". Mad dog.

DAY 46 (THURSDAY).

MIND SHIFT.

"Why do you always sit with your crotch protruding?" Drake was sat on a stool, leaning back on it.

"I do it for you, Egbert."

"Why don't you just sit on a normal chair and not look like an idiot?"

Well, that was Form. And then I can't recall what happened in first period. And I can't remember what happened in second period. I can't remember what happened in third and fourth periods. The only thing I remember was walking past Gladys the English teacher, who was making her kids line up outside her classroom. She was pissed off with them and doing the routine stern voice, bollocking every kid for any benign issue. ID cards. Top buttons. Slouching. Gladys is an interesting character, she's tall and thin and copies Julia like she is the messiah. As a result, Gladys is a very teacher-like-teacher. She fucking loves it. There was this one time when I was in my classroom alone and Julia came in with a student, just to use a quiet place whilst she asked him some unusual questions. Turns out that she was after the name of a kid who had thrusted at Gladys whilst she was bent over at the front of her class. It's a pretty stupid thing to do, but when I heard this student say "pretended to hump her" I was struggling to keep my shit together.

What I did notice today was that... well, it can't have been that fucking interesting because I forgot. I could describe a plain piece of A4 paper better. Actually, the ratio between the lengths of the edges of A4 paper is pretty interesting, it involves $\sqrt{2}$.

The kids went home at lunch because, like every Thursday, we have our teacher CPD meetings. I've told Margie there is no chance I'm doing my PLT research anymore. I don't even know what PLT stands for, but it's what SLT are calling this research project bollocks for CPD and they pronounce it "platt".

"Totally no point if I'm quitting, should I tell Cleo?"

"No, because she'll ask why."

"I'll say I'm leaving. She can't make me do it."

"Yes, but save the hassle and just don't do it and let her find out at the end."

"Fair enough."

I have work to do but I feel unmotivated. I remember having sex last night and it gives me a bit of motivation.

The second half of the CPD session is the well-being group meeting, which is online since us teachers are still not meeting in person. Alice does an ice breaker, asking questions like what's your favourite noise, smell, food and so on. I pencil down my ideas, deciding to take part and do it properly... But, I ended up not saying a thing in that meeting. Not one single thing. It's not for not wanting to, I just was not given the opportunity to take part, as if I wasn't even in the meeting.

On the bus home the driver did a cock-up and we ended up going over the big Valley Bridge. It's got anti-suicide railings on it, but if someone was determined it wouldn't stop them. I have a mild daydream of being the hero and grabbing someone just before they jump or just after they jump, grabbing their belt through the railings. I'd tell them that's OK and we can work it out. I tell them that they can come back from this.

That thought is now glowing in my mind. I've come from being the one thinking about jumping to being a hero and stopping someone jumping.

Isn't that fucking something.

DAY 47 (FRIDAY).

THE DREAM.

I had a dream last night and it's really fucked with my head. I don't usually dream, well, remember them, apparently we always dream but it's the remembering we don't do. Since I don't do it very often, when I do do it really fucks with me and I struggle to separate emotions and memories from dreams and reality. In my dream last night I was at the Royal Society. I think I must have been invited to an event because I wasn't working. It was night time and I really needed a piss so I was out on the terrace that looks over St James's Park, pissing all over some marble columns that don't exist. It was just me out there and I was spraying it about like a cat marking its territory. A woman walked out and caught me, I think she was some of the catering staff. I apologised for pissing but didn't stop. She said she didn't mind and liked my attitude. Then there was the weirdest little nonsensical time skip and we were holding each other. She was tall and thin with pale skin and straw coloured long hair that went past her shoulders. Before, on the terrace, her hair was tied up and it was dark so I couldn't see what she was wearing. It was something that made me assume she was catering staff, but now she was wearing a long black sleeveless jumpsuit that had little straps over her shoulder. We were laughing and I picked her up. She pulled the top of her jumpsuit down and we laughed some more. We were still at the Royal Society, it must have been the same event but the next year and now she was my guest. We had fallen in love in a dream. I have no idea who this person was, for all I know I made her up. *But can the brain do that?* Maybe she exists somewhere. Maybe there is something make-believe happening in dreams and she is a real person who had the same dream but from her perspective. Now I'm awake I remember falling in love with this person who is a construction of my subconscious mind.

The dream affected my morning quite a bit as I needed to take an extra long shower and didn't have time for breakfast or to get lunch. So I was in Sainsbury's at 7:30am buying food and I saw a triple pack of Jaffa cakes that I decided to buy for my Form. I left it in their common room with a note saying:

To the best Form in year 13 xx

It made me smile; they are the only Form in year 13, it was a small intake that year.

I've not got a chance to properly see my Form this morning, as we are all in assembly. What I'd love to do is to a play drinking game where every time an assembly refers to Greta Thunberg or book burnings, you take a shot. The only assemblies I enjoy are the ones from Frank, he just tells a story and it has some sort of moral direction, but he says it in such an interesting way. This assembly is about Earth Day and, I must admit, I did just learn something. Greta Thunberg's mother represented Sweden at Eurovision 2009. *I can't believe it*. It seems that no one famous has plebs for parents.

Alice is doing this assembly with her teacher voice. It's so fucking annoying, I don't know how students are meant to listen. It's high pitched, rather patronising and she emphasises every other word. The WORDS she CHOOSES are LIKE they're FROM a CHILDREN'S book. She has a drama background, she always reminds people of this, so why doesn't she change her voice? It's not difficult, you just breathe differently. Her PowerPoint is amusing too. The usual low resolution, wrong aspect ratio images. Greta's head is a trapezoidal prism.

My lessons today go with a ridiculous speed. I was constantly busy, gassing away whilst the students worked. For year 13 Maths I decided to cover an entire unit in one hour. We did it. It's crazy mad when you can do that. Period two, I wrote the goals on the board and told them to get on with self-learning. Again, with me leaving I need them to learn how to do this. I circulated the classroom, checking their work and guiding them. They're getting the hang of doing this. There's still those few students who I'm struggling with, though, and I'm still not sure what to do there. Mathematical Engineering was just going over practice questions. In the middle of the lesson, however, my back started to ache and my legs began to immediately sweat from the pain so I went to get painkillers mid-lesson. When I came back Rudy had taken over the board work I was doing and was teaching the class so I said nothing and sat down in his seat and watched, letting him get on with it.

I did all my lessons entirely on the whiteboard today and never touched a computer at all. To me, it feels great to be able to do that but I know every other teacher would think that's a bad thing. That it makes me a bad teacher for not using technology. There is one aspect of not using a computer that I'd agree is bad, though. At lunch, because of my back hurting, I went for a short walk in the sun and smoked some weed. When I came back in, the receptionist asked if I could complete my registers. I'd not done a single register today. That's probably a personal best. Registers are important.

I wish I got into a routine with my year 12 Maths class earlier. I feel like lockdown hasn't helped them transition from GCSE but, more importantly, it takes time to get to know a class. Each one is different and so your routine is going to be different each time. There is also that maturity jump that happens from GCSE to A-Level, however it doesn't all happen at the same time, so you almost have to wait for it to happen with each student. A good teacher would be able to make a routine very quickly, but it won't be the class's routine it will be the teacher's routine. There's a subtle difference there, the class routine is one in which the class feels ownership to and that makes them try harder and take more pride in their work. Well, at least for my style of teaching it does that. When I first started teaching at this school I got my classes to make revision notes on the wall using dry-wipe pens. It was a simple trick to make them feel comfortable with me and with the classroom. Thanks to the pandemic I've not been able to do it with this year 12 group as I don't even have my own classroom. There's a lot of things I wish were different with this year 12 group, but I'm pleased with where they are now, as a majority.

That dream, though… it's still fucking with my head.

DAY 48 (SATURDAY).

GROSMONT.

Went for a walk around Grosmont. Saw a fella doing the Coast to Coast walk with a teddy bear the size of Fuchsia on his back. This is his last day. He's done it in seven days for charity. It took me and Curlos 12 days.

I wanted to get a photo of the man and send it to Curlos but I didn't want to push my sudden enthusiasm. I woke up in a terrible mood and had been trying to fight it all morning. Fuchsia had been trying to help, but we had just been pissing each other off. I didn't realise how much it was bothering Fuchsia until we were driving to Grosmont in the morning and I was playing a game of chicken with an oncoming car. I won, but it scared Fuchsia. So I didn't really win. Once we parked up we had a little chat and were able to put some of the bad moods behind us. The novelty of seeing and talking to a man with a bear on his back really helped.

Walking along past the couple of shops, some people in a car waved at us and pulled over. It was Benjamin and Becky with their child in the back seat. They were driving around trying to get her to sleep.

DAY 49 (SUNDAY).

NOTHING.

We stayed in. Did nothing much at all.

DAY 50 (MONDAY).

CALCULATORS.

I had an email that had the subject "DT" and I have no idea what that means. I presume detention, but that doesn't really make sense.

In the maths office we spoke about the exam papers that the year 11s recently sat for their TAGs. Margie says that the students have done too good. I ask if there is a reason for this and what the action is going to be. She says the grades will probably even out over the next few papers as it was higher than it should be as she let the students use a calculator despite it being non-calculator. I said how I wasn't a fan of this idea. I understand why she did it because she hadn't covered as much non-calculator techniques, but I still said I disagree with it. It belittles the purpose of the assessment and the efforts of the students, i.e. my year 11 Nomad class, who can smash these exams without calculators.

This day is a drag, I barely have any lessons for some reason. I have work to do but I sit and stare at the wall pretending to work, not feeling any motivation to do anything else.

In period five I have that special moment where I am double booked to teach both my year 11 and year 10 Nomad classes. Because of mixing bubbles and risk of infection, SLT won't let me put these nine students in the same class together so I leave the year 10s with their dumb-dumb ordinary class and focus on the year 11s. The year 11s have that assessment to be doing for their TAGs that Margie mentioned. We focus on practising whilst Piper, who missed a lesson last week, finishes her exam. I'm not entirely sure how to assess this Further Maths class as they all joined at separate times. Marcel can do everything, but Piper on the other hand joined right near the end and, despite being really smart, has only been taught one unit. So am I meant to give each of them a different assessment? We are only meant to assess what they have covered in class, it's government guidelines.

Piper finished this exam early, it was only a normal Maths one and not the more difficult Further Maths one. Whilst talking to them about the work, I can hear myself breathing. *Am I hyperventilating?*

DAY 51 (TUESDAY).

BROMCOM.

The bus was cold. I didn't have the right coat today for it as I was running late and the girl on the opposite side didn't close her window. I don't know how she wasn't also really cold but I couldn't be arsed to ask her, since she had headphones in. It was the first time it had rained in about two weeks and it was nice to see. But it was so fucking cold that I struggled to roll a smoke on the bus. It was like a short fatty.

Today got kicked off by getting a WhatsApp message in the Group Chat:

    [08:36] Unknown: Would you rather fight one horse—sized mouse
    or 100 mouse—sized horses?

I didn't even notice who it was from but I take the piss and say "phone box full of my own shit", since that seems to always be an answer to this kind of bullshit. But my honest response is the horse-sized mouse. What enjoyment is there in killing small horses? At least I'd get to feel like an ancient gladiator facing a kill-or-be-killed situation against a fast, sharp-toothed monster, rather than stamping on 100 retarded horses as if they were a bag of spilled Wotsits. I reply and say this in the chat, but no one replies. *Am I being annoying again? Maybe.*

I take the question to my Form who were already in the classroom as I was running late again. They have some interesting ideas, but nothing surprising.

"Tiny horses are easy to kill."

"Can't you just leave them alone?" *Yeh, I get it too.*

We then end up talking about the book I started reading on the bus, Rich Dad Poor Dad, and the part where it talks about the fear of not having money. It made me feel good to read it since I've already quit but I don't really know why I'm reading the book. A student suggested it to me a few years back and I downloaded a PDF of it and have been occasionally reading it on my phone. I figured stealing the book was within the theme of getting rich.

*   *   *

Bertha walks into the maths office whilst I'm pretending to work and asks if she can borrow some calculators. I would say yes but it's getting rather annoying, people coming into this office to borrow basic equipment. Really they are Doc's calculators and so I say I can't make that decision. She says she is making an executive decision and will take them. Bit of a fucking weird way of saying it, it comes across with an air of "I'm a Director of a subject, so I am very important and will just take them". I don't really care about the calculators, I care more about the sickly perfume smell she has left in here after leaving with the full box of calculators. The smell reminds me of some crayons I had as a child.

I'm struggling to take anything seriously today. I'm pretty much sat waiting for the day to end.

I decide to try and get on with some admin work and marking books. In one book it looked like the student had found and copied a mark scheme line-for-line, number-for-number. It's just lazy cheating. I gave up and replied to an email from the Director of Engineering. It was quite a serious email asking for me to update a grade tracking spreadsheet for Mathematical Engineering by adding my class data before the people from the academy trust *(was that what they said it was it in the meeting this morning?)* come to visit next week. Since the subject of the email was "Tracking Sheet", I started thinking about sheep driving tractors so I replied by sending a picture of Shaun the Sheep in a tractor, no text. The reply I got was rather amusing.

```
From: Ricky
To: DEAD

Hi,
```

Thank you for the light-hearted picture, however, please update
your data as to their current performance and progress by COP.

Regards,
Ricky

To which my reply was a little more thought-out than previously:

From: DEAD
To: Ricky

I thought you'd like it.

Ricky, I honestly have no data to put in that spreadsheet. I
have been doing very little assessment with the class as I am
currently focusing on trying to get them to learn by rote to do
three exams in the coming weeks.

Bear in mind that since the autumn term I've had a total of
nine lessons with them as per timetabling.

DEAD

It's true, I have only had nine lessons with that class in four months and he
expects me to have done meaningful assessment in that time. All I've been
able to do in those nine lessons is teach by rote. That's when students do
the same work over and over and over, and eventually they have done it so
much that they know how to answer a question without actually
understanding the concept behind it. It's not great, and I hate doing it, but I
want them to pass.

It took me ages to figure out exactly how many lessons we had had too. All
our registers, timetables and student information are on a CMS called
Bromcom. It's a stupid system like they all are. Schools pay money to
developers who release CMSs especially for schools. One of the most
popular ones is called Sims, the one we use is Bromcom. There are others,
but those two are the only ones I've ever used. Bromcom has a nice
interface and can be accessed through a browser but unfortunately I think
it's a requirement that school CMSs have to be clunky, hard-to-navigate
pieces of shit. I was trying to find exactly how many lessons Mathematical
Engineering had done since the start of the academic year. On paper, I
calculated it to be 28. After about ten minutes of digging on Bromcom, I
found that it should be 27. But I could only find it by seeing the attendance
figures of individual students and going by the largest number of lessons a
student had been in. That method is flawed, however, as not a single

student had 100% attendance, which I found suspicious. Maybe a lesson got cancelled?

Bromcom is used for a lot of things, despite my difficulty in using it. On the homepage it has your current class information, decided by the time of day and your timetable. If you want to choose another class, there is a drop-down menu which will take you to your upcoming classes for that day. But that will only show you information like the register and the time it is at. If you want to find information on the class as a whole, it doesn't seem possible from there. So when I wanted to see the attendance over all time, it wasn't on that page and I had to click to an overview page where I could show attendance pie charts of each of my classes. The pie chart is kind of nice, but completely overkill as all that you need is some bare-faced numbers. It feels odd trying to describe this system which doesn't have one thing wrong with it, it's more an overall sensation I get when I use it. My face feels hot and sweaty and I start to quickly get annoyed. Using it to log positive and negative behaviours for example, I still haven't got my head around it after three years, so I don't do it. It's too time-consuming.

From what I know, there are five methods that should let you log a behaviour event:

1. On the home page, click on the behaviour button from the drop-down menu. This takes you to a page where you can overview the behaviour of a particular class and it will show some sort of graph in the centre of the page. None of my classes show a graph because of me not logging anything. But you cannot add a behaviour entry from here.

2. On the home page, click on the behaviour button at the top of the page. This takes you to a page where you can also overview the behaviour of the whole school over the last five days. It shows a pie chart, two bar charts and a scatter plot of behaviour broken down by gender, year group and as a timeline. But you cannot add a behaviour entry from here.

3. Search for the particular student using the search bar at the top of the page. Go to the student's details page and click behaviour. Here you can see all the behaviour entries for the student since they started at the school, from all teachers. But you cannot add a behaviour entry from here.

4. Go to the modules page, click behaviour, click event records. The filters don't work so you can't search for a particular student to look up their

behaviour data. You can add a new entry here by writing what student you are doing it for and you can also, if you wanted to, enter it under the name of another teacher. Seems like a bit of a security issue to me. So you can add a behaviour entry from here.

5. On the home page, click on overview and use the drop-down menu to select the class that you want. It defaults to the next lesson that you have with them, however, you can ignore that and scroll to the class list. Select the student(s) you want, click action and select new behaviour event. This brings the pop-up where you add the behaviour details, the same as in four, above. The problem here is that the date defaults to the next lesson so, unless you change that, you are adding a behaviour event for the future. So you can add a behaviour entry from here.

Of those five ways you would expect to log a behaviour entry, only the last two work and they give you different options. If you successfully found the behaviour event pop-up, a mandatory field to complete is "Event", which is a drop-down menu of 43 different items chosen by SLT. About a third of these are negatives, most are written in codes of acronyms and abbreviations, as usual, and I don't know what they are.

All behaviour entries get belittled, anyway. Sometimes I see that students have had a positive behaviour comment from their Form tutor for "having a pen today", yet that gets put on an equal standing as if I were to give them a positive for "solving a fuck-massive equation". You're also meant to write the reason for the behaviour comment but not all teachers do that. All too often a student will get three negatives, giving them an automatic detention, but no one knows what the student has done wrong. How are they expected to encourage the student to behave differently? Sure, that's the fault of the teachers who do it as they are meant to tell the student and log it in the behaviour entry, but there is never really time to log it properly in lesson. Most teachers spend their breaks logging all these little issues or even staying late at the end of the day, sat typing away on this clunky, hard-to-navigate piece of shit.

```
Pudge forgot his pencil.
Piper needed the toilet twice and didn't have a note.
Hugh farted.
```

That last one genuinely isn't a joke. The teacher Gladys replaced once told me in the staff kitchen that Hugh had just got up in her lesson, stood on his chair and farted. Pretty disgusting in all honesty, and I can guarantee that when someone goes into teaching, they don't expect to have to metaphorically wrestle a student into reading An Inspector Calls, rather than stand on their chair and fart. Oh and by the way, there's nothing wrong with that kid, he was just being a cunt. It's no surprise that the teacher just got up and left one day. A shame as I got on with her, she was honest.

My lunchtime cigarette was neither at lunchtime nor a cigarette. I've been getting so bored I find myself sitting and staring at the wall and I thought a small bifta might help me concentrate. It didn't. But I somehow eked my way through the last two lessons of the day.

I was glad to be home and had been mentally preparing myself to exercise all day. Unfortunately, I was in glorious back pain again, so I took some pills, drank some Jack Daniel's and ate biscuits. The night became one of leisure and pleasure with Fuchsia, eating mushroom burgers with a rocket salad.

DAY 52 (WEDNESDAY).

PRINTING ERROR.

Last night me and Fuchsia had a fairly large bifta and watched a film. It was Zoolander, which is not my type of film at all, but it made me laugh. Anyway, it meant that Fuchsia still has my lighter in her pocket. When I got off the bus at the train station, I asked the first smoker I see to borrow their lighter. It was a man in high-visibility workwear and he didn't say anything, he just passed me a lighter. He didn't look too happy, but I didn't care, it was probably just his face. But the lighter wasn't working and I struggled to get it to spark. Once I finally got myself lit, I took a big inhale, passed the lighter back and blew a big cloud of smoke in his face. I quickly scurried off laughing out loud to myself.

By the pond I saw a seagull that amused me. It had a wad of grass in its beak and was shaking it about like a dog would shake a toy. I was a bit confused. I think the seagull was too. Wake and bake Wednesday, as usual.

In Form there was only five students, I have no idea where the rest of them were. At the best of times we don't do any proper Form activities, so with only five we played a game of cards. The students had to teach me the rules and I was very honest saying "I'm a bit of a spaz", and it took a few goes for me to understand. It was essentially a game of highest card wins, and you can choose to swap your card with the person on the left of you. Alice walked in about halfway through Form to talk to Bianca. Throughout their conversation, Alice's eyes kept flicking to our table as if someone had just done a shit on it. Clearly she did not approve of the card game, but I couldn't believe the look on her face, as if she was about to explode with disgust but was reigning it in so she can be more reserved when she brings it up.

She's done with Bianca, let's see how Alice plays this out.

"Have you done the theme of the week?" She says.

"Yep, we do that on Monday." I hadn't and I hope she doesn't ask about it, calling my bluff.

"Isn't there anything else you can be doing? The quiz?"

"We do quizzes on a Thursday and there are only five of them today, so they are teaching me how to play this card game."

She left with an "oh, OK."

As if this is even a problem. The students have explained a game to me, communicating and teaching the rules of a game and then playing with each other and myself. Jesus, it's not like we were playing strip poker.

This day was an absolute drag. First lesson was slightly interesting, with the year 10 Nomad class. I was checking their work and one student had done all the questions but couldn't do one. And neither could I. It looked to me like there were an infinite number of solutions since there is an infinite number of Pythagorean triples. I said I'd get back to him.

It turned out that it has to be a printing error in the exercise book as there is an infinite number of solutions. Only the kid who got full marks on an IQ test has ever noticed this.

DAY 53 (THURSDAY).

MARY WAS A CHILD.

It's pretty good, really, I get to do maths as my job. It's fun, but I don't feel like I'm doing anything with my life. I feel like the maths is a distraction from the fact that outside of the window of the classroom, the world is moving and changing and I'm not a part of it. As a teacher, I'm helping the next generation get out there and be part of it.

A random thought popped into my head. *How old was Mary when she supposedly had Jesus?*

Turns out she was between 12 and 14. *What the fuck?* I'm really struggling to understand this, this morning. She was a child. The mother to the saviour of the most prominent global religion was a child?

In Rich Dad, Poor Dad I read a piece about getting assets and it made me wonder about creating digital assets. So fuck off all the property wankers, what about YouTube property?

DAY 54 (FRIDAY).

MARCEL.

Nothing really happened today other than I got a pretty sweet checkmate against Marcel, even though I lost my Queen. Not sure I've ever said that I regard Marcel as the smartest person I've ever met. And I've met three Nobel Prize winners, each for different fields. What makes him so different is that he is both academically smart and socially smart. That's something rare. And he's into sport too. He's even a national kickboxing champion for under 18s. And he happens to be the only EAL student in the entire school. Übermensch comes to mind.

In the evening Fuchsia suggested we get an Indian takeaway. There was chicken in my veggie vindaloo. I got them to replace it but it disturbed me, I thought it was a lump of potato.

DAY 55 (SATURDAY).

EMAIL.

BAS emailed. They said no.

DAY 56 (SUNDAY).

SLEEP.

I slept.

DAY 57 (MONDAY).

GODMOTHER.

It's bank holiday Monday so I'm not at work. I popped in to see my parents and my dad was asking me about Fuchsia and the money. I tell him I don't want to talk about it but he still does, asking and annoying and irritating me. I leave and go for a walk but it feels meaningless and I end up driving the country lanes too fast, too bored. Dreaming about crashing, about wrapping my van around a tree.

I know I'm starting to lose my shit.

I pull over on the road to Maybeck. I like that place, I'm sure it will cheer me up. It doesn't.

I decide to go look at war graves and find my godmother's son. He died in Afghanistan at age 27. Blown up by an IED. The perspective helps a little and I start to cry.

The graveyard is near Audie's and I did ask if she wanted to join me for a walk. She didn't.

DAY 58 (TUESDAY).

EXAM CAGE.

I've woken up with something really smart to write down so I grabbed my phone and started to make a note in Notes. When it came to writing it, however, I've noticed that I've forgotten it. Either that or it never actually existed and all that existed was the thought of a good idea. I have a memory of it having something to do with time, me waiting for time or time waiting for me. I don't know. It's 25 minutes until my alarm goes off, I should really get up as I have a lot to get ready, but I can feel my eyelids rocking themselves open and closed as I try to fight being tired.

It was a grotesque morning but I somehow got to work and didn't even have a cigarette. I'll need one later, mind. In school the heating isn't on and it's really cold. I manage to ignore it and for some reason I feel productive so I put my tie and jacket on, do a COVID test and print out the exam papers for period one, all before the 8:30am staff briefing online. I don't recall what was said in the meeting, something about the Ofsted inspection from a few years back and that we should all stay calm whilst the visitors are in. *Like I give a shit.* Doc gets up as he's heard someone at the door. It's Piper and she says an elongated "Siiiir". I turn to her and ask "which sir?" but it's obviously me. She says "you" and explains she can't make it to our second period lesson. I say that's OK and we'll figure out another time when she can do that assessment and thank her for coming to let me know. Getting up to leave for Form, I hear Doc mention something about isolation, so I ask him what it was. Turns out that all study cover periods, where you are meant to sit in the breakout area helping sixth formers study in their free periods, are now covering the isolation room, watching the naughty kids be quiet. Great. I have a full day now.

In Form I decide to do the actual Form-time PowerPoint since it was so ridiculous. The theme of the week is "exams". There is some bullshit artwork on the slides to talk about and some stupid facts about exams, like stress levels are higher in exam periods and drinking water helps. *What a disgusting welcome back after the three-day weekend.* It bugged me that Cleo was in the classroom, pottering about whilst I was doing the theme of the week. The last time she was in a classroom with me was around March last year. Remembering this, I glared at her whilst feigning a smile.

She was observing my lesson that last time, as my induction tutor for my NQT year. To transition between training and being a full-time teacher, DfE require teachers to complete an NQT induction year to be able to teach in state schools. Despite training and gaining QTS years ago, my NQT year was delayed due to employment contract technicalities. Also, this isn't technically a state school, it's considered a free school, so it wasn't mandatory I had to do it. But to work anywhere else, I would have to complete it and so it makes sense to just get it done. When doing the NQT year you have a slightly reduced timetable so you can put evidence together to show you are a good teacher in the eyes of DfE and the Teachers' Standards, just like during the PGCE. The whole process is a little convoluted and in simple terms, at the end of the NQT year, your evidence is used in a final assessment where the school will make the recommendation to DfE that the NQT year has been successfully completed. As a member of SLT, Cleo was my induction tutor, which is someone who's supposed to help guide you through the year, giving you regular support and observations. Well, she didn't do that.

Instead of support and observations from Cleo, I had support and observations from Margie and various external maths education organisations who do this kind of thing as their main function. Throughout the year, everything was going great and I was getting great feedback. And then, at the end of the year, Cleo came to observe my lesson. Not only did she fail my lesson, she failed my lesson so badly that she said the school cannot recommend me to DfE to pass the NQT year. It was game over.

After the lesson when she told me this, I went straight outside and smoked a bifta. You see, if you fail your NQT induction year, it is essentially game over as a teacher. You can't retake the year and, although you still have QTS, you can no longer be legally employed as a teacher in any state school. I ran through my options of teaching, about quitting there and then so I could default out of the NQT year. I wouldn't pass, but at least I wouldn't fail. It would mean only teaching in none-state schools forever, and I started making a plan of applying to the independent school near Robin Hood's Bay. Thankfully Margie came along, striking thunder in her wake. She called out Cleo for her lack of involvement as the induction tutor and unrealistic observation feedback. I always thought Cleo was a bit of a charlatan, but all of this made me sure. And thankfully, I did pass the NQT year, getting a PDF certificate emailed to me a month later in a design that matched my QTS certificate.

So with Cleo hanging about like a stale fart, I couldn't really say what I thought during Form. It's kind of her classroom this one and we just use it for Form-time. I did express myself about the artwork, however, as it was on two different slides in two completely different aspect ratios. *In education, do they just stop giving a shit about this kind of stuff?* Egbert asked me about the money situation, and I explained why he shouldn't ask me. Basically, I'm trying to not think about it whilst we're waiting to see what the bank does. I tell them the story about my dad from yesterday and then we talk about the football protests, whatever they were.

On the way to the first lesson, Mathematical Engineering, I go to borrow a box of calculators from Doc's classroom. I know there will be some students who don't have calculators, despite them knowing I'm giving them the first of their TAG exams today. Even Doc knows they'll need all the help they can get. Whilst picking up the box, I hear a familiar "Siiiir" and I quickly glance the classroom and notice I'm the only teacher in there. *Why is Piper in this class?* She says she can now make period two to do the exam. *OK, this is good, but my back is seriously hurting today. Was it from being in bed too much at the weekend? Perhaps I'll need a wheelchair soon.* I can feel my mood slipping a lot.

Walking into my classroom, all the students are waiting at their desks already, and I immediately notice a table is missing. Then I take in the rest of the room and experience the dirty, disgusting state of it. Bam. My mood hit the bottom. I calmly flipped a table near me, explaining to the class that I can't deal with looking at the dirty stains all over it. One student starts to question the exam we are doing today.

"Why is it this long? Why are we doing three?"

Yap yap yap. Shut the fuck up. I ignore him mostly and explain that we are doing it this way because this is the best way of getting a pass for a class who have had a total of nine lessons this calendar year. I add that since it is an exam, I don't want to hear any noises from them otherwise I will give them a zero. Bam. Job done, now I can write an angry email.

```
From: DEAD
To: Monty; Quinn

Hi both,

I've flagged this before but it's becoming a bit of a joke now.
In a Friday enrichment, I don't know what CCF do but classroom
nine is again left in a disgusting state and I don't have time
to clean it. Not that I should have to anyway.

Today there is a table missing, coffee stains on most of the
others, rubbish on the floor and inappropriate drawings on the
whiteboard.

I would ask if we can make sure cleaners do this room on a
Friday, but really can we make sure CCF are not treating a
classroom like this. It's not right.

DEAD
```

I hope it changes something, it probably won't but at least I feel a little better.

I hear a student sniffing and worry if any of these students get sad because they can't answer any questions in the exam. *What is the point of this education system?* We put kids who are good, reliable people in bullshit situations that stress them out. It's good to feel stress in life, as it's part of life's learning curve, but it's not good to waste their time. Schools are so preoccupied with getting numbers in the classrooms that they seem to ignore what is best for the kids. The one who sniffed isn't the brightest in the room, but he is the most polite and has some really good suits. Plaid ones. I like talking to that kid. But it's the "bums on seats" situation, as most teachers call it. *What do I think that kid should be doing?* Training to be a joiner or a mechanic, or a chef, something where he can use practical skills. There's someone knocking on the door and I can't figure out who it is from where I sit, so I get up and see. It's Pudge, he apologises for being late and says he missed several buses. This is weird.

"Pudge, we don't have a lesson right now."

I hear people in the class laughing a little, so I remind them they are in exam conditions. Pudge looks confused, I wonder if he knows it's Tuesday and yesterday was a bank holiday. He scarpers and I go back to sit down. *Not long left on this exam.*

Throughout the day I've recorded one-second videos with the aim of piecing together some sort of a representation of a day in teaching. I only really get chance to film between lessons, though, and I'm starting to feel a little manic anyway. In period three I had to monitor the isolation room, now it's made its comeback. We stopped having it whilst COVID was rampant as it's a small room without windows. Now SLT don't care about that and have made a timetable for staff to be in the room with students, meaning what would have essentially been my one free period today is here in this small, cold room. There aren't even any students when I start my shift. Walker turns up after 15 minutes, he just got up and left his geography lesson. I don't blame him, with a teacher like Monty. As he walks to a desk I ask him if he needs to give me his phone. He says no, which I accept as an answer even though he's meant to hand it in. If he's sly about using it, I really don't mind. I'm going to be on my phone whilst marking anyway. When it comes to the end of the hour I ask him what he's done for the last 45 minutes.

"I've been reading." There is a geography textbook in front of him and I hope he hasn't been wasting his time with that.

"But on your phone, yeh?"

"Yeh," he confirms.

He says he's sick of being here and doesn't see the point of it anymore. I tell him I agree and that I'm in the exact same position, to which he asks if I'm leaving. I look at him and silently nod. He asks the usual question of what am I going to do afterwards, and do I not like teaching. The point that people struggle to get is that I don't dislike teaching, I just don't like it enough. I ask what he wants to do and he says about going to a college to learn to do joinery. I sympathise with him, saying how I would love to do something like that, something where I'm busy using my hands and can be outside if I need to be. We are both on the same page here, in the thought that being here is like being in a cage.

Even though I've been popping pills, my back hasn't stopped hurting. I go outside and smoke a bifta at lunch and lie on the dry, warm pavement.

Period five was amusing, I started to teach when I heard a knock at the door. In a moment I looked, recognised and understood. It was Stitches from the year 10 Nomad class, I'd forgotten to set work for them. It's one of those fucked up periods where I'm meant to be teaching two classes at the same time.

DAY 59 (WEDNESDAY).

NO FREES AGAIN.

I keep thinking about self-harm, suicide and just running; packing a bag and leaving. Maybe I should stop drinking and doing drugs because the thought seems to happen more afterwards. But I feel like it is brought on by work, by being locked away in the days after feeling so free. It's been good to feel slightly active again, though, and I wonder if I'll have that when I'm not teaching, when I don't have to do anything. That will be a problem of self-motivation.

I'm getting ahead of myself, I need to focus on not walking out right now with a bag on my back and a map in my pocket. Things at home are strained again but I don't think Fuchsia knows it. It goes with that feeling of being stifled. Last night I edited my video together and posted it to Instagram. When I try to be active with my own hobbies and interests, I hardly see Fuchsia as a result and she doesn't like it. She doesn't say but she doesn't need to, I can tell. Perhaps it's just because she was unwell and needed a bit of support, but I needed to be alone. Maybe I wish I was alone and not in a relationship. I'll need to talk to her about that feeling before I end up ripping the plaster off. My disregard for my life is reminiscent of when I ended my last relationship, it's very concerning. I'm listening to Michael Nyman to calm me a little. He did the soundtrack to GATTACA, and that's one of my favourite films. I like the dystopian future vibes and that Vincent achieves his dreams, despite the destiny his DNA and society gave him.

I smoke my bifta on the walk from the bus stop.

Period one is an A-Level Further Maths lesson and I actually enjoyed it, but I don't know if the students did. I liked what I was teaching and think that the method of differences for finding the sum of a series is nice. It's useful. It's thought-provoking. It's simple, yet challenging. Marty described it as tedious, which I liked because he usually says the work is easy and this is his way of saying it isn't. Pudge was asking some really good questions too, he was getting the hang of it. I think I taught it fairly well. Going from that period one into the isolation room for period two was a bit of a downer. Again it was cold, didn't even get any students and the chair made my back ache. It's a free period that I've just fucking lost for no reason. I wasn't able to work as I didn't have any work to mark with me and was not in the mood to make something productive on my laptop. Instead, I sat and looked at rings and kimonos I'd like to wear. It sounds like a free period, but it's not the same.

In the afternoon I ended up covering a Computer Science lesson as Cleo was ill today. This meant I genuinely had no frees at all today.

* * *

The money is back!

DAY 60 (THURSDAY).

DOING TAGS.

I woke up in a positive mood, I had had a nice, stress-free dream for the first time in ages. I was exploring somewhere in the UK and found an old concrete road bridge that was huge. It was pretty well decayed, as if it was in some dystopian future film, and the surroundings were green as far as my eye could see. Some people were walking nearby on what looked like a well-trodden path that went beneath the bridge. It was a dusty brown track in the middle of the gorgeously green grass. I was viewing from the perspective as if I was a drone flying around looking at the bridge and the landscape. And then I wasn't the drone, I was on the drone. It was a drone the size of a dining table, with two seats on it. I was in one seat and someone, I don't know who it was but it was someone I was with, was in the other. The pilot was on the ground and we didn't know them, but we were putting our trust in them. They started to fly faster and faster towards some high trees, swooping us through the branches unharmed but thrilled. My stomach was in my heart. I was scared and excited, it felt like being on a roller coaster. We dived, we looped, we skimmed the ground and shot to the clouds. And that was how the dream ended. I woke with back pain but a smile on my face.

The bus ride was strange. I didn't read, sleep or listen to music. I just sat and I remember nothing else of it. Yesterday I had planned to get off the bus this morning and buy alcohol from the supermarket and drink it whilst at work today. But I completely forgot, just buying some cheap dental floss and a CBD drink. Ben Howard was playing in my ears and I realised how much I've been listening to indie folk this last week. The last time I did that so much was when I ended my last relationship. *Fuck*. I had a cigarette and went into school. I don't want to end this relationship, I know I'm just getting swept up in self-destruction and a changing direction.

In the maths office the floss frayed and got stuck in my teeth. I had to get a pair of scissors to free it, and the rest of the roll went in the bin.

My Form were pleased when I told them that Fuchsia got the money back. They really were pleased, it was nice. We started talking about cars and vans a little bit and I mentioned that I'd like to spray my van pink, it's so rusty right now. Chai came over and showed me a video of her friend who has a racing bike. It's actually the dragster kind of racing bike and has a big anti-wheelie bar out the back of it. Her friend wants to spray it pink. Alice comes in and explains to the students that we have visitors in and they might come into the student's lessons. It's just a little warning but it comes across so seriously, I don't know why the students even need to be told. The students are always suspicious of this kind of behaviour and some even speculate that the school is being bought out, which it's not. SLT just want to merge with another academy trust. When Alice is gone, I tell my Maths students that I'll explain more about the visitors in first period.

Bianca wants to do a quiz so I pull up one from the Cosmopolitan website and we squeeze in 20 questions. I don't think they really liked the quiz, it was kind of dumb, but we did it anyway.

In the first period I explained that if we get the visitors this lesson whilst they are doing the TAG exam, then they need to make sure they are in strict exam conditions. I then position the whiteboard in front of the door, so if someone came in, it would be a few seconds until they see the students. Halfway into the exam I notice Monty walk past the door, looking at me through the glass, but he couldn't see the students. He then bursts through the door and marches straight towards me. *Fuck, he did that quick.* Out of the corner of my eye, I saw all the students quickly rearrange their desks. It's obvious they have just shit themselves and hid anything that shouldn't be on their desk during an exam. As it turns out, Monty's doing a TAG exam with some GCSE kids next door and wanted some help with one of the maths questions they're doing. *Is anyone doing these TAGs properly?* I make a note of the question and tell him I'll pop in in a second. It wasn't a difficult question, I just couldn't do it with Monty leaning over me, breathing into my ear. All those numbers describing sweets and flavours and ratios were meaningless with him there, sounding like Darth Vader. When I go into his class I put the piece of paper with the workings out on his desk face down. A student looks at me and asks if I've done it. In all honesty, I was a little shocked by the abruptness of the question and just replied with "I don't know what you're talking about". They should really be a little more subtle. Back in my classroom a few minutes later, Monty walks in again saying that I'm clever and that I should consider being a maths teacher. Then he picks up the pencil I stole from him when he came in first time and left again. I wanted that pencil.

Before they started the exam I went to get some water for the students from the staff kitchen, meaning I had to walk through the management suite. As my hand went for the handle, I clocked one of the school visitors through the glass in the door: a Vice-Principal of a local school was sat in there and she clocked me back. I recognise her because we got into an argument two years ago when I was at an NQT meeting at her school. She was giving a presentation on how to give a presentation to SEN students and was ignoring all her own rules in that very presentation. And it wasn't on purpose. There were different colours and sizes of font, over lapping text and images, poor resolution images, images with wrong aspect ratios. It's like she played bingo with what not to do and got a full house. I made a point that she had no right to assume that an adult doesn't have an SEN.

She didn't like my point and we got into a heated argument because she refused to be corrected by some little pleb like me. I really hope she doesn't come into my lesson, given the look she just gave me, she clearly still doesn't like me either.

* * *

All day the rain has been coming down heavily. It's like rain, hail and snow all mixed into one. In period four it's Mathematical Engineering and everyone in the class, including me, was sat staring at the windows like we were toddlers watching the Teletubbies. It was a shared feeling of awe, so maybe more like toddlers looking at something fucking awesome, I don't know what toddlers think. But we all had that dumb look on our faces. The students in this class have one lesson left with me after this exam they're doing. No point in keeping coming to lessons when you've done the exam, and we all agree that we're fucking sick of this course and the pandemic has done us a favour. There is so much to learn in so little time that this Engineering unit is an absolute joke. Mathematical Engineering is just a mandatory module in a wider Level 3 Engineering qualification. The exam board expect students to be able to learn a syllabus which is like a watered-down A-Level Maths, but in 60 hours of lessons. For this school that works out to be three lessons per fortnight for only one year to get students who scraped their GCSE Maths capable of doing calculus. Impossible. Half of the kids in here can barely expand brackets. This is actually the course that I was teaching to Billy, the kid who gets on the bus. Thanks to the pandemic, he passed the module and got the full Engineering qualification. When I marked one of his exams last year I was surprised to see he found the right answer on a basic algebra question and so I asked him about it. He said he did trial and error. He looked pleased. I was gutted. Trial and error isn't the most useful of skills for an engineer. It's the kind of shit that gets people killed.

Since it's Thursday the students have gone home at lunch again and we're all working on TAGs this afternoon instead of CPD. Margie will submit the TAGs to the exam boards, and they submit them to the government. I think that's what happens, SLT haven't really been that clear. My concern is that the exam board are expected to randomly ask for copies of the student's TAG exams for moderation. I really don't want that to happen to mine, it could cock-up everything. Unfortunately for me, in this morning's meeting, where I didn't pay attention as usual, they said that the internet is off this afternoon. So I sit down to mark some exams and find that I'm going to have to do the exam myself before I can mark any, as I don't have a mark scheme. It's not hard, but it's more time and effort than I'd prefer to do. After marking half of the tests, Quinn comes in and mentions how the internet isn't off. Turns out there was an email earlier saying the internet isn't down. But why would we be checking our emails if we thought the internet was down? What a fucking joke. Another example of shite communication.

Me, Doc and Margie just got on with marking, having what teachers like to call a "marking party". I had to put in my headphones, though, because I couldn't concentrate with their music and talking, and I kept adding up marks wrong or losing count. I opt for something mundane to drown them out.

* * *

What would it feel like to get a Stihl saw and press the disc into your skin? Will the rotation catch on the skin and flick away or will it dig into the bone? I kind of want to try. I can imagine doing it and feeling it cut hard. I think it would be OK.

Me and Fuchsia went to the gym together for the first time in over six months. It felt weird, like I didn't know what to do. It was fairly busy with the bro-club on the weights, all grunting and groaning and hogging the equipment. I chose to start on the treadmill, taking a while to re-familiarise myself with my pace. I ended by running at a four-minute pace for a kilometre. I was pleased, but I still felt weird.

DAY 61 (FRIDAY).

CHANGES.

I slept like a log and didn't want to get up at my alarm, although I did get up in back pain and took painkillers in the night. Running late I decided to not have breakfast and made a peanut butter sandwich to have on the bus. At the bus stop, I realised my breakfast was still in the kitchen. I'd fucked up already. And then by some grace of god, the bus passes me from the left meaning it's running late. At that, I'm running down the hill back home to get my sarnie, and then back to the stop.

I'm out of breath, it feels awful. *Why can't I run like this?* Maybe I should stop smoking, but I'm on the bus now eating my peanut butter sarnie reading Rich Dad, Poor Dad. The sun is shining strong and it's not so cold. I even take my jacket off.

I get tired of saying "morning" to all the students in the morning. Everyone I pass seems to say it this morning. Morning. Morning. Morning. Morning. MORNING. MOOOORRRNINGGGG!!!

Spike sent a video to the Group Chat whilst I was sat in assembly and I watched it. It was a guy putting a vacuum on his dick. I laughed nervously. *Why the fuck am I watching this?* The assembly was actually quite good, Frank sat on a chair at the front and told a story about why he came to work at the school and about his first experience at a specialist school like this. The first he ever went to was the same as the one I first went to, in Liverpool. I went there whilst working at the Royal Society and it was amazing, all I thought was that this is what schools should be like. They let me onto the roof when showing me around and you could see the iconic Liverpool skyline and the old cathedral right near the school. That was the first time I had been back to Liverpool since my spectacular departure after my first year of university. Spectacular because it was my first real episode of depression, but I didn't know it at the time. I packed my things and just left. Didn't even tell my friends.

*　*　*

I'm overseeing the kids in isolation and, instead of silent working, we're all sat having a debate about whether water has taste.

I keep getting flashbacks from the weekend and remembering something new. This time it was picking up Hopper, who's more than 20 stone and trying to squat him. I fell over and he flattened me. I'm such a dickhead, this is why my nose has been hurting on the bridge all week.

I found a job to apply for and I've started filling out the application form. The job's pretty good, it's 0.6 of full time, decent pay, working from home, still doing maths education but from the side of teacher training, supporting schools and teachers. It's a little like what I did at the Royal Society but specifically for maths. The problem is that I don't know if I want a job. I'm pretty sure I don't and I don't want to compromise the plan, but if I run out of money, then the plan is also compromised. I'll apply and do a decent application and see what happens. Realistically I need to think that there is no shame in doing the job for a few months and realising it isn't for me. I can quit and that would be OK.

* * *

Since chess club has now merged, I'm sat with Julia in book club. Stitches comes over to talk at us. I ignore him as I've got the marking to do, but Julia stops what she is doing and listens to him. She starts to make me laugh from the looks of desperation she flashes me. Another student notices and tries to save her by asking if Stitches wants to play chess. I'm still laughing at Julia, it made me lose count of my marks and oddly attracted to her.

DAY 62 (SATURDAY).

PIERCING.

Went to Middlesbrough. Got pierced. I'd been wanting this for about ten years and figured now is the time.

It felt so uncomfortable to have a needle go through my bellend but not necessarily painful. I was proper scared, but it was OK. I finally have a Prince Albert after all these years. Albeit wrapped up in handfuls of bloody tissue.

On the way back to the van we saw a huge new charity shop that had opened and we poked about at books in it. Some old woman was having a conversation with the cashier and didn't realise how hilarious she was being.

"All I have is coke… coke, coke, coke, that's all I have… can't go a single day without coke…"

I was losing my fucking shit and so was Fuchsia. I assume she was talking about Coca-Cola, but we could never be sure. I found the Ladybird Book of the Mid-Life Crisis in really good condition and decided I wanted it and a Foo Fighters Greatest Hits CD. That's the album which Wheels was released on and I love the dreamlike harmonics. At the till Fuchsia got a message from Audie, saying she wants to break-up with Al and is going to tell him to move out tonight. *Fuck, I'd not heard from Audie in a while, is she screwing up inside?*

After getting lunch at Nando's I finally braved going for my first sit-down piss. It was traumatic, there was blood everywhere.

On the way home we popped in for dinner at Fuchsia's friend's house and I mentioned my new piercing. Becky and Benjamin didn't seem too impressed, which disappointed Fuchsia a little bit. When I went for a piss, since it was taking 15 minutes, I decided to message Audie and tell her about my new piercing. She wanted a photo, so I sent her one. She said she liked it.

DAY 63 (SUNDAY).

LAST WEEKEND.

I saw an article that came out on the Guardian website today: "We're all marking late at night: teachers on England's new grading system". I didn't have the patience to read it properly, but got the overall vibe. TAGs are expected to be better for the students but not for teachers. *This, I know*.

After last weekend, I decided to stay in today.

Speaking of which, last weekend, here's what happened on the Saturday. Audie and chums came around to ours and we played cards and drank outside. Spike was around too and it was awkward as fuck, I'd not seen him since I messaged him about choking Audie. When we all decided to leave and go up to Audie's, Spike revealed he was leaving altogether and we hugged it out. Was still fucking awkward. We walked along the Cinder Track, Audie was wearing a black North Face hiking outfit: black North Face tights, black North Face t-shirt, black North Face beanie, with a black North Face shoulder bag, and some walking boots. She looked good in it.

It was a long evening from there on. Once we got to Audie's the sun was still shining so we decided to go to the Brewery. I ran there so everyone else could fit in a taxi. We drank loads, met with Hopper and his friend then went back to Audie's and took a load of coke. I was so drunk it was ridiculous, but the coke kept me being able to function so I was just doing ridiculous things, such as trying to squat Hopper. He came with me to the toilet when I said I needed a shite, I don't know why, and he ended up being sick. A bit over the top but I did say I needed a shite. Everyone started to leave or go to bed and it ended up being just a few of us chatting and listening to music, with me and Audie touching each other under a blanket whilst we sat on the sofa. At the time it felt good, but the memory is a bit cringe now. We kept drinking into the next day and I told Fuchsia that, unlike the last time where I left and ended up ruining my jean shorts with blood, I wasn't leaving until she decided it was our time to leave.

Eventually, we did go home and I slept the rest of the day.

This Sunday, however, the only constructive thing I did was make some more of my clothes.

DAY 64 (MONDAY).

APOLOGY TO THE PAST.

Woke up at 2am in breath-taking pain from my back. I tried adjusting my position several times in bed but it was no good. I got up, took painkillers, had a piss and went back to bed. But I can't sleep, the pain is still there. Why is it so bad, I have no idea. I'm good to my back, although maybe I don't drink enough water. *Fuck this shit, I need to get up and stand under the hot shower.*

I don't know how long I was there, perhaps 30 minutes, maybe a full hour. But I eventually started to feel better, and wide awake. I get an alert on my phone that the ISS flyover is in 30 minutes so I start to get my camera and clothes ready to go out for a walk. I imagine the police stopping me if they see me. I wouldn't blame them, someone walking around at 3am in jogging trousers, hood pulled up and a big bag. I look out the window and realised I may as well stay in. There's not a single star visible right now. Complete cloud cover.

* * *

"I think he was dead. I couldn't see he was breathing. But I've got a lot of marking to do so someone else can clean that up... did you see my onions?"

This was Monty's reply when I asked him about my message this morning. On the bus, coming up the hill out of Robin Hood's Bay, I saw a man lying on a bench, not moving. It was a cold morning and I was concerned about him, so messaged Monty and asked to check on him on his drive-in. He'd only have needed to pull over, prod him, and see if he moved. Instead, he just looked at the man out his car window, decided he didn't know and kept going. He's got marking to do after all, but he was interested to know if I saw his onions in his allotment next to where the man was lying, potentially dead.

I don't have my watch on today, it's really annoying to not be able to see what time it is at the flick of my wrist. *How else can I sit and watch time tick down?*

Speaking of down, the internet is down today.

I am so bored. So bored I'm even messaging my mum. It's always hard work though. I'm impressed that she can use her phone, she was so reluctant at first but now she WhatsApps me, buys from the internet, all sorts. But she still can't fucking use grammar, it's like trying to decipher verbal diarrhoea. Here is the last message I got from her on Saturday:

```
[10:47] Mother: Hello thank you for the money I have the
500bill for electric on Wednesday I didn't ask dad to put in
yours he forgot are you out for ride out nice day are you off
Monday given heavy rain Monday just been tili OK brother's like
a jungle dad getting the lawn mower from your sister's to cut
next week
```

I don't know what "tili" is, nor the rest of the message. So I replied by commenting on today's weather. It's fresh.

* * *

"We're going to learn how drugs were discovered." *Fuck me, Bertha's lesson sounds good.*

"Some drugs are illegal because they are too harmful. Each of the drugs below say if they are medical, recreational or illegal."

I want to sit in this lesson and write it all down like a shopping list. *Not long until it's mushroom time now.*

I overhear all sorts when I'm in this isolation room and have the door open. One thing I hear that really fucks me off is when teachers call other teachers "Miss" or "Sir". God, it's fucking gross. It's like when parents call each other "Mum" or "Dad". What an ultimate cringe. *Just use my fucking name.* I like it when staff say my name in front of the students, it normalises us as people. Most of my students call me by my first name, anyway. There are some who still don't, as if they think it is taboo or they aren't part of the crowd who are allowed to.

The science technician is talking to a cleaner. What a fucking berk the technician is, he doesn't stop talking and it's just shite what he says.

The internet is back on. I can stop rinsing my mobile data now.

*   *   *

I tucked my shirt in and knocked the end of my dick. It hurt. It bled.

It's been a really fucking tiring day. Doing all these TAGs is exhausting as I'm on constant watch and support, trying to cram in as much information into the students, trying to keep them focused and motivated.

Taking an emergency pee and blood cleanup, I had to get the later bus. My penis is wrapped in so much tissue it's like it's been mummified.

On the bus home I decide to message Audie. We did message at lunch briefly, when I felt like I wanted a return for sending her the photo of my dick on Saturday. I simply messaged "show me your boobs". She replied with a photo showing from her chest to her lips. It looked as if she had just gotten out the bath, with her hair wet and a towel draped over her. I was nice but I wanted something explicit. I felt disappointed as if it wasn't a fair trade, and also that she didn't take the photo for me. I wanted something that felt impulsive, taken at work now. She did look nice though.

So that was at lunch and now, on the bus, I decide to send a message to put it on the record that we are to just be friends. To make it clear now that we shouldn't ever go any further. But I don't. I know I don't want to say it. Although I believe it, I just don't want to say it, so I ask her about her day instead. Her answers are short and to the point. She's a little cold, really. I get concerned that she's not OK and I tell her this.

> [17:36] DEAD: Is there anything I can do to help at the moment? You seem not OK, I'm concerned about you.
>
> [17:37]: Audie: Erm. I'm OK…

Shit, the penny might have just dropped that I'm inventing this. Inventing it like I do with Fuchsia. I'm inventing that she is not OK, when really it's me that isn't.

Fuck. That's much worse.

I message back and apologise for what happened between us and she ignores it.

Fuck. What am I doing?

As the bus lulls into Whitby I play a game of fate. If it pulls over at the next stop, I'm getting off and walking the rest of the way home. My back is starting to ache and the walk might help.

It pulls over and I get off, walk over the big bridge and take a photo of the river and woods below. It's nice. I don't have my jacket on and the wind is blowing my hair about.

By the time I'm home, my back feels like my muscles are bubbling in pain under my skin. They scream and spasm and I strip naked, and lean on the radiator, warming my back. I talk to Fuchsia, but about nothing particular and take some painkillers. She goes upstairs to the toilet and I decide to unwrap my dick to air it. The tissue is bright red and damp, falling apart in my hands. As I put scraps of the deep red tissue on the table, the wooden surface goes red. Blobs of blood start to collect on the end of my dick and on the new ring that threads it. I cup myself to catch the blood and shout up to Fuchsia to get me more tissue. She didn't hear. I ask again, with a little more urgency in my voice.

It took about ten minutes of lying down on the sofa with my hands cupping my tissue-wrapped dick for the bleeding to stop. Apparently this is normal for this kind of piercing. My back is now hurting more so I go back to the radiator, rubbing my back with a towel like it's some scratching massage. The painkillers still haven't done anything and I crouch on the floor, my arms wrapped around my knees.

As the pain started to simmer back down, my brain scrambled back to the penny that dropped on the bus. I don't know how the conversation started, it got underway so quickly, I think I apologised to Fuchsia for being "not very good at the moment". She knew what I meant, which was in a broad sense of boyfriend, person to be around, person in general. As we spoke, words poured from my mouth, swept along by a current of emotional confusion that's been living in my head rent-free.

We spoke for a long time, I felt like shit for feeling so different to what I did in my 20s. For having different morals and seeing that 20-year-old me as a different person. I felt bad for him. Apologetic.

I went upstairs and cut my hair because I wanted to feel like a different person. Fuchsia corrected me that it's feeling like a different version of me. She's right. She's incredibly emotionally smart.

DAY 65 (TUESDAY).

A BANANA.

I sleep with my dick wrapped in tissue and my boxers on. Still, blood had seeped through and marked the bed sheets. It was the damp blood that woke me. But I slept really well and was relieved to have not gotten up with back ache in the night. When my alarm went off moments later at 5:30am, the room was already bright and I got out of bed without pressing snooze, going straight into the shower. There was plenty of time to get ready, but my body moved slowly and I had so little appetite I only took a banana for lunch.

* * *

The internet is off again.

DAY 66 (WEDNESDAY).

GETTING SUPPLIES.

Since it's Wednesday I send my "Happy Wednesday" message to the Group Chat. I do this every Wednesday like something between a tradition, obsession and grasp for attention. The image with today's Happy Wednesday was the camel from Camel Cigarettes, sat smoking in a swimming pool in Hollywood. The reference is hump day. On the bus, I go for the other Wednesday tradition and roll a bifta. The tobacco I have left is pretty much just dust and when the bus went over a bump, it all flicked out of the paper onto my jacket and the floor.

It was a gorgeous walk-in and I smiled without effort. The sun was shining through the trees, at a height just above the Valley Bridge from my perspective. The grass was an apple green, perhaps so bright from all the rain we've had recently. It is nice to not see it raining, even though rain is still forecast for the next two weeks. I stand and listen to the birds, I don't know what they are but it sounds good.

With the internet still being off, we had an in-person staff briefing in the hall, which we haven't done for almost a year. I sit there, I'm not really listening, my legs stretched out in front of me. Apparently the visitors were very impressed with what they saw when they came in, which I was pleased about. The other schools in the area have undeserved opinions of our school, just because when it first opened all the other schools sent their shite kids here. So at first there was a lot of struggling and management systems that needed working out. For example, when I started here there was no detention system or isolation room – Leopold said he wanted teachers to "grasp the nettle with both hands" but thankfully us teachers agreed that we didn't and a teacher-signed petition went to SLT asking for change. Now it's going fairly well and I seriously doubt the other schools in the area are as good as this one. That's not to say this one is perfect. A big talking point among staff this past week is how tight the school is financially, although it's got about half a million pounds worth of engineering equipment sat doing nothing but taking up space in the workshops. I'm talking milling machines and lathes, laser cutters and pillar drills, welders and a forge, and all these things I couldn't tell you what they did. It's all very impressive, but not really relevant to a student's education.

*   *   *

"Form is wank now." We're playing hangman and Egbert is bored.

"I know, Egbert. We all know." Honesty was my only answer.

*   *   *

In isolation I was talking to Benedict, a year 11 student, about education and how we both agree that you learn a lot of pointless stuff and they should learn useful skills instead. It's never going to be right though. He would like to learn to lay bricks, but you know that someone else, like one of the nerds, would hate to do that and would want to do something with computers. You can't get it right for everyone, but there must be something we can do better. The education system is so arcane, it's disgusting.

In the Group Chat, Spike says he has some pills which we can take at the weekend. I can't recall if he knows they are ecstasy or just thinks they are. The funny part is how he bought them. He said he was in his car in Middlesbrough when some lad on a bicycle came up to his window and asked him what he wanted, so he asked what the lad had to offer. He had some pills. *Fucking hell, I need to go to Boro.*

Me and Fuchsia want to get some more drugs in and we're thinking about getting a stash of coke for ourselves. So I ended my day messaging people, trying to get some drugs for the weekend and trying to buy some from the internet. My bank blocked the purchase, thinking it was fraudulent. Fuchsia said hers worked, which concerned me because of the recent actual fraud. Anyway, £100 for three grams. I'm happy with that. She owes me rent so I tell her to take it off of that.

DAY 67 (THURSDAY).

CONVERSE.

I've woken up before my alarm again. I'm wide awake so I get up. Whilst in the shower my alarm goes off and I have to press my wet hands against my phone to silence it. I had so much more time to get ready that I just went slow and ended up not really having any more time than usual. But eating my breakfast was hard work, I just had no appetite and was pretty much forcing it into my mouth. *No appetite again, fuck sake.* I don't take any lunch but decide to go to the shop from the bus and buy something.

One extra good thing this morning is that I'm not hungover. *Kind of want to fuck though.* If it wasn't for my Prince Albert, I definitely would have had to do something about it.

Walking around the supermarket I'm listening to Antemasque's one album from 2014. This band is a supergroup formed by, most importantly, the guy from The Mars Volta. I can't remember how I found out about them, but got sucked into their music straight away. They did some gigs around London when I was living there and I tweeted about them, saying how I was going to go by myself. This was at a time when I was still with my ex-girlfriend, who didn't do gigs, and I didn't do gigs by myself yet. The band's account liked my tweet and followed me. I felt pretty fucking special, they didn't follow many people and I was one of the chosen ones. I had some good followers on that Twitter account, but don't use it anymore for fear of getting unfollowed and so I made a new one.

*   *   *

I can't deal with this shit right now. Had a conversation in lesson with Tammy about her wearing Converse. *Really can't be arsed with this, I want to walk out. I feel like smashing things.*

I went out for a cigarette and wanted to kick over all the motorbikes as I went. I avoided the students, I don't want to look at them.

In the next lesson I have past papers for them to complete, so I can sit in silence and try to calm down. My back has started hurting again, I wonder if it is stress-related. I spoke a little bit about leaving a cardboard cutout of me for my class when I leave. I started talking about that because Monty walked in and looked about the room saying he wants to redecorate it for CCF. I said he should get cardboard cutouts of himself for each of the walls. *Or was it a student who said that?* Anyway, I told the class that I might leave a cutout of me and they replied by saying they'll use it to summon me back when they get a teacher who isn't as good as me. I said I've set the bar pretty low, so it's OK. Then Nate asked if there was a way to still contact me, and I explain how I've told Margie that I'm happy to do free tutoring for them. They seem pleased at that.

The thing is that I really think that I'm a crap teacher and I've failed them, but I'm wondering what their take on this is. They seem to enjoy my lessons and think I'm a good teacher, but I know that recently I've given up completely. I just can't do it and I think it's for the best for me to leave as soon as possible. I know I want to make it to the end of the academic year, to have finished a full term and to get the money, but I can't cope right now. God, my back is aching.

Benedict said something good in isolation today, about student-teacher interactions. He said "talk to them in a way you want them to act".

DAY 68 (FRIDAY).

BLAND PORRIDGE.

Woke up at 4am with my back again. I went and showered, rubbing a spiky massage ball on my back. It didn't really help, but I was desperate to get rid of the pain without pills. After an hour, nothing was better so I popped some ibuprofen and got my bag ready. Still having no appetite I made some porridge in the hope that something nice for breakfast would help. Pouring maple syrup on, I think there must have been mould in the jar as my porridge was coated in what only looked like mould. Maybe it was a layer of sugar, I don't know, but I didn't want to eat it so I scraped it off the top of the porridge and rinsed it down the drain. After one spoonful of the bland porridge I looked at the bowl and immediately scraped the rest into the bin, picked up my bag and went for a long walk to get the bus from a different stop.

* * *

Fell asleep on the bus and hooked my foot around my bag.

Had school photos in the hall.

Couldn't buy drum kit for Fuchsia. Bank card has been blocked.

Apologised to Tammy.

The year 13s have actually done well in their TAGs.

DAY 69 (SATURDAY).

EMPTY.

Empty.

DAY 70 (SUNDAY).

EMPTY.

Empty.

DAY 71 (MONDAY).

FUCKED TIMETABLE.

This is a Monday. *What happened over the weekend?* It's a bit of a blur, I just slept. Right now I've just got off the bus but I've left my headphones on it. I saw them through the window as it drove past, I'll have to walk to the bus station to get them.

*   *   *

It was a full day teaching, with isolation cover.

The timetable is so fucked that no one came to cover me in the isolation room at lunch. I sent an email to all staff describing the fucked timetable and how I've got zero breaks today because of it, then walked out to the balcony and shouted down to the staff table in the canteen below. Monty came up and watched the room for 15 minutes whilst I scoffed some rice and salad and had a smoke.

When I got home I was flicking my tongue into Fuchsia within ten minutes of walking through the door. She came loud.

We had tea and went for a long walk around town.

DAY 72 (TUESDAY).

DECAPITATED.

Apparently Bertha was moaning about not being able to go to the toilet yesterday because she had a six lesson day. Margie didn't understand it and neither did I. If I need the toilet in lesson, I go to the toilet. I'll get someone to cover if needed or just go. Doc said he's done several number ones and a number two today already.

*   *   *

I took out a Double Dip as an end-of-day treat but the dipping stick was snapped. I poured the sherbet substance straight into my mouth, I used to do that as a child. Turns out it's not the same as an adult. I coughed, spraying powder across my desk and instantly felt like my teeth were rotting. This was no alternative to a fag so I grabbed my stuff and fucked off, rolling up as I walked for the bus.

On the way back there was some cunt at the front of the bus, looking like he was in his 50s. A kind of nondescript man in a grey t-shirt, wearing AirPods. He keeps turning around, looking about the bus. *What a fucking arsehole.* When I got on, the bus was almost full and I had to sit on the top deck right behind someone. It was disgusting being so near someone. And then it stank like someone died, I thought I was going to be sick. Someone else got off and I was able to move seats, further away. Being at the top means I get more sensation of the bus toppling over and I imagine it. I wish it. Maybe the train to Manchester will derail in a few weeks. What if Fuchsia got decapitated in the crash? That would be pure trauma. I'd hold her head and lay her down with my jacket over her. *Would I get my job again? Maybe I'd have lost an arm or a leg too. Would I move away? Maybe I'd just fuck off and not tell anyone.* Would need to get a new home for my snake, though. My nephew could look after it, but that would mean having to tell them I'm fucking off. Maybe my ex-girlfriend would, she liked snakes, but that would mean talking to her. *I'm thinking about this too much.*

DAY 73 (WEDNESDAY).

COLDPLAY.

My only memory of the daytime was at lunch when I heard Monty shout at a student "tuck your shirt in, you scruffy little oik".

In the evening me and Fuchsia went to a pub. I was tweaked and I don't know why. God, I was in an awful mood. The woman serving tables at the Black Horse was acting like an irritated mother. Whilst we waited outside for her to clear a table, since it's table service only, I crouched on the floor and vocalised that she was pissing me off. I wanted to go but Fuchsia didn't want to, she could see through me. When we got to our table, the seats were still damp from the disinfectant spray and Fuchsia got a piece of tissue to dry it. The woman explained it was already clean and I nearly shouted at her, if only Fuchsia didn't ask what I wanted. I knew I was getting a Guinness, Fuchsia looked through the gin menu, commenting on the different flavours. The woman cluttered and banged around us, spraying tables, moving chairs. The entire room smelled like a disinfectant advert. Clinical, like a mix between a hospital and an old people's home. At least it's better than the Abbey Wharf which we went in for a moment before coming here. That place had plastic sheets hanging all over, it was like walking into that scene from ET where the government have taken over the house. Fuchsia ordered and encouraged me to go have a smoke outside by myself. It seemed to help because I came back in a better mood, apologetic.

We only stayed for one and decided to go up to the Brewery to see what was going on with the event up there. There were messages on Facebook in the day saying there will be fireworks so pets should be made aware, although I didn't tell my snake. A few of our friends were working at the Brewery that night, so it turned out quite well. Spike was serving tables, took our drink order and said that's £8. We just stared at him like children waiting for someone else, a grown-up, to talk for us. Thankfully Hopper explained that we didn't pay, and that was the start. Coldplay were performing in the Abbey grounds and, although we could barely hear them, they had loads of fireworks and lighting which made it fun to watch from behind the wall. We stayed for hours drinking free beer, topping it up ourselves and smoking like the industrial age. There was a lot of people stood on the road listening to Coldplay, but they were all too tight to come into the Brewery. I started getting slightly drunk. Slightly lairy. I don't think I was really even that drunk, just having a fucking good time, living on that natural dopamine of being around good company. Viva la Vida and all that.

As it started to thin out, my thoughts started to come back in and I thought about the Group Chat and how I think it's total shite, full of dicks. Since I didn't do the Happy Wednesday message today I decided to take a photo of my dick in the toilets and send it to the Group Chat with the caption "Happy Wednesday". I don't really know why, but I like the look of my cock at the moment and have been feeling a nihilistic mania creeping in for the past week. No one really replies to the message, what was I expecting them to say? *Ha! The fucking dicks.*

Me, Fuchsia, and Spike walked back to town with beers in our hands, all heading the same direction. On our round about route home, we walked passed Spike's house and ended up going in and smoking weed in his attic room, listening to music, chatting shit. Well, I mostly just drank and smoked whilst stroking that fluffy dog they have. No idea what breed it is, but it's big and fluffy. Their house is a bit dirty, though, like it needs a good clean-out. Between that dog and their three cats, there is fluff and fur everywhere. It's also cluttered with all sorts. Stacks of books, random tools, motorbike parts, musical instruments, clothes, ashtrays... A few plants are on the window sills and they actually look healthy and well watered. One is a bonsai tree, Spike says he doesn't know what type it is and I tell him it's a Chinese elm. A fact I know because I was going to sell bonsai trees after finishing university, but was too broke to buy stock. He looks like he doesn't believe me but I don't care and continue stroking the dog.

Stella was in bed whilst we were there and she came up to ask us to turn the music down, had a fag and then fucked off back to bed. It was surreal, like a scene out of a film. I couldn't wake up, have a moan and a fag and then go back to bed. She says she's up early in the morning, which is fair since it's 2am now. She said she gets up at 7:30am to work in the shop down the road. I keep quiet about being up at 5:30am to do a full day of teaching. It's all relative.

At 3am we are back home. I go to bed but don't really see the point.

DAY 74 (THURSDAY).

GROUP CHAT POLITICS.

This day was difficult.

Nihilism has a neon sign in my mind today. I wanted to leave the Group Chat and wrote a message saying "I'm leaving". Then deleted it. Wrote "I'm leaving the chat". Then deleted it. If I leave, they'll ask questions. If I write a message to explain, it's not going to be what I really want to say. What I'd really like to say is "I currently think you're all dicks and would find myself better off not being in this group right now". Instead, I decide to just ignore the group. Don't read anything. If I read it, I know I'll reply because someone will piss me off. Just ignore it.

It's been ten days since me and Audie last communicated. What a fucking arsehole, I prefer it this way, though. I'll have to check in on the Group Chat in a few days just to let the read receipts go through, otherwise it'll look like I'm trying to get attention. *Fuck me, why am I thinking about these politics so much?*

I've got an interview for that job tomorrow, so today is my Friday because I've taken the day off for it. But I need to make a presentation to give: ten minutes on how to encourage wider participation in A-Level maths. I wish I cared enough to write it.

DAY 75 (FRIDAY).

INTERVIEW.

It must have been the sleep catching up with me, I fell asleep last night and didn't work on my presentation at all. I didn't even do any interview preparation, figuring it was better to just get a good sleep.

I showered early this morning, put on my white shirt and grey suit trousers and perched at my desk to finish the presentation. I've tried to keep it simple. I'm not even sure I want this job, but it's starting to eat me up a little and I'm getting nervous and agitated. Fuchsia is going out for a coffee whilst I do the interview, it's only on Microsoft Teams but I'm telling her she needs to leave now.

* * *

OK, so the interview went OK, but not great. The presentation was shite, but I realised that ten minutes to explain how you would like to try and solve inequality in maths education is rather pathetic. I just mentioned general things, spoke about data, referenced some reports. *Yada yada yada.* And then went slightly over time. When it came to the questions part, I had three people asking questions and me responding with a vague kind of verbal trash, I don't know what I was really saying. In hindsight, I struggled because it wasn't a particularly challenging interview. The job wouldn't be particularly challenging, you just fucking get it done. Talk to schools, talk to teachers, build a network, disseminate good teaching practice, record data, feedback loop. It's not fucking hard, it felt like they were interviewing me for a job at GCHQ and I wish I said that at the time. *Although Derwin...* Anyway, the guy that would be my line manager at the university looks a little cold as an individual and that concerns me. I asked some good questions in return about the gender split at the university and their response was interesting. And then near the end of the interview I started to feel as though I wasn't going to get it, which is a shame because I'd like to get money for sitting at home on a part-time job. But I am slightly concerned about how seriously I'd take it, if I were to do it. I'd probably give it the same existential cold shoulder that I'm giving everything at the moment. So I said to the interview panel at the end that I "appreciate the opportunity, enjoyed researching for the presentation and regardless of who gets it, I hope they do a good job of it". In an instant I felt like I gave away that I'm indifferent about getting the job, so added "of course I'd like it to be me", but it felt like someone else said it.

In the afternoon I went up to my sister's house in Stainsacre. The other day when I tried to buy the drum kit and my card got declined, I asked her if I could use her's and transfer her some money. So I went to see her as that's where the kit got delivered. I put it together, it looks nice, then stashed it all in the back of my van.

Before going back home I went to my parents' house in Hawsker to pick up my new bank card that had been delivered. I still use my parents' address for my bank, I've not changed it since opening it when I was 16. I don't see the point. When I pulled up back at home in Whitby, my dad rang and said he'd found my bank card on the street. I checked my pockets, even though I knew there was only one answer. Kind of dumb of me.

Fuchsia was in one of her online meetings, so I decide I may as well stretch my legs and actually move.

*   *   *

I can hear the ocean ring through my ears. A red rose is discarded on the wet sand. The tide must have been in only an hour earlier, I wonder who left the rose. I have an overwhelming feeling that I'm dying. On the beach where the tide doesn't reach, the sand is spongy and pleasing to walk on. That cigarette I had on the walk was long and I feel it on my lungs and in my throat. I can smell salted chips. It's comfortably busy out. Fuchsia messages saying she's done and will come to meet me.

We pop into Poundland for rolling papers.

"Do you have any ID?" I'm at the checkout and the staff ask me.

"No." I do, but I'm not getting it out for something you need to be 16 to buy.

"How old are you?"

"31." I'm still actually wearing my shirt, suit trousers and, for some reason, lanyard too. She laughed. I stared. *Cunt.*

"Can I have your date of birth?"

I told her and she types it into the screen. I don't know why they need this personal data. I feel violated just for buying rolling papers. They are liquorice flavour, I hope they don't taste like shite.

This reminds me of last year when I was ID'ed here for WD40 and had to get my sister to buy it. I said "I'm a 30-year-old teacher" and the same checkout woman said "maybe you are". I almost smashed her in the face with the aerosol can.

At home, we listened to music, smoked weed and drank rum and coke.

DAY 76 (SATURDAY).

EUROVISION.

Walking in the forestry alone, I didn't see anyone and smoked a bifta left over from yesterday. Everything was so green.

It was Eurovision in the evening. I've watched it every year since university. Fuchsia said Switzerland's entry looked like an autistic cowboy. It cracked me up. UK came last with no points. I commentated it all on my Instagram stories.

@DEAD1.414: I want Israel to win.

@DEAD1.414: Not Miley Cyprus, though, she sucked.

@DEAD1.414: OK, now I want Russia to win.

@DEAD1.414: So far three people have worn this sequin dress.

@DEAD1.414: Serbia sent on some Bratz dolls.

@DEAD1.414: He had a year to lose weight. He looks like Tyrone from Snatch. It's not terrible. Sounds like royalty-free music. Let's have that bifta. Go UK!

@DEAD1.414: This is great to watch whilst sat next to a professional VFX artist. Thanks, Greece.

@DEAD1.414: What was this, Spain? It was shite.

@DEAD1.414: Number four in sequins. Moldova.

@DEAD1.414: I thought it was great when it started. Germany.

@DEAD1.414: Finland reminds me of Linkin Park, but shite.

@DEAD1.414: I missed a song about ALS or something. Don't know who it was.

@DEAD1.414: Lithuania seems to have a boy band made of Louis Theroux clones in power suits.

@DEAD1.414: This is what I imagine Sartre looked like whilst writing Nausea. France.

@DEAD1.414: Azerbaijan were on stage and that's all I remember of that.

@DEAD1.414: This is like a scene from Zoolander… So hot right now. Is that Blue Steel or Magnum? Norway.

@DEAD1.414: I did like seeing Suzy Quattro as an Italian.

@DEAD1.414: This last song is like the credits from Street Fighter. Sweden.

@DEAD1.414: OK, this is the last song. Meh. San Marino.

@DEAD1.414: My prediction is Italy or France. UK last.

Italy won. Måneskin with their song Zitti E Buoni.

DAY 77 (SUNDAY).

FEAR AND LOATHING IN LAS VEGAS.

Walking on the beach alone, there was no one in sight and I used my binoculars to look at boats. It was 8am.

On the way back home I met Fuchsia for breakfast in a small cafe called Java. Our first meal out together this year.

I changed the living room layout again, moving the sofa so it makes an L-shape in the corner, rather than the middle of the room. Al came around to watch the Formula One in Monaco. There were no overtakes, it was boring. He showed me how to spar in the backyard. I didn't expect it to be so exhausting punching each other, he was really good.

Me and Fuchsia watched Fear and Loathing in Las Vegas in the evening. I'd not seen it before and found it an unusual film to watch right now, at this point in my life.

DAY 78 (MONDAY).

DDOS.

I took a photo whilst in the isolation room of myself. It's quite a nice one, almost hot if I felt comfortable making such a comment about myself. Which I don't. I'm in my grey suit, twirling my moustache showing my pink fingernails and my beard looks awesome. I sent it to Fuchsia and she wants me to bring home my suit jacket, which I usually leave at work.

Walker came in with Quinn for a few minutes, to get Walker some proper shoes to wear rather than his trainers. He says he's a size 12. I look at his feet, say "you're never a size 12" and leave Quinn looking in the cupboard behind me for shoes. It took her a while to find some size 12s, but Walker finally changed into a pair and went off to lesson.

Then my isolation fun got interrupted. Seven students in total got sent in, and they were all from the same lesson, leaving as many in isolation as there were in the class now. *The fucks*. At first I ignored them all and they sat silently staring at the wall whilst I marked. Then I got interested in the work they were missing out on, it was science, and I started to talk about Brownian motion and mercury thermometers. They were pleased to have learnt something and even said they learnt more with me just now than six weeks with the other teacher. The other teacher is supply and he just tells students to leave his class if they are annoying him. Unfortunately these seven in the isolation room now all started to talk to each other. *I started this*. I didn't care too much really, some of them had no work to do and one of them even complimented my pink and black nails, which wasn't expected. It was from a kid I'd never spoken to before called Hamlet. My concern here, however, was if another member of staff walked into the room and found them all talking, then I'd have to deal with SLT being an arsehole to me. But we got through the remaining ten minutes without disruption before I told them to fuck off to their next lesson. They were talking about some shite: bending another student's mother over, smoking, drugs. All of the shit. *God, fuck off, kids.*

I was about to get up and go get another coffee when Graham appeared in the room to check the rota. He's not on isolation duty today, which made him pleased. Then he started talking to me and I had no idea what he was on about until he mentioned the name Joey. In the short stint that I saw Margie and Doc this morning, they actually mentioned that on Friday, when I wasn't in, it was revealed what had been causing the internet downs. What they said didn't make sense, but now it all clicked. It was this year 10 student, called Joey, doing a DDoS attack. *Fucking hell*. Graham was now talking about it, saying how he was trying to teach his year 13s last Friday and being unable to because of the internet being down. But this kid, who had some reason been sent to work in his classroom, was sat doing the DDoS at the time. There had been rumours going around that it was a year 10 student, but Leopold said it was a virus. They've had loads of people in looking at the server and related hardware, buying new bits, trying things out. Turns out it was just a simple DDoS attack from a year 10 student, who then boasted to his friends. I actually recall Chai saying last week that Cleo accidentally displayed her IP address in a Computer Science lesson weeks ago, and that a student was using that to cause havoc. I didn't believe Chai because Leopold said it was hardware and virus related... Well, anyway, Graham says it's cost the school tens of thousands of pounds, not to mention been a real ball-ache for students too. Some students even had to cancel interviews, Marcel for example who has applied for a scholarship. Internet issues was actually the reason I gave for needing to do my interview at home last week. In Graham's lesson last Friday, he had left his class for a moment and when he returned he said Piper was in the room threatening this Joey with violence. Good on her, but I don't even know who this Joey lad is, so I'm struggling to imagine it. Apparently he has a reading age of eight, which implies he's a bit of a fucking numbskull. Probably a YouTube watcher.

I've run out of scran already so may have to have a cigarette as compensation.

Oh, I put that photo of myself on my Instagram story and keep checking to see if Audie has seen it yet. Fuck, she still lives in my head, maybe I should block her. I'll go have that cigarette.

Next lesson I had the pleasure of gypsying around the building in search of an empty classroom to teach my year 10 Nomad class, whilst they followed me about like sheep. It was nice to teach in what was my old classroom that I had when I started here, in a room with proper desks, rather than workbenches in the workshop. Inspired, I decided to go all in and teach calculus. It was good, for about half of them. The other half checked out, but I decided to ignore it and keep chugging away for the benefit of the others, like Stitches who was excelling. It's not that fucking difficult anyway.

In the canteen I saw Walker was back in his trainers and I mentioned it to him, pointing out he's back in his size sixes. He corrected me and said they are actually 11s. *Fucking knew it, that's an old trick he pulled.* Never mind, that's up to him. I wanted to tell Bob, who was walking next to him, that I had a go at sparring yesterday and I was crap at it. Bob is the one who knocked the student's tooth out the other week, so I maybe shouldn't encourage him. That reminds me, apparently the other kid had taken coke that morning. Doesn't surprise me, his eyes were wild at the time. Mad dog.

Whilst I sat in the maths office listening to Rush, some students walked past the door pushing a large bookshelf along and into the boys' toilets. I just sat and looked. It was Bob and another year 11 boy. I took out my headphones and asked what they were doing. They said they are blocking Hugh in the toilets.

"I don't know who that is." I did know and was only using it as a way to show my lack of emotion and interest.

"He's the short one who used to have long hair."

"OK. You know that door opens inwards?" This was to demonstrate they are stupid.

I left them to it, I can't see them from my desk anyway. Hugh must have found the shelf soon after, as I could hear struggling and laughing. Then I heard another teacher asking why they weren't in lesson. I hid in the corner of the office not wanting the teacher to see me, otherwise they'd come and ask me about the students. The teacher must have been a right dope as they didn't notice the shelf blocking the door and fire exit route. When they had gone I popped out and pushed the shelf back to where it belonged. I could smell crayons.

The song Tom Sawyer is playing now and my ear hurts a little. I think I poked at it too much. *Ear wax is gross.*

*   *   *

Who gives a shit if Måneskin used drugs?!

DAY 79 (TUESDAY).

NO-MAN'S LAND.

I don't feel sexy. I just feel like the whole world is pathetic. I'm urging it to do something stupid, just to prove my feelings. I can't feel sexy when the whole world is so pathetic. And that's why I'm in a dry patch. I just don't want it.

I was in a bad mood this morning, as soon as I got out of bed. It didn't help that I found my towel folded over the side of the bath, meaning that half of it was soaking. *I didn't put it there.* I had to use a different towel, which bothered me. Then when I went to find a shirt I stood on my Gorilla Pod and snapped it. I just wasn't feeling it this morning. Sitting on the bus, I have my coat pulled up around my neck, it's so cold. My plan was to go to the supermarket from the bus to get some breakfast, but I'm not feeling it and roll a fag instead. I'm starting to run out of tobacco again. I did have a quick look at flights to go somewhere like Gran Canaria to buy cheap fags yesterday, but I don't feel confident with international travel right now. I could bring back 2000 fags if I did, though. That's a saving of about £70 from a rough calculation, which would make the holiday a lot cheaper. Maybe I could just do a day trip and save on accommodation.

As soon as I walked into school, Monty said hello and asked about Friday, wondering where I was. I said it was an interview and told him a little about it. I wish I could keep my mouth shut sometimes, I don't like people knowing what I'm up to, I really piss myself off. Now I'm sat in the maths office eating my lunch even though it's only 7:30am. Also, Audie hasn't seen my Instagram story yet. I feel like it's suspicious, she usually sees it within the hour of posting. *Why am I checking?* God, I wish I didn't care, but I do. I'm trying to not let thoughts like either of these bother me, but I have little else I want to think about.

I'd like to write a book where the main character is just sat on a beach. Try and make that one interesting. I think this thought has been fuelled by reading about different narrative techniques on Wikipedia. I don't know how I got onto that page, I just kind of dumbly stumble about on Wikipedia, clicking this link, clicking that link, opening extra tabs. Then I'm somewhere I've never been before and have 40 tabs open at once.

In the staff briefing, Doc asked if I was wearing nail paint. I showed him.

"Yeh, pink on the left. Black on the right."

He seemed surprised, I don't know why. *Doesn't he know me?*

In my year 12 Maths class, I'm not in the mood. On one side of the class, I've got students who I couldn't confidently expect to solve a quadratic. Then on the left, I've got students who have been studying independently and are on year 13 topics. In the middle, it's no-man's land, where no one belongs. Students like Tammy and Pudge are in no-man's land. All this variety means that I can't teach the class properly, there is just too much variation. It's like trying to have a conversation in three languages, and I'm not the fucking Rosetta Stone. I hate teaching this class and this half-term has been horrible. Granted we got off to a negative start with me announcing I'm leaving, but it went completely downhill from there. At the start of this year I asked if I could split the class, knowing what it would be like from GCSE results and because my timetable had the space. SLT said no.

Marty has asked me a question about the work he's doing, so I take a quick look to mark it. *Fuck, it's all wrong.* This is meant to be the smart side of the class and it turns out he can't do it. I'm broken, I can't think. *What am I meant to fucking do here? What's the right fucking thing to do?*

*   *   *

All day I've been hungry, I should've gone to the shop this morning. Now I'm hungry, cold and my back aches. It's also raining so I can't go for a smoke or a walk to the shop to get food or painkillers, without getting piss wet through. I'm sat in my suit with my coat on trying to not think about the miserable mood I'm in. I look back at the window and the sun is now shining, as if someone has just turned off the rain. Within seconds I've rolled a cigarette and I'm outside walking to the big Tesco.

It's stressful in Tesco. People are just milling about in the middle of aisles, their shopping trolleys barricading me out. *Why is it so busy at this time of day?* I shove them out of the way as I wander around wondering what to get. I found some vegan wraps in the meal deal section and got two. They actually cheered me up.

DAY 80 (WEDNESDAY).

TIRED.

Wow, I am tired. I fell asleep several times on the bus, waking up each time with a jump, scared.

Nothing really happened today. Hamlet said he likes my tattoos and nail paint again.

Graham said he likes my look whilst I was stroking my beard, to which I figured he meant my beard. Several hours later I realised he was talking about my nail paint too.

I asked Margie where I'm meant to put the TAG data on the system. She says she's already done it. Fair enough.

DAY 81 (THURSDAY).

FORM MEAL.

Having driven in, I was the first in the car park. I sat and rolled a cigarette whilst I saw Leopold's car park-up in my mirror. Whilst fiddling with the filter, I saw the Principal appear at the passenger window of my van – the driver's side being pressed up against a hedge. *He said something, what did he say?*

"This is a private car park," he repeats. *It doesn't surprise me, this, I kind of expected it.* I wave at him, trying to signal it's me.

"This is a private car park." *Fuck sake, can he not see me?* I lean over and open the door a little.

"It's me," I say.

"Oh, is that you?" *You're a fucking idiot.*

"Yeh, can you not recognise me? I've driven in today." It's kind of obvious that last comment, but I feel like I'm talking to a child and I even imitate steering.

"No, I can't see through the glass." *You're still a fucking idiot.*

We have an awkward moment of silence.

"Well, good morning," I say, and he turns around and walks off. I slide back over to the driver's seat, roll the window fully down and light my cigarette. My arm hangs out of the window between drags.

I think Fuchsia is still in a shite mood this morning. She messaged with what feels like cold, short replies to my customary "I'm at school now". I don't know why I send that every morning, it's kind of just become a routine because she usually asks or gets annoyed if I don't tell her these kind of things. This is especially the case with coming home at the end of the day. She'd be annoyed if I walk in unannounced, even though I pay the fucking rent and bills. Piece of shit. Anyway, I was pissed off with her last night for being in shit mood again. It's so exhausting, I really would rather not be in a relationship right now. And she often says that she doesn't feel like we are in a relationship, we are just housemates. Well, it's hard to feel romantic when your partner is always in a shit mood. Last night she was in a shit mood with me because I shrugged her off when she tried to hug me. Issue was that I was in ridiculous back pain whilst we were at the gym and rather than her asking me what's wrong, she got in a mood and fucked off. I don't help the situation ever though because I can't deal with people being like that and I want her to explicitly say what's wrong, rather than just be a dick to me. And I know it wouldn't get resolved until I say something along the lines of "I'm sorry for being grumpy, I was in back pain". But how about she just fucks off. How about I say "I'm too tired of this bullshit, fuck off". It doesn't help with how caught up in my family she is, especially when my mum says things like how much she likes her. And when my sisters say how great she is. I swear people only hang out with me so they can hang out with Fuchsia. Fucking hell, I was in an OK mood this morning until she messaged back with those cold, short replies. What do I say back, "hope you had a good sleep"? Well I fucking didn't have a good sleep, I was awake for hours and then when I finally fell asleep I woke up again in back pain. Fuck it, I've said it to her anyway. It will break the tension.

* * *

Marked all the year 12 work. Had a fairly good lesson. Spoke to Lucky and Tammy. They said they think I'm a good teacher. I said only for students that get it and we laughed about a time when Nate said he didn't get it and I said "OK", then ignored him and walked over to see Lucky's work instead.

* * *

A while back I suggested to my Form that we'll all go for a meal just before they leave. That idea got out among staff and now I'm sat in my van, it's 5:30pm and I'm early. Some of the other teachers and SLT are coming to the meal as well, it's at an Italian in town and that's why I drove in today. I rolled and lit a bifta whilst I waited in the car park at the back of the casino. I had the windows up, hot boxing, and it was getting rather smokey in there. Think I put too much weed in too.

The meal was weird. The seating arrangement, the... OK, well, that was about it. I think I was just mega-stoned. Bianca took a photo of us together and put it on her Instagram and also set it as her wallpaper. After the other teachers and SLT fucked off, the rest of us made our own way to a pub on the outskirts of town. The students like it because they can get served there. I was feeling really socially anxious, but it might have just been the weed, I don't know. As I drove into the pub car park I was on loudspeaker to Fuchsia. Egbert and Chai came over to see me and said hello to her.

There were some really creepy men at the pub. Scabby-looking fuckwits that looked like they'd just come from a building site. There's nothing wrong with being a builder, what was wrong was them being paedophilic scumbags, perfectly content with talking and acting inappropriately to the students. They may be getting served but they are obviously just kids. I chose to not say anything as the students are sort of engaging with it and even encouraging it. And I felt completely socially awkward. It seems that the students have met some of these fuckwits before and it's currently harmless. Although, Bianca is sat on one of their knees. I don't hang about for more than one drink. Was nice to join them, though.

This end-of-Form meal went a lot differently to that one two years ago. I didn't ring any students and call them a dickhead, and this definitely feels like the end of something bigger.

DAY 82 (FRIDAY).

THE END.

This was the final day of seeing my Form. It was emotional, they got me a card and in it they had written:

Thanks for being our Form tutor and friend, and making us laugh every morning. All the best to you and Fuchsia, we wish you many years of happiness.

Hopefully we will meet again.

Lots of love,
your favourite Form.

PS don't forget to invite us to the wedding.

They all signed it. It meant a lot to me.

It was another emotional day. Like saying goodbye to an entire family forever. But it felt more strange because I knew I'm not going to get a new one. And that it really was the end.

PART THREE

HALF TERM (ONE WEEK OFF).

DAY UNKNOWN.

MANCHESTER.

We have gone to Manchester to stay with Rosie and Raymond, Fuchsia's friends who are mine also by extension. Nice couple. Professional couple. Roll strong biftas. I got crazy high and couldn't figure out which way was forwards on Mario Kart.

DAY UNKNOWN.

BIRTHDAY GOLF.

Fuchsia's birthday. The four of us went to Ghetto Golf. Was fucking mint. She sussed out I got her a drum kit, just from the drum key that I gave her. I was impressed. She will have to wait until we get home though.

DAY UNKNOWN.

FALLING APART.

Hvdfph cbjkchbkl xcvbkjh shhag;lxchfbcfkzhbv xzvzo hvxzohi kjavhjksv vkjcvxhjkndvt

I wish I was dead. I wish there was some switch that I could flick and I no longer existed. It's the last Friday of half term today and me and Fuchsia have fallen out. I can't help it from happening now, I say things without thinking and then later I know I should've kept my mouth shut and my feelings inside, pretending this was some happy version of me. But I don't like lying and I don't like keeping my feelings from Fuchsia. So here we are. She said she wishes everything wasn't shit anymore. Then gets upset that I walk off like I'm some robot who can just take that being said to me. I sit downstairs. I'm thinking, trying to string thoughts together as fast as I can. *Why is it all shit now? What has happened?*

To me, it feels like there is only one explanation: how can I care about making this relationship work when I care about nothing at all?

DAY UNKNOWN.

PUFFINS.

Went to see puffins at Bempton Cliffs. It's an RSPB nature reserve. It was the gannets that were the most impressive, didn't realise they were so fucking big. I've wanted to go to these cliffs for years, ever since a student in my old Form told me about them.

Then the evening was a little jumpy. Went to Audie's to say hello. Felt weird. Went home. Thought about getting washed and going back. Went for a walk in town to the Captain Cook monument. Bumped into Spike and Stella outside a pub on the quay. Joined them for a while. Went back to theirs and listened to music. Came home. Watched Mrs Doubtfire and ate noodles, finally going to bed at 5am.

SUMMER TERM (SECOND HALF).

DAY 92 (MONDAY).

TIME WASTERS.

I wish I wasn't here today.

Monty got on the bus this morning, which disrupted my routine but it was almost nice to have something different.

I'm sat in the isolation room now. It's near the end of lunch and I have two lessons straight afterwards. I don't want them to happen, I'm sick of it.

Cleo has just emailed me.

```
From: Cleo
To: DEAD

I've got a load of employer video material that needs editing
by COP — do you have time to help put it together?
```

I reply.

```
From: DEAD
To: Cleo

As tempted as I am, because I like video editing, unfortunately
I don't have any free time until I leave.
```

She replies straight back.

```
From: Cleo
To: DEAD

Has your timetable been restructured following losing year 11
and 13 classes?
```

She knows I can edit videos because she's seen my YouTube channel. In fact, she actually asked me to remove one of my videos last year, saying that flicking off a police car isn't appropriate for a teacher to do. Anyway, I'm not responding to this email because I really want to point out that I was being polite and the real reason is that I don't want to spend my spare time at work editing some bullshit video on a four-hour turnaround. *Fuck that shit.* I close my emails.

* * *

On the bus home, I message Spike. *How do you encourage your fat friend to not be fat?*

And my sister. *Watching YouTube is not a fucking hobby, especially for a 19-year-old, and existential dread in a child is bullshit when you do fucking nothing. He says he wants to film animals but doesn't know anything about filming and doesn't even go to where animals are.*

And then Audie.

Oh. I've just remembered that I said I'd give a copy of ZAMM to someone else. Who was that, Raymond? Maybe. He'd appreciate it, he's a hidden philosopher. I presume he reads.

DAY 93 (TUESDAY).

TACOS.

There was some dude on the bus taking up the entire back seat by sitting in the middle and spreading his bags out over the remaining eight seats. Four on either side: two facing forwards, two backwards. I ask if I can sit at my usual side. He says sure and gets up and sits nearer the front, taking his bags with him. A little unnecessary.

*   *   *

Sat in the hall for staff briefing, my legs are stretched out straight and wide in front of me. I'm slouched on the chair with a coffee in my hand and my head tipped back with my eyes closed. I'm listening to what the Principal is saying but I'm not interested. It just sounds like the adults on Snoopy that talk like a horn. *Wah wah wah.* My old boss at the Royal Society once told me that I should pretend to pay attention in meetings. It was worse at the Royal Society because all the meeting rooms had glass walls so everyone could see me not paying attention. But I just don't care enough to even look like I care.

*   *   *

Sat in the maths office, wasting time, I watched a video of Amy Schumer as I read her name earlier and didn't know who it was. She said something about "the shocker" so I looked it up. Made me laugh. By the way, that coke me and Fuchsia bought on DAY 66 (I checked back to see when it was)... Well, it didn't turn up.

*   *   *

Walking to the bus stop I found some shite, unartistic graffiti that said "FUCK THE SYSTEM". I don't know how I'd never seen it before.

*   *   *

Walking back from the bus stop I put Arcane Roots on and air guitared to You Are, all the way over the big bridge. I felt in a good mood, enjoying the walk, looking at the traffic and trees.

*   *   *

Walking down my street, I put out the recycling bin and then open the door. Immediately a smell of spices erupts out the kitchen and Fuchsia smiles at me, stood at the cooker. I walk into the living room and, in hindsight, that good feeling I had had completely left me. Done an Irish goodbye. It was almost like it was never even there.

Fuchsia had made dinner and set the table in the yard. She had made tacos, and I was not in the mood. I struggled to look anywhere but at the floor and table whilst I ate, making a conscious effort to not cry. But I kept winding myself up because I didn't know why I felt this way and didn't want to put it on Fuchsia.

All sorts of things started to get to me. The salt was too crunchy. The tacos were slightly burnt. The water was flavoured and really sweet. *And how the fuck do you eat a taco?* What a stupid invention, I just crunched it up and mixed it with the bean chilli.

Obviously, she did pick up on my mood and asked if it was her that made me feel this way. I said it wasn't but I didn't get any time to wind down from getting in the door, we are straight to having a meal together. Although I know that can't be the only reason, the feeling of depression must have been waiting and hiding for me and then suddenly got triggered when I walked in, as if it were a sensory overload. I struggled to articulate this to Fuchsia.

It didn't take long until she got swept up in my feelings, put her shoes on and said she's going for a walk. Whilst she was inside getting her shoes, I picked up a taco and threw it across the yard. The chilli inside it made a wet splat on the brick wall. *Why am I like this?* She came back outside and I had lit a cigarette and was staring into nothing. She had her backpack on and was looking at me. She says she doesn't know what to do and I ask her why she would go for a walk. I didn't really care for the answer, I just wanted to try and show some interest. The truth was that I didn't want her to leave me alone and I didn't want to go with her. By some miraculous turn, maybe the cigarette, I managed to look up at her and she came over to hug me. My eyes started to leak. *What the fuck is wrong with me?* Having made up to some extent, we went inside where it was cooler and darker. I laid on the sofa and pulled a blanket up and over my head, and stretched out my hand to grab Fuchsia's.

I woke up an hour later with a start. *Fuck, I felt awful.* I said it to Fuchsia, but it was a kind of groggy, guilty, awful feeling; no longer that despair and depression episode that overcame earlier. What happened next is some sort of surreal dream memory now, almost like it was a dream. Fuchsia went for a bath, whilst I sat and theorised about panic attacks but with the emotions of despair and depression. *Despair attack. Depression attack.* And then I felt like I needed to fuck but had no energy. Phone in my hand, I scrolled through Reddit on r/gothsluts and r/ahegaogirls. I just scrolled. And then had a bath too.

DAY 94 (WEDNESDAY).

PAIN AND PLEASURE.

At 2am I was squatting at the top of the stairs bollock naked, eating a flapjack. I was trying to stretch my back a little and help the painkillers get rid of the bubbling, frothing pain that engulfed me. It died down after about 30 minutes and I went back to bed.

Three hours later I was woken by my alarm, my weird dreams drifted through my being and I only remembered the feelings, not the content. My thoughts shifted straight to those subreddits I was looking at last night.

I went for a walk after getting off the bus and had a cigarette. It made my stomach hurt. But was that actually my abs aching from exercise? Or maybe something else entirely?

Right now I'm waiting for my second and final lesson of the day, sat listening to Pure Pleasure Seeker by Moloko. It's the song that was on an advert where a puppet sloth was dancing on a bed or sofa. It's got a dirty bass trumpet-like noise to it. I like it. My vape is on the desk next to me, thankfully I stuffed it into my bag this morning. *God, I only have a few minutes left.* Gossip have come on, it's Standing In the Way of Control and it's made me smile. I've not heard this in ages. At least I have work ready for this lesson.

I have a bit of my vape. *I think the coil is burnt, it tastes funny but still like custard cream.* I did look for the spare coils last night when I got out the bath but couldn't find them. *Man, I have no idea where they could be. I think the vape gives me numb tongue.* OK, time to let the class in. *Skolliwol.*

DAY 95 (THURSDAY).

CIRCULATION.

My tooth is starting to hurt. Last night I was chomping on some late-night cereal and a filling came out. Was a fucking huge filling too, from a wisdom tooth on the upper right. Although it might not be a wisdom tooth, now I think about it, I thought I had that one pulled out years ago. Anyway, the tooth feels sharp on my tongue and now the tooth itself is starting to hurt. It has left a proper big hole, it's rather gross, I can feel right into the hole with my tongue. I've just booked in for an appointment at the dentist and the closest they can get me in is six weeks away. God, that's so far away. At least I actually rang the dentist though. That surprised me.

Well, I'm feeling slightly more upbeat today, I hope it lasts. I messaged Fuchsia and she is too. I thought about messaging Audie because I was thinking about how she spotted I have Raynaud's last week. In fact, I don't think I wrote any of this down...

The other week, during the half term, on the day we came back from Manchester I was in a bit of a shit mood and didn't want to leave the house. When it got to the evening, I decided to venture out to stretch my legs and get my back moving a little, it was painful. At that point, I started to feel really shit that my job makes me miserable but my mum won't tell my dad that I've quit because it will stress him. They want to pretend that I'm still in this respectable job forever and ignore how unhappy it makes me. (That last sentence gives me a really strong feeling of anger towards my family, and I struggle to describe the reasoning in writing.) Anyway, I was on the beach walking and thinking and I sat down on a rock, lit a cigarette and took a photo of the sea. I must have intended to put it on Instagram because I was on the app and saw Audie was having a drink with some guy I didn't recognise. Knowing that she has an open relationship I wondered if that was a new person on her scene. And in an instant, I felt angry and jealous. And it was then that I realised that I needed to block Audie and avoid seeing anything from her, let alone messaging her.

So when I got home I did the following.

- Unfollowed Audie on Instagram and removed her from following me. We both have our accounts set to private so that does that job.

- Blocked her on WhatsApp and blocked her from adding me to group chats. We hadn't messaged since the day she sent the photo, I was actively swerving her.

- Messaged the Group Chat saying I was leaving the group and to not take it personally. I sent it with a gif of Bing Bong's death scene from Inside Out when he fades away, it was the first time I had messaged the group in over a month. Then I left the Group Chat.

- And finally, I blocked everyone who was in the Group Chat on WhatsApp because I didn't want to hear from them individually, except for Fuchsia.

The plan was fine, I was feeling quite relieved and then the very next day, me and Fuchsia went for a drink at the Brewery. She mentioned that Al and Audie were going there later that evening, but I said it's fine as we'll be gone by then. I even joked that if I saw them, I'll get up and leave. (Fuchsia had realised I had been avoiding everyone from the Group Chat, but didn't question why.) Unfortunately, I had my back to the entrance and after only two drinks they turned up and sat straight down at our table. Audie in front of me. I almost shat myself but managed to keep myself together. Over the next hour or so, Audie locked her eyes onto mine a handful of times and I instantly remembered how beautiful they are. From behind her sunglasses, they had a green tinge to them, but I couldn't ever hold her look back for more than a second before I would turn away. They didn't stay long, and they left when two of Fuchsia's other friends turned up. But that was when she looked at my hands and asked if I have Raynaud's disease. No one has ever noticed that before. Later that night I was drunk and broke the messaging silence.

    [21:04] DEAD: Hey, I want to break the silence.

She sent a gif of a "virtual hug" back.

    [21:16] DEAD: I'm sorry.
    [21:16] DEAD: I've missed you.

[21:17] Audie: Sorry?

[21:19] DEAD: Never mind.

[21:19] Audie: You don't need to be sorry.

[21:24] DEAD: I've been trying to avoid you.

[21:24] DEAD: But tonight it didn't happen.

[21:26] Audie: You can't get rid of me.

[21:27] Audie: I'm here to stay.

[21:31] DEAD: You haven't messaged me in a month though.

[21:33] Audie: I haven't really spoken to anyone recently.

[21:42] DEAD: I'm struggling to see my phone…

[21:49] Audie: Why have you been trying to avoid me?

[22:05] DEAD: Because I don't like feeling things.

[22:07] Audie: Did trying to avoid me help?

[22:16] DEAD: No.

[22:16] Audie: Then stop it.

[22:41] DEAD: I want to meet when we are both sober.

[22:42] Audie: To hang out?

[22:46] DEAD: Yes.

[22:49] DEAD: Why haven't you messaged in all this time?

[22:52] Audie: I don't know.

[23:09] DEAD: Maybe we shouldn't message then.

[23:09] Audie: Why?

[23:10] DEAD: I have feelings for you.

[23:11] Audie: Maybe we shouldn't message when you've been drinking.

[23:12] DEAD: Never mind.

[23:13] Audie: You beat yourself up about this stuff when you're sober and then avoid me.

[23:13] DEAD: We should avoid each other.

[23:13] Audie: No.

[23:14] DEAD: Why?

[23:14] Audie: It won't solve anything.

She messaged me the next morning and we moved on, shelving that as a drunken conversation.

Anyway, today I didn't message Audie. And we are meant to stay at work until 4:30pm, even though CPD isn't on, but I got my bag and fucked off at 4pm. I've been doing shit all anyway.

I'm trying to not smoke at the moment and have my shitty little vape with me again. Pretty sure vaping gives me spots, it's why I gave up on it years ago in London. But I haven't had a smoke today so that's a good thing. In fact, I think this is the first day I've been teaching and not smoked. Well, that's an interesting achievement.

* * *

I've not wanted a cigarette as much as right now for a long time. The last time was when I was working at the Royal Society, two weeks after I had run the London Marathon. I'd quit for the marathon and, I can't remember what caused the thought, I looked up at the top of the Royal Society building and wanted to jump off it. Right now, I have lost my erection and feel totally shite.

DAY 96 (FRIDAY).

THE RACE TOWARD DEATH.

It's Julia's book club. She is reading Night, by Elie Wiesel, with four students and I'm sat listening, doing my own work. She is a very inspirational teacher, I think she's great.

She asked them what they would ask a god, an all-knowing person, if they were to meet one. They talk about existence and death and the afterlife. Julia says how we don't know any of this is real, but if you think about it too much, it can get you quite down. *Fuck me, she knows.* She does a nervous little laugh and talks about the holocaust and a sense of purpose. I wonder if she's had depression, maybe even existential depression, and been able to move on?

She is a very inspirational teacher, I reiterate that.

Stitches is loving the discussions. He says that the holocaust wasn't just about religion and faith, it was about blood and DNA. Ethnicity. In the book no one believed the Jew that escaped from the concentration camp, Julia asked all four of them why they think that happened. They say denial; that it was so horrific that others cannot believe it is happening. I think for a moment about how this is maybe happening in the world right now. *How the fuck can we know?* Julia mentioned about Nazis throwing babies in the air and using them as machine gun practice as if they were clay pigeon shooting. It's hard to believe.

There's a line in the book that Julia wants to revisit:

"…tears, like drops of wax, flowed from his eyes." *S*he perfectly enunciates and emphasises in slow motion, provoking thought about the line even deeper. The words echo.

Then, quickly in harsh contrast:

"Why is this so good? Are the tears going to run out? Are the tears burning? Do they feel hot, heavy and sticky?"

They made me think deeper about the line too. And in a flash, I'm starting to feel anxious about doing something with my life. To achieve something. Almost excited.

Julia points out another line about the German control of a Jewish city, reading it aloud in the same way:

"…from that moment on, everything happened very quickly. The race toward death had begun."

The words echo.

Fuck.

DAY 97 (SATURDAY).

WALK.

We went for a walk in the woods and went to my sister's in Stainsacre.

DAY 98 (SUNDAY).

FOOTBALL.

Watched the England-Croatia game at home.

DAY 99 (MONDAY).

WAITING.

I am tired. I do not want to be here. I am bored. I have one lesson. And I don't want to teach it. I will just give them revision tasks.

Also, we are out of coffee pods in the maths office.

* * *

I've hidden for most of today in an empty classroom, waiting for the end.

DAY 100 (TUESDAY).

BIRTHDAY PLANS.

Again, I have only one lesson. So my focus today is to research how to better livestream on Twitch for fun. I've done it before but I didn't really know what I was doing, I just kind of clicked at things and it didn't work very well.

* * *

It's my birthday in a few weeks and I felt a bit shite in the evening when I found out that my friend is having a party of my own, meaning I can't have a birthday bash. Stupid thing is that she asked if she could do a beach party for my birthday. Fucking stupid situation and why I'm saying "a friend", I don't know. It's Audie.

So I was in a shite mood and didn't want to be in a shite mood, particularly because Fuchsia wanted to have sex. So when Fuchsia went for a bath, I messaged a few people to try and lift my spirits up a bit. Audie was the only one that replied, so we chatted about doing something for my birthday. She's polite and said we can still do something, but I replied by saying it's OK and it doesn't matter. Because it doesn't matter. And that realisation made me feel a bit better. Not like I was suddenly amazing, but like I could stop spiralling.

And eventually… Fuck. Squirt. Cum. Shower.

DAY 101 (WEDNESDAY).

BUS WOMAN.

Again, I don't know what happened today. Essentially nothing again.

Marked some tests for year 12 Maths. Most got U's. Lucky got full marks, Marty nearly did too.

My morning walk was nice along the cliff top. Bit of a different route. Made me appreciate how beautiful the world can look.

Right now I'm sat on the bus on the way home and I'm fascinated by this woman sat in front of me. She's sat next to her partner and for some reason, part of her butt isn't on the seat. It's hanging over the edge but not because it's big, which it isn't. She must find it more comfortable. She's in hiking clothes which for a woman is always tights, t-shirt and walking boots. No hat, though, she's got a lot of brown hair scrunched up in a small knot at the back. I just enjoy looking at her.

I messaged Audie to say thanks for replying last night, as she wasn't the only person I messaged, it's just the others didn't reply. We chatted for a while. She said she was upset yesterday and cried in the bath for two hours. I thought that was mental.

Went to the gym in the evening.

DAY 102 (THURSDAY).

HOLLOW.

Fuck me, the soap dispenser in the fabled disabled toilet has been fixed. The one I broke three years ago.

I think I've realised that I no longer do anything because I enjoy it. I do things because I have a reason to do it. Like I wouldn't play chess because I enjoy it, it's because I want to get better. Or that I don't read because I enjoy it, it's because I want to learn from what I read. Most of my hobbies are oriented to have some ulterior motive or goal. And I don't have sex because I enjoy it, it's because it's necessary to clear the mind of sexual desire.

When I was downstairs at lunch I saw a girl that a lot of the boys seem to like and I realised she looks rather weird. Hazel's a bit tubby and has her hair tied up like a troll all the time. It's odd that the boys seem to like her, but I've noticed it seems to only be the boys who smoke and are generally a nuisance, like Hamlet and Benedict. Vicky Pollard comes to mind.

I can hear the conversation at the teachers' table as I walk through everyone eating. Bertha says she often ends her lessons early because she comes to a natural end to the lesson. Doc says he naturally doesn't start his lessons. I smiled.

At the Royal Society I once asked Bill Bryson if he had any inspirational teachers as a child. After his initial no, he said that his advice to teachers is to not forget the magic of why you got into teaching. His reply eventually made its way onto the Royal Society's Twitter for World Teacher's Day. Doc must have some magic of his own, but I have no idea what it is.

* * *

We went to see my mum and dad in the evening. It's Dad's birthday, but I only got him a card. He's a hoarder, so what do you buy him? I think it's more important to spend time with him and chat shit, which we did.

On the way down our road, driving home, a baby seagull waddled out in the street in front of us. At first it was cute and amusing. But then it became an issue of "it's fallen from its nest, it's probably going to die now". The chick itself was quite cute until I went to pick it up, at which point it turned into something that more resembled a velociraptor. I wanted to just leave it, not caring that it would probably die, but Fuchsia was adamant that we did something about it. Long story short, we contacted a friend who works with an animal sanctuary, borrowed a huge ladder, caught the seagull and put it on a roof so it could have a chance of still being tended to and surviving. I carried the ladder back through town myself, mainly because I didn't like driving with it in the van, and we continued on to the pub.

I know it was an eventful day but writing this now, laying in bed, it feels hollow as if nothing really happened. I'm wondering what my godmother did today. It was on this day ten years ago that her son died in the IED explosion in Afghanistan. His funeral song was Snow Patrol, Chasing Cars. It was also his wedding song.

DAY 103 (FRIDAY).

BLUE SKY.

Frank says he has some socks he can lend me. God, it's boring, people always pointing out that I don't wear socks. But the thing is that I do wear socks, it's just that they are small invisible ones because socks with Toms look daft. It's warm, I wear Toms with small invisible socks, roll my trousers up a couple of times and it looks great. But people really struggle to accept it, even though it's essentially identical to what all the women wear. Gladys even wears Toms without visible socks.

*　*　*

Book club with Julia.

"…all this under a magnificent blue sky." She stops reading and looks up at the students. The words echo.

The sentence was thrown in the middle of Jews panicking to leave their ghetto. Stitches says it shows that it's humankind and not nature making these terrible events. Julia agrees and continues to the main point that shit things can happen even in wonderful weather. We are used to bad weather meaning bad things, but that's fiction and this book is real life.

I sit and think about what they have just said, eventually tuning back in to hear Julia finish by saying this:

"being equal can be scary as there is no one to look up to."

Fuck.

DAY 104 (SATURDAY).

EMPTY.

Empty.

DAY 105 (SUNDAY).

EMPTY.

Empty.

DAY 106 (MONDAY).

WEX FACE.

It's the summer solstice, but really it's just another fucking day where nothing happens and my face hurts. Wait, I've just realised I didn't write anything for the weekend. *Fuck.* I'll talk about it here.

Me and Fuchsia went for a pizza and a few drinks on Friday evening. Then at 8am the next day, rather than wallowing in the post-drinking anxiety, I suggested we go swimming in the sea. It felt great. We felt great. And so we went drinking again. We'd been drinking ages until we bumped into Spike and Stella again. Then we kept fucking drinking. In one pub, Fuchsia really wanted to talk to an older goth couple, thinking they looked interesting. She had been talking about wanting to talk to them for a while but whilst she was in the toilets they started to leave. I jumped up and said hello to them. Spike said hello too. Fuchsia came back and everyone was talking, I gave her a triumphant smile and then my ears pricked. Spike was getting the fella's number and he says my name. The thing is, I know Spike doesn't actually know my real name. But he definitely said it. Turns out the fella had the exact same name as me and it blew his Geordie fucking mind. So they stayed longer and drank shots with us.

At some point Fuchsia was talking to a chick with a green mohawk, saying that she fancied her. I was OK with that.

We left and went to another pub. Stella and Fuchsia had disappeared and Spike looked at a table of blokes and said he'd love to find out what men like that talk about. Being in a chatty, drunk mood I got up and asked them exactly that. The first guy I spoke to looked angry as fuck, like I'd just stamped on his child's kitten's neck. He told me to talk to the guy on the other side of the table because he was the chatty one. I did and I sort of knew him. Friend of a childhood friend. We had a good chat.

Then it was throwing out time. Me and Spike walked ahead and when we got to his place he ran upstairs to the toilet and, I don't know how, I smashed my head on his carpet. He came back downstairs and I explained I had hurt myself somehow.

"Yeh, I can tell." He said, with his eyes not quite meeting mine and looking slightly to the left.

"Shit, I need a mirror." I needed to see what he was looking at.

Looking through the dirt, dust and clutter obscuring the mirror over the mantelpiece, I saw it. A big fucking carpet burn down the side of my face. At this point, Fuchsia and Stella turned up and I showed them.

Fuck. I was OK for about ten minutes and then I was curled up on the sofa bed in their attic room, spewing my guts into a bowl.

When I woke the next morning, Fuchsia was next to me and I got up and left without seeing anyone else. An hour later she turned up at home too. She had a story for me though.

She said that on her walk from the pub, Stella had pinned her against a wall and kissed her. Then once me and Stella had gone to bed she stayed up drinking and talking to Spike, who suggested they go for a walk to the bandstand, down near the pier. She figured this meant Spike knew what had happened so she mentioned it to him. Unfortunately, he had no idea and was really upset. He started asking her about how I would feel about that and had she considered me. From what she said, it sounded like he was upset a lot. They came back, had coffee at 6am and then Spike said he really likes Fuchsia and began rubbing her back. That was when she realised she needed to go to bed.

And so we spent the rest of the weekend hanging out our arse, me with my neck and face hurting.

On this Monday at school, however, it's the first day of a virtual work experience. It's been talked about in meetings for a while, but it didn't really make sense to me. *I don't understand how work experience can be done virtually.* Since today was the introductory day for all students, I thankfully didn't have to do anything. Instead, I sat in the maths office all day. Doing what, I don't really know.

DAY 107 (TUESDAY).

WEX PIGEON.

So today I'm overseeing some stupid virtual work experience made by a national company that does this as their business. It's pretty shite. The good thing is that the school is supporting it with talks from local businesses and they are vaguely interesting.

I was sat in on one of the talks when, ten minutes before it was expected to end, a pigeon flew in. It was pretty exciting until it flew into the wall.

The pigeon had flown in through the fire exit, which was open because it was so warm in the hall. I was sat at the back enjoying the slight breeze when the pigeon flew in over my head. It panicked a little and flew beak-first into a wall, giving off a surprisingly loud, dull thud. All the students laughed but I felt a bit bad for it. It appeared unharmed and flew up onto the top of the projector and sat there. Probably a little dazed.

Leopold and Ricky immediately went and stood near the fire exit like they were bouncers and were going to catch or bite any more pigeons out of the air that dared come in. It was so fucking stupid, the Principal and the Director of Engineering standing there like that. Since I was sat right in front of the door, I turned around and looked at Leopold and Ricky to show them what I think of them. Leopold looked back at me. He gave me a look as though it was my fault that the pigeon came in and his eyes flicked to the left side of my face. I stared him in the eye with the sensation of being Jack's smirking revenge. He looked away. *What a pair of fucking dickheads these two are.*

I enjoyed the rest of the presentation, it was a video tour of the factory that Cleo had filmed. Turns out this is what she wanted me to edit.

*   *   *

I wanted to write more here and to write about walking back upstairs to the maths office, but I have no idea what happened that made me want to write. *It must have been something.*

Fuchsia has messaged to ask when we can talk on the phone. It's a worrying thing as that is usually when something is wrong.

We spoke, it was just for a chat. She was feeling a little strung out from the weekend and especially from the interactions with Spike. We messaged a lot throughout the rest of the day about various things, such as agreeing to go to see Hopper at the weekend for his birthday and to fuck off Audie's party for sure. I'm happy to boycott a party that stole my chance of a birthday bash. Not that it matters.

I didn't bring lunch today, but in the afternoon I was told there was a leftover free school meal that was vegan. For some reason, the student didn't pick it up. It consisted of a lettuce sandwich, a dry falafel sausage roll, a slice of rubbery cinnamon bagel with jam on, and an apple. It was depressing.

DAY 108 (WEDNESDAY).

WEX MARKING.

I'd love to tell you something interesting about today but there was nothing. My one session of working on that bullshit work experience was swapped out, so I had a day of full admin. What kind of admin, I can't even fucking remember.

Alice did remind me that I had to mark the submitted work from the WEX sessions I oversaw yesterday. I say remind, but I actually had no idea that I was meant to do this. Apparently she "mentioned it in the training last week". So she mentioned it, but gave us no training on how to actually mark it? I can mark maths easy peasy, but have no fucking idea how to mark a script talking about a fictional CV, or a poster for a shite company celebrating its 60th anniversary. I think I'll just pass or fail them with no feedback. This week has no educational value anyway, it's just so SLT can say they did work experience for the students. And they will lie and say it was a huge educational success.

DAY 109 (THURSDAY).

WEX FSM.

Marty wasn't let into the presentation because he wouldn't take his hoodie off. When Alice asked him, he walked over to his locker near the hall, started to take it off and stopped. Then he came over to me and said he can't take it off because he put an old shirt on underneath and it isn't long enough. He looked very sincere about it, but I said "don't tell me, you need to tell the Vice-Principal". So he did. She was having fucking none of it.

I had to walk off because it started to piss me off and so I went upstairs to rant at Margie and Doc whilst I dug out my carrot sticks. They're the only food I have today. Doc understood and voiced that it's Victorian. *Which it fucking is.* And he continues about the... I didn't hear what else he said, I had to run off to the first session I was covering.

*   *   *

Well, what another pointless day of the work experience. And also a pathetic cock-up in terms of staff communication. Because I was with all the students all morning, teaching the work experience shite, I missed an email saying that the school was sending a runner to buy all staff lunch. It meant that by the time I had read the email, I had missed my chance to put an order in. So everyone got free fucking lunch but because I was the only fucker working, I didn't. Quinn tried to ring up the runner and get me something to eat but it was too late.

As I didn't get chance to bring any proper food with me today, it was an extra blow to the shite mood I found myself in. Not wanting to sit and stew in a self-pity pot, I went to the big Tesco to get something nice to eat. It's a bit of a rush to get to the Tesco in a lunch break, but I wanted something good to eat and they had good choices last time. And there's not enough time to get to Sainsbury's.

On the way, I had barely left the car park, some year 10s asked if I wanted a cigarette. They were milling about, as if they want to be seen smoking. I said no, but borrowed their lighter and lit one anyway. My lungs still feel a little rough from smoking so much at the weekend so I only had about half of it, I am trying to cut back anyway. I stubbed it out on a wall and lobbed it down a drain.

At the big Tesco I was starving and excited to get a nice wrap or sarnie only to find there fucking wasn't any. In fact, there wasn't a single vegan lunch option in the entire supermarket. I got well fucked off. Absolutely fucking nothing. No sandwiches, no pasties or pastries. Nothing. God, that fucked me off, so I went back to the corner shop in desperation. Obviously fucking nothing in there either and I bought an energy drink in the hope of it compensating for the lack of food I was about to get.

Sometimes I don't mind not eating but today it was just fuelling a whirlwind of negativity in my mind. By this point I was 20 minutes late for the afternoon CPD, but I didn't care.

Going past the front desk I spotted the vegan FSM was available again. The students have left at lunch, as every Thursday, but they still get FSMs to take. I took it, went up to the maths office and ate half of it. Then I wrote a reply to Quinn's email, first thanking her for ringing the runner, and then going off on one.

```
From: DEAD
To: Quinn

Never mind, thanks for asking though.

I popped to Tesco and they were all out of vegan sarnies, so I
grabbed the leftover student lunch. It makes me wonder a few
things, and I hope you don't mind me raising these.

Is it actually vegan? There is a slice of brownie which I
didn't dare have, some sort of spread on the bread and the
pastry on the pretend sausage roll tasted a little milky. (This
might be me being paranoid, however.)

But putting my paranoia aside, is that meal the best we can do
for the students? I don't know the ins-and-outs of funding for
free school meals, but I'd say it's quite low quality. I know
there are some issues with it being a takeaway lunch, but shops
are doing really good vegan sausage rolls and cakes and meat
alternatives. It's just a little concerning and I wouldn't feel
comfortable not saying anything.

Thanks,
DEAD
```

The reply I got was good. Quinn isn't a fan of the food service either and they are looking to change supplier. She even seemed pleased to hear my feedback, but she also said there aren't any vegan students. I looked at the food bag that clearly had "vegan" written on it. So the cooks don't even have a fucking clue what vegan means. I feel slightly violated, such is the psychology of being vegan.

It's only food, but it's also a symbol of the pointless bullshit we are subjected to. It's these kind of things that make you just want to bang your head against a wall until everything sorts itself out or you lose enough brain cells that you no longer care. Either that or you just drop dead.

The thought of all the other staff chomping into a nice lunch that was bought for them whilst I eat a pathetic sandwich after marching about town trying to find some food, well, it just added to the pile. I didn't go to the CPD, I couldn't be fucked.

DAY 110 (FRIDAY).

WEX ASSEMBLY.

"No man is an island… or woman." *Well corrected, idiot.*

"University is a career route." *No one cares.*

God, this assembly is shite. It's meant to be the end-of-work experience assembly, but it feels like I'm at church and Alice is the priest.

The prizes are nice, even though they are shitty pieces of promotional tat from local businesses, the students appreciate being recognised.

Lucky has won the CV award, which is good since I essentially wrote his for him. (There was absolutely no guidance beforehand for the students so I had to teach everyone in the 30 minutes I was covering that session.) Marty won something too. And Stitches has won the backpack, I wasn't listening and don't know why he won it, but he's genuinely pleased. He's smiling and clapping as he walks (runs, Stitches runs everywhere) to the front of the hall. It's kind of like in an 80s game show when the contestants clap themselves at having won a new dishwasher or microwave. This has really made me smile, I hope he uses it, his bag is falling apart.

The Principal is such a dick, he's now giving an end-of-ceremony speech even though he's been involved in none of this. What a wanky pretentious piece of shit. I don't even know what he's saying, I can't stomach listening to this cunt. No doubt he's preaching the career ladder and being a money-grabbing turd bag with the social skills of a fart in an elevator.

Fuck, I'm glad it's Friday.

*   *   *

I'm on the bus coming out of Robin Hood's Bay looking at my work emails. Why is it that we sign off emails with a comma and then your name? Doesn't that mean you're talking to yourself?

    Have a nice weekend, DEAD.

    Thanks, DEAD.

    You're welcome, DEAD.

It's like an ironic message to yourself at the end of your emails.

    You're doing great, DEAD.

But it wouldn't work so well when you send angry emails.

    Fuck you, DEAD.

    Get cancer, DEAD.

    I wish you were dead, DEAD.

You know, I'm not a great fan of the insult "get cancer" because it's too real. The statistics are that one in four people get cancer. I have three siblings, all of who have children. Looks like I'm going to have to be the fucking hero and take one for the team. *Fuck, I hate being the morally adjusted one.*

At least with "get cancer" you're not wishing someone actually were dead. They might survive.

Tomorrow I'm driving back this same route for Hopper's birthday barbecue.

DAY UNKNOWN.

CATCH-UP LATER.

I have had weed, mushrooms, coke and alcohol and just sat down on the toilet. I don't need it, I just need to sit away from everyone. So I've put on an Animal Crossing play through on my phone. The sound and the familiarity of it is really nice. Comforting. It's been a weird day. Lots of emotions, lots of talking, lots of social awkwardness. I'm going to go and will catch-up later.

DAY 113 (MONDAY).

JULIA.

I'd be surprised if I give a fucking shit today. When I open my laptop I see that I was last reading about uniform policies in school and how there is no evidence to suggest that it aids learning. However, there is the argument that it helps to embed a school ethos and manage behaviour, which in turn can aid learning. I'm not a fan of uniform, but I am a fan of wearing appropriate outfits. There is always an outfit that is more appropriate for a given situation and students need to learn how to realise this. Last Friday when Marty got up in the assembly to accept an award, he was wearing a zip-up hoodie over a shirt and tie. The shirt wasn't tucked in. He looked like a fucking idiot and I felt bad for not helping to tidy him up before going into the hall.

Julia has come in to talk to me whilst I'm typing this. I'm currently sat at the desk in the isolation room. There aren't any students and it's not likely I'll get any when it's this late in the school year.

"Do you want me to cover this isolation period?" She asks.

"No it's OK. I can just sit for the two hours and get my head into some work."

"OK, then. I'm just outside if you change your mind."

She turns to walk out the room. *God, my stomach fucking hurts.* I missed breakfast and so bought a porridge pot from the supermarket after getting off the bus. I read that it had milk in it but decided to risk it. After two spoonfuls the pot went in the bin and I went to the toilet. *Think I'd like to be sick right now.*

"Are you OK?" I don't know where that came from, but I asked it to Julia's back.

She turns and comes back to talk to me. We ended up having a conversation about how she had to chase down a student to tell him to put his lanyard on. I understand that because once you ask a student to do something like that, you can't back down and let them get away with it. If you do, it lowers your status and you'll lose control of your classes. It was funny that she mentioned this as I saw her and Gladys on Friday being uniform nazis, telling kids to put lanyards on, tie top buttons, tuck shirts in and so on and so on. Funny thing is, though, that it needs to be done for the reasons of letting them learn about appropriate dress. I'm not asking students to do anything that I wouldn't do.

My mind is starting to wander and I can't decide if I'm feeling down or not. Sometimes I get down when I think people I care about are down, such as Fuchsia, who is down at the moment. At least I think she is. Maybe I should forget about it, as I can't do anything about it right now.

Al messaged earlier to see if I was OK with what happened. Makes me wonder if Audie said something to him. Right now I don't think I feel anything about it.

DAY 114 (TUESDAY).

REBIRTH.

I've pulled another interview day from school and I'm getting two tattoos right now.

The first tattoo today is a big feathery one on my ribs inspired by the Caspian album Dust and Disquiet. I bought this album on vinyl when I went to ArcTanGent festival on my own after my ten-year break-up. Evils keeps asking if I'm OK. I'm so thin you can count my ribs by sight, but it actually doesn't hurt. I first came to him for my skull and crossbones tattoo when I first started teaching at this school. It's like a standard skull and crossbones, but the bones are in the mouth and have been bitten in half. It's a design I came up with when I finished my degree, based on a nihilistic feeling for having paid tens of thousands of pounds for a piece of paper.

The second tattoo today is a small crucifixion cross under my left eye. I'm not religious, but I like the idea of faith, especially in yourself. To me, this is my rebirth.

Me and Fuchsia spoke a little bit about the weekend. I told her how it meant nothing to me and how I found that feeling strange. She said she did wonder why I hadn't talked to her about it. I reiterated, it's because it meant nothing to me.

DAY 115 (WEDNESDAY).

GIGGLING AGAIN.

Haha. I give so few fucks today.

Monty and Doc lost their shit when they saw my face. Doc saw it first, it was just me and him in the maths office and he laughed. I still have to keep the pretence that I did an interview yesterday, even though Margie found out it was my birthday. It was surprising really, the Principal's PA came into our office and gave me a birthday card for yesterday. And that was how Margie found out.

Monty saw me later on and asked why I had drawn on my face, then asked if it was tattooed. He shook his head and I enjoyed his dismay.

What makes today extra hilarious is that I keep looking at my Tuesday timetable. I am only three hours into the day and students have had to come and remind me of every lesson. I give so few fucks it is really making me laugh.

I thought of what happened at the weekend and started giggling to myself in lesson. Then I started giggling that I was giggling in lesson. I've just remembered it and started giggling again.

DAY 116 (THURSDAY).

GASSING.

I gassed for like three hours solid in my lessons. It was like I was lecturing. Felt great but tiring.

DAY 117 (FRIDAY).

CHESTER BENNINGTON.

I've decided to do something in memory of Chester Bennington. He died on 20 July 2017, and that's the same week as the last day of term. The only logical thing to do is to run to work that day and fundraise for the Campaign Against Living Miserably. That's how my brain works. So I have three weeks to go from running two kilometres on a treadmill to running 22 miles (35 kilometres). Yes, I've been working on pace recently, only running on a treadmill and only running two kilometres at a time. I've been doing good though, can run two kilometres in less than seven minutes now. Still a slower pace than London Marathon winners. It's crazy to think that.

There are things missing in the class I teach my year 12s in. It always happens near the end of the academic year.

```
From: DEAD
To: all staff

Hello,

Can I ask teachers to refrain from being as light-fingered with
classroom equipment at the moment.

I know people are getting excited for room changes, but I keep
finding my equipment missing from classroom nine and have spent
```

the first ten minutes of the lesson waiting for students to
source equipment because full drawers are missing.

Thanks,
DEAD

So why do I want to do something for Chester Bennington? It's not just him, but he is a symbol of what I want to care for. Here are some of the names that come to mind.

- Kurt Cobain (1994)

- Aziz (2011)

- Robin Williams (2014)

- Rollo (2016)

- Chris Cornell (2017)

- Chester Bennington (2017)

Rollo was the father of my ex-partner, the ten-year relationship one. He hanged himself too.

* * *

There's a man next to me on the bus. Short, maybe in his late 40s, kind of stocky-dumpy and he's in full khaki with an army backpack like he's going hiking. It's rained so he's a bit soggy like me. Unlike me, though, he's talking to himself. He keeps having angry outbursts that I can't really understand. Occasionally I can figure them out.

"You don't know... fuck them..."

He could be on the phone with a headphone in his left ear that I can't see. But the pauses between the outbursts are too random for it to be a conversation. And he's now gone completely silent. It's a little unnerving with him in his army wear. I still think I could take him if need be, I'll fight dirty just to make sure. His backpack is big and well packed, the contents look soft as the bag looks inflated in the way that something like a sleeping bag would cause. It gives me the feeling that he isn't carrying an arsenal of weapons and isn't going to try and kill us all. But he still might. Now his silence is unnerving. *What the fuck is he doing?* Originally I assumed he's going hiking, maybe he is. Or maybe he's going to go kill people. *I'll put my headphones in and forget about him.* OK, he's started babbling again.

"No one's listening…"

He's definitely fucking bonkers. I could talk to him but really can't be arsed. *I'll spit out my gum into some tissue and find those headphones.*

"Risk it…"

Risk what? Jesus Christ, this man is crazy. Also, I can smell weed. *How much do I have in my bag?*

OK, headphones are in now so I can't hear him. Although he has started gesturing as if giving someone directions. This is great, I actually am enjoying it. We're turning off to Robin Hood's Bay, I reckon he'll get off here.

Fuchsia has sent me some photos to look at. I've messaged her and said I want to fuck her. Odd bit of contrast to this situation.

Not what I expected, he's not got off. And I can still hear him talking over my music.

"No point in existing… ignore you… shut up, don't tell me… leave me alone… I'll start sounding like… you judge me… yeh, I have seen that… people looked at me … not always right…"

Listening to him talk this demented bullshit out loud to himself is starting to annoy me. I might talk to him.

OK, so I spoke to him, I said I assumed he'd be getting off to go hiking and he just looked at me and said "no". I had nothing else to say because he looked away.

Maybe I should ask who the fuck he's talking to.

"They tell you what to do…"

But I don't. We're going through Hawsker now, I've not long left so I'll try ignore him and think about the weekend ahead. No one else on the bus seems to be bothered by this fucked up Gurkha, anyway. In fact, no one else really even seems to be aware of him being there.

DAY 118 (SATURDAY).

RAIN STORM.

It wasn't long ago that I was in the park trying to feed squirrels with peanuts I found on the ground. At that point, the tab of acid was starting to work. I'd love to recall what happened after that, but I can't right now. It involved more acid and more weed. It's going to be Sunday soon.

There were many thoughts that happened earlier in the day and two of them I wanted to write down to say to Audie. One was whilst listening to The Beatles, I Want to Hold Your Hand, where I simply just thought of Audie. Two was whilst thinking that I've always been OK with ditching friends and never being in touch with them ever again. I've done that several times; I get tired of them, sever ties and move on. I've been thinking of doing that with my current friends, but my thought was that I wouldn't want to do that with Audie, and she is the only person that I have felt that about. We're ignoring Fuchsia in that of course. I figured that Audie's greatest asset, and also downfall, is that she is too unique. Irreplaceable.

Those were two of the many thoughts. The only two worth writing down and explaining.

*   *   *

I'm listening to Boris Brejcha.

I'm outside and can see the air moving.

There are patterns in the patio.

I'm inside and can see patterns in the bricks through the window.

There is a fox looking at me in the bricks.

*   *   *

I came up again. If I had colouring pencils I would try to draw that fox.

Fuchsia wasn't seeing as much visuals but we spoke about it quite a lot. About how it's not like seeing fairies, it's just visuals. And the difference between me and Fuchsia is that she had contacts in and I wasn't wearing my glasses. The music was good.

What is this weird feeling I've got on my tongue?

It's 3am, I'm laid watching Scott Pilgrim vs the World, a film that I view as one of the ultimate romance stories. Plus, I have always thought Ramona is amazing. Anyway, Fuchsia is laid next to me with her eyes closed trying to sleep and I get a message. It's Audie sending a picture of the thunderstorm from her bedroom window.

She was alone at home with her children. We messaged for over an hour.

DAY 119 (SUNDAY).

WAVE PATTERNS.

I didn't sleep very much and I woke with back pain early, so I showered and decided to see if I could grit my teeth and run through the pain. I ran to Sandsend, four kilometres along the beach splashing my feet as I went. It hurt. It was hard. But I did it.

I didn't want to run back and so walked the four kilometres home in the sea, occasionally stopping to look at the patterns the waves were making on the pebbles, and wading out to my knees. By the time I got into Whitby it was 9am and I went to see what shops were open. None. It's a Sunday. Costa was open, however, so I got me and Fuchsia a coffee and walked home to take it to her whilst it was still hot.

My neck was hurting when I got home and Fuchsia told me that it's potentially to do with tensing up and restricted blood flow from acid, so I should take some magnesium supplements. They left a disgusting taste in my mouth.

DAY 120 (MONDAY).

ANIMOSITY.

An interesting point to note from checking my emails this morning, I only had three and they were all from students. Students rarely ever email and they were all "I saw this and thought you'd like it" types.

I watched the video from Marty, it was long and about the system of units we use, and the video made a new system of units based on using the speed of light, the calorie and the frequency of a middle C. It was interesting, I watched all of it.

OK, what the fuck am I doing here again? I got this tattoo, actually two tattoos, the other day to have faith in myself and I'm ignoring them already. Wow, you can do better than this. Here is the question, what do I call myself when I finish teaching? Something gender neutral and not unique.

At 8:54am, I sent an email to Margie and Alice listing the times I want to run extra maths study sessions for sixth form.

At 11:36am I got an email from Alice, copying Ricky and Margie in it. She may as well copied Bertha and Julia in too, then she would have had all the directors of subjects. *Cunt.*

```
From: Alice
To: DEAD; Margie; Ricky

Hi all,
```

Thanks for the information RE these extra maths lessons. It is important that <u>no students miss</u> other lessons.

```
Week 1
Monday — N/A
Tuesday — 1 — PHYSICS CLASH
Wednesday — N/A
Thursday — 4 —  No Clash
Friday — 4 — No Clash

Week 2
Monday — 1 — PHYSICS CLASH
Tuesday — 3 — ENGINEEERING CLASH
Wednesday — 2 — ENGINEEERING CLASH
Thursday — 2 —  No Clash
Friday — N/A

Regards,
Alice
```

It fucked me off. The bold text, the underlining and the capitals especially fucked me off. And that spelling mistake on engineering... *wow*. I reply all with this:

```
From: DEAD
To: Alice; Margie; Ricky
```

<u>There is no physics clash on week 1 Tuesday period one.</u>

<u>Why are the other engineering classes even studying now?</u>

> How about we forget about it. I have a lot to do in these three weeks and to-ing and fro-ing on a timetable is not really a priority. They are only intervention sessions that I wanted to provide on the basis that there are some students behind and a very thin maths department next year.

DEAD

And that was that. I have now given up on the idea of running extra maths study sessions for sixth form.

We bumped into each other later on in the day. It was awkward and Alice was making an obvious effort to be nice and clear the air. It made me feel a little bad, but I also knew I was right to have been angry in the first place. I'm just trying to help these kids. Sure there are timetable issues, but it was just drop-in, optional lessons and all I'm met with is animosity.

*   *   *

Went for a little run.

Did a live stream in the evening, but my laptop nearly took off from overheating. In the stream all I did was finish writing my JustGiving page for the "22 Mile Suicide Run". URL extension is "dead-calm". I think it's clever.

DAY 121 (TUESDAY).

JUST GIVING UP.

A long day. In the morning I made the JustGiving page live, got annoyed at emails again, and spoke to Doc about drugs. He knows a lot more about drugs than me and he's done a hell of a lot more. In his younger days he was training to become a Medical Officer in the Royal Navy. Then one day whilst docked in Denmark he got some shore leave and went to Roskilde Festival. I don't know if it was drug-encouraged or what, but he had some sort of epiphany about life and never went back to his ship. Years later he did prison time for going AWOL, then eventually retrained to become a maths teacher by doing a humanities degree. He said it was the easiest route. I don't really understand how though.

Margie wasn't in, her child was ill. I spent the morning bumbling about until my mum messaged me.

> [10:44] Mother: It says on Facebook the Whitby dentist practice closed that where you go

```
[10:56] DEAD: Yeh, why is it closed?

[10:56] DEAD: Just for a couple of weeks?

[11:14] Mother: No for good I rang about my tooth

[11:25] DEAD: How can they just close? I have an appointment in
a couple of weeks.
```

She sent a screenshot of a conversation on Facebook, reiterating what she had just told me, but with punctuation. Randomly my dentist is closing in two weeks and the other dentist isn't accepting new patients. *Fuck my life.*

With the JustGiving page now live, I sent an email to all staff with the subject "End-of-Term Fundraising".

```
From: DEAD
To: all staff

Hi all,

Two weeks today I'm running the 22 miles from my house in
Whitby to school, in memory of Chester Bennington (singer of
Linkin Park).

I'm fundraising for a mental health charity called the Campaign
Against Living Miserably, who work in suicide prevention. And
if you didn't know, 23 July is my last day working here as I'm
moving to a new direction in life. A little donation to the
JustGiving page would be the best leaving present ;)

So attached is my JustGiving page, dead-calm.

It's going to be a difficult run.

Thanks,
DEAD
```

Only Graham replied, saying good luck. And then two hours later Ricky sent an email with the subject "Sponsored Walk". He wrote six long paragraphs about a sponsored walk he's doing and gave a link to his JustGiving page.

God, that fucked me off. He's not even doing a proper challenge, it's just a wanky little walk. And Ricky is fucking minted anyway, he always talks about how much money he has. Why doesn't he just donate himself and… I don't know, it's not sat on me well this one.

* * *

I bought myself a running belt from the Sports Direct near the bus station. It can fit my phone in it. I put it in and listen to Chester singing Sharp Edges live. The live version has more meaning to me, it resonates more.

... sharp edges... consequences... find out ... myself.

The words echo.

DAY 122 (WEDNESDAY).

CRACKHEAD.

I've been messaging Audie every morning this week as it's the first week at a new placement on her course. She studies dentistry of all things, but not anywhere nearby.

I don't know why I'm doing it, I think it's just because I know what the first week of a placement feels like. When teacher training, I found it really difficult. All I say to her is "I hope it goes well today" and every day she has replied and we have a little conversation. It's nice. Once I got to school this morning I unlocked my phone and the conversation with Audie is still open. I notice it says she's online and without thinking I message. It was almost like Tourette's, it kind of freaked me out a little.

    [07:11] DEAD: it says you're online. Are you slacking?

She replies and says she's sending changing room nudes. My response is a generic laugh emoji.

And there we go, it's fucked with my head that she sends other people nudes. Maybe we don't have anything for each other. Although maybe she is scared to send them to me because we do have something for each other. I think that most guys would ask for a picture, but I don't. I don't like to ask for those kind of things, but I am curious as to who she sends them to.

Anyway, this is sitting on my mind and it's only 8:30am. Doc comes in and so I tell him of the emotional predicament I'm in, but don't go into the details of the nudes. It's nice to hear me say it out loud. It's another one of those cases where, once I've said it, it all sounds a little stupid. He was a little shocked, or rather, he was worried... He actually said he was worried about me.

My lesson was good, as I know what I'm talking about. Then I was covering isolation, which was a drag and I just spoke to Benedict about cars.

After lunch I covered Monty's lesson and the students were talking absolute shite. Just waffle. One kid asked if I'm watching the match tonight and I said "Not relevant, shut up". It's harsh but I need to close them down as I get suckered into talking to them.

Hamlet came to talk to me as I asked him about his name whilst reading out the register. Turns out BromCom has his name wrong. That is, the school records have his name wrong. I can't believe how normal this kind of shite is here. He asks about his behaviour entries on BromCom and we take a look at them. There was one that I couldn't help but laugh at, written by Gladys.

Calling another student's parent a "crackhead" and further insults along this line.

Below it was another one by Gladys.

Called another student a "gay boy". Explained how this was inappropriate, homophobic, unprofessional etc. Hamlet was not apologetic and said "he knows it's a joke, he isn't crying".

* * *

Fuchsia's made a big group chat for an 80s music night at a bar this weekend, to see who's around for it. I messaged the group.

[17:30] DEAD: I LOVE FUCKING 80s MUSIC!!

[17:37] DEAD: I also could have said I love 80s fucking music.

[17:38] DEAD: And Fuchsia can vouch for all the times I've been singing Girls Just Want to Have Fun whilst she's bent over the sofa with me behind her.

[17:38] DEAD: Wait, who's in this chat?!

It was for my own amusement. Then I shared a link to my JustGiving page. My sister replied with a thumbs-up emoji.

DAY 123 (THURSDAY).

BULLSHIT, TAGS AND SEXSOMNIA.

How are we meant to teach when you can't be comfortable as you are? Teaching isn't difficult, the difficult part is putting up with all the bullshit whilst still having some belief that life is worth living, because you can't let the students know that you know existence is pointless.

What is this bullshit that I talk about?

- It's the mundane irrelevant shit like saying I can't teach without socks on.

- It's having posters about rules, like sitting up properly and how every answer should be "framed".

- It's having to use PowerPoint when I have no need for it and it has zero additional educational benefit.

- It's having to tell students they are wearing the incorrect outfit. And if I don't, SLT having a go at me in front of the students, asking me "why are they wearing Converse?" Or "why are they wearing a jumper?"

- It's being told the school is open to diversity but a male student got sent home for wearing a skirt.

- It's assemblies and the "theme of the week" that seems to be on a cycle of Greta Thunberg, book burnings, the holocaust and LGBT.

- It's an environment that thinks it's professional but can't make a spreadsheet or a presentation that doesn't look like it was made by a primary school student.

- It's about being called "Miss" or "Sir", like I'm better than these students.

- It's about not getting a moment to just talk to someone because we are all "too busy".

- It's being told about different educational theories when there is always evidence for and against something.

- It's about very little freedom in anything you do.

- It's all the things you force yourself to forget because they peck at your mind and soul if you don't.

174

I can't even continue this list.

By the way, Margie said that AQA got back in touch about moderating all my TAGs. It's all fine apparently. My year 13s will get the grades I put them in for. At least there is some relief there.

*   *   *

OK, so here is the problem about fundraising: I don't believe in charity as it doesn't make a problem go away. But for something like mental health, I don't think that is ever going to go away. I'm not against charity, it's just I'm fully aware that it only makes a problem more tolerable, rather than fixing the problem. But not all problems are fixable.

When I did the fundraiser in December last year, the marathon row on a rowing machine, that was just for the charity that the school was supporting that year. That fucking hurt that challenge did. Physically and mentally.

*   *   *

I don't remember what happened tonight, I was so tired. I think I grabbed Fuchsia and dragged her to my side of the bed. Within a matter of minutes she was bouncing up and down on me. She looked beautiful on me, although I wasn't really awake. That was sexsomnia. I've not had it in years.

DAY 124 (FRIDAY).

BEST MAN.

I'm in isolation and I can hear Bertha teaching nuclear physics wrong.

Benedict is stood outside of his class, he's been sent out so he decides to come sit in isolation with me instead. He's got a lot on his mind and I let him vent some gas.

He gets ill with anxiety, which stresses him and it makes him more ill. Teachers seem to be picking on him unnecessarily and he is very vocal about not taking shit, getting him in more trouble. For example, recently Cleo told everyone in his assembly to leave and he stood up, but apparently he wasn't supposed to yet. She shouted at him, saying "that's a detention", which was like lighting a fuse. Making it worse is his home life, as his mother is really ill and hears a different story from him and the school. A lot of the staff think he is taking drugs and that's why he gets the train to school, but Benedict tells me the train is £30 cheaper a term than the school bus. That's just simple maths.

Doc pops his head into the isolation room and shows me a YouTube channel of some guy who rips on a bong and records it. We sit and laugh about it. That's how this guy makes a living.

* * *

Remember when you played snap as a child and you held your hand on the card as you put it down in case it's a snap, just so your hand was there first? And then you start shouting "nap" because it's quicker than pronouncing the S in snap. Could you imagine seeing adults doing that at the pub or in a cafe? Shouting "nap" and arguing. Nearest you get as an adult is playing Ring of Fire. And the last time I played that I actually passed out.

When did we grow up?

Why did we grow up?

I remember when I was a child and everyone called their pets Jet. I want to call a dog Shet, just to confuse people. "No, it's shet, as in 'who's done a shet and not flushed it?'"

I'm curious, was Jet a popular pet name or am I making it up?

A quick search on Google found a list of the most common cat and dog names from the last ten years. The data is from insurance policies, so it naturally only really represents middle-class families. Apparently the most popular name given to a cat last year was the same as the most popular name given to a dog last year, and it's the same name as Audie's youngest. I message Audie and tell her the fact, saying it's her own personal Friday fact. She just says "excellent fact". Jet wasn't on the list though.

* * *

Some uneventful hours passed featuring me binning shit from my desk in the maths office and a randomly overwhelming desire to have sex. I contemplated having a wank in the toilets but I really don't want to cross that boundary.

When I left I put my jacket on, even though I didn't want to wear it, it was so warm. Bertha left the building at the same time as me. I knew what was coming and it fucking did. It took her about two seconds to start talking about when she lived in Cyprus, gobbing off about how she doesn't wear a coat anymore, it was so warm there. *I know, Bertha. I fucking know, you talk about how you lived there all the time.*

Just out of the alleyway on the way to the bus, I bump into Hazel and Hamlet smoking near the graffiti. I have some time and we talk. About smoking. About how I'm cutting back for running. About the run. Then I mentioned I'm out this weekend, so may end up smoking a little bit. To which Hazel says "get them down you". I laughed.

On the bus I decided to message everyone I know about fundraising. Felt like a dick, but I'm not doing this fucking run without more donations. It gave way to some some interesting conversations with people I haven't heard from in ages. For one, Fauna's mother-in-law has just died. Fauna is the person that I bought that really nice dark blue-grey suit with black lining for. I did say that she's married now.

I also asked my mum to share it with the aunties and uncles, since I don't have their numbers. Half an hour later Mum rang me. I was half expecting this, but I didn't expect her to be so much of a dick. It was about me mentioning my ex-partner's dad on my JustGiving page.

If I can explain this, I'd be surprised. Whilst he was alive, there was a lot of mixed opinions of him and allegations of him doing some quite bad things, one of which involved my sister. He was never convicted of anything as far as I'm aware. But regardless of what I or other people thought of the man, I saw what his suicide did to his family. And it still affects some of them now. My mum didn't understand this and so I deleted his name from the page, it's not worth the agro. But I wish people would understand that it's not about what they think. I wish they would just fuck off. I can't be myself around these people.

At home I got changed to go to the Brewery with Fuchsia. Our little date night to just sit and talk. We'd been there about 30 minutes when Audie messaged me and asked what I was up to.

    [19:11] Audie: What you doing?
    [19:12] DEAD: At the Brewery.
    [19:12] DEAD: You joining?
    [19:13] Audie: We're out in Sandsend.
    [19:13] Audie: How long will you be there?

```
[19:13] DEAD: Until close prob. Lol.

[19:17] Audie: We'll come join.

[19:18] Audie: Wait, who's with you?

[19:19] DEAD: Fuchsia.

[19:19] DEAD: That is all.

[19:19] Audie: Good.
```

They turned up about 30 minutes later getting out of a taxi, meaning that I had to drink two more pints. I don't know how that logic works but it fucking did and I then suggested we go into town.

We got up to leave, Fuchsia and Al leading the way, Audie and myself walking together further back, holding hands. It felt nice, like it was natural and meant to be. She looked pretty good, although not in my style in all honesty. She looks different to Fuchsia.

In town we went to the cocktail bar. We sat on the balcony, I smoked a bifta and asked Audie to be my best man. She said yes. Then we spoke about us, about what we are doing. Then she said that I'm the one that messages her and I'm the one that chases her. It pissed me off, but I laughed and pretended it didn't. It made me wonder something uncomfortable about her.

DAY 125 (SATURDAY).

80S NIGHT.

It's 80s night, it's like Phoenix Nights here. I've taken acid, no one else knows that. Fuchsia and Audie haven't come, they are too hungover from last night.

I've gone on Instagram for some reason and noticed Diana has put a picture of herself on her story. She's dyed her hair pink, it looks fucking awesome and so I tell her.

```
[00:01] DEAD: Oh my god, your hair is amazing. I am in a full
pink outfit right now :D

[00:01] Diana: I feel like a new girl.

[00:03] DEAD: It looks really nice.

[00:04] Diana: Thank you :P
```

[00:04] DEAD: Remember what I said about that girl ages ago?

My mind flicks to the few months we worked together and the long and deep chats we'd have at break time. She once suggested I move to France with her. I was tempted. Maybe I should have.

[00:05] DEAD: Well, it's all weird now.

[00:06] Diana: Strange, I was just thinking about that.

[00:06] Diana: Why's it weird?

[00:06] DEAD: I don't think I could articulate it.

[00:06] DEAD: I've taken acid :D

[00:07] Diana: Fabulous news.

[00:07] Diana: How's that going for you?

[00:10] DEAD: Pretty good.

[00:13] DEAD: Are you up for a drink, a week on Friday?

[00:14] DEAD: For my last day. 23 July.

[00:20] Diana: Yeh, sure!

Everyone has left, leaving Spike, Stella and myself outside having a cigarette. They are talking together and suddenly start arguing. I don't know what started this domestic, but clearly something petty. Stella turns around and leaves abruptly. Spike stands silent, looking out towards the sea and then towards a couple walking near the cliff. I'm jumping on and off a wall, minding my own and yet fully aware of my surroundings. Randomly, Spike says he's following the couple. I stumble on the wall and ask if he was joking. He says the woman looked scared and the man was being threatening. I stand and stare at him. *He's being fucking weird*. I didn't see anything of what he said, it made zero sense to me. I explain there is no fucking way I am following a random couple. And so he walks off in their direction leaving me stood on the brick wall, alone.

I don't want to be alone.

I turn and run to go and catch up with Stella.

We walk and talk about their relationship, me throwing my opinion in. *They are fucked*. My opinion is to not drag a relationship through shit, relationships aren't worth that. She says they are both a-sexual. I laughed and say they definitely aren't and she just needs a good fuck. I looked at her and laughed again, she was in a shit mood.

179

"Why would I kiss someone whose breath stinks?" She says, more to herself than me.

"Why would I want to have sex with someone who doesn't exercise?" Again, more to herself.

"End the relationship then." It's all I have to say. Most people don't appreciate the nihilistic side of relationships, specifically romantic relationships, and wouldn't say this. But I don't see the point of beating around the bush. However, I don't mention about how she also doesn't exercise.

Stella goes quiet. We walk in silence. A minute passes, probably.

"He always says how he thinks I'm autistic." She definitely isn't, but I say nothing. *Is he gaslighting her?*

"I think he has ADHD." *Is she gaslighting him?* I also don't think he does, but I remain quiet.

She goes quiet again. Another minute passes, probably.

Her phone rings. It's Spike...

It unravelled quickly from there, into hours of running about town looking for him.

He was annoyed I was with Stella. He hung up. He messaged. He rang again. He wants to be left alone. He rang again. And then again. He's on the cliff. Why haven't we come to meet him? Where are we? He messaged again. He's outside a pub. Why aren't we there? Eventually we found him. He was confused as to why I was worried, he's not going to do anything. And eventually we went our separate ways. I left them near the big bridge, they walked towards their home and I turned towards mine. On the walk back I message him.

        [03:10] DEAD: I'm sorry I left you.

        [03:11] DEAD: You are one of the few people I regard as my
        friend.

        [03:12] DEAD: And yes, I was worried about you doing something.

        [03:13] DEAD: Because I worry about myself in the same way
        every day.

        [03:15] DEAD: It was still a good night.

        [03:26] Spike: I'll see you when I see you.

And then I started to cry.

Here I am, high as a fucking kite and crying. But it's about Audie and what she said last night. I thought she was my friend, I'm so sick of trying to be friends with people when they don't care about me in return. Is that the kind of person I am? One who cares, but isn't cared for? Regardless of any other feelings I may have, I just thought she was my friend. But she isn't. I feel so alone.

DAY 126 (SUNDAY).

GODSPEED SUNDAY.

I've woken up and decided how to finish this book. A slight hinge in this problem is that I can't make a note of it now because I feel like shite. And you may remember that night when I tried to write when feeling particularly down and ended up ruining a perfectly good pair of jean shorts. Anyway, I'm at peace with the idea of how to finish the book.

I feel like I'm feeling things for the first time ever. As if I had shut off a large section of my emotions and now the door has opened to them. Well, at least some of them, there may be more doors in there. It's not great though. There is so much shit in my head that nothing emotionally makes sense. And I feel as though I understand why those doors were shut. But what if I can sort through these new feelings? What if I can unlock more doors and make sense of it all?

I've gone for a walk. Just me in a pair of shorts and my trainers. I decided that will help my mood today, so I aimed along the Cinder Track and towards Stainsacre Woods.

On the walk towards the viaduct I can hear a lot of noise and I recall a sign I saw a few minutes back that said something about bungee jumping. I didn't really register it at the time, but I suddenly appreciate why it was there. *Are they bungee jumping from the viaduct?* It turns out they are. There is a big scaffolding rig set up which people are launching themselves from. There is quite a lot of people working on it, people queueing for a go and people just watching. I look over the edge and can see a small boat in the river and a man scrabbling up the bank. His legs look wobbly, he must be the one that just jumped.

I can't quite imagine the appeal of this bungee jump. The tide is out so the river is low enough to just look like a collection of brown sludge. The thought of potentially the last thing I see being brown sludge if something went wrong is not what I would want. I walk past everyone, feeling their eyes on my naked torso. I have spots on my back today, but there's not much I can fucking do about that.

I continue up the Cinder Track, just wanting to smash things. That feeling of getting a bulldozer and driving it into a random house. Smashing car windows. Getting a baseball bat and standing on the bonnet of a police car whilst sinking it through the windscreen, making beautiful warped splits in the laminating. This is that feeling of existentialism. I've lived until now suppressing those feelings and now I see no point in existence, I should just do them. I can imagine my parents wondering what went wrong. *Fuck them. Do what you want.*

This gives me a thought, the naughty kids in school who don't care about consequences are really just existential doubters. Maybe that's what everyone does, those who are in prison don't know why they exist and so they lash out. Do the wrong thing. Amplify that and you'll ask yourself if this feeling has caused wars, destroyed nations and ransacked and raped our Earth? Was Hitler an existential doubter, playing a little game of war for the sake of it? Why else does it matter to them that they purge ethnicities and religions when they are going to die and cease to exist? Is it because they want to feel like they do exist and so challenge that feeling by doing something outrageous?

Now on the way back, I sit on a bench at the other end of the viaduct and my phone buzzes. It's Spike thanking me for last night and adding that him and Stella have broken up.

* * *

I'm listening to Godspeed You! Black Emperor. Drone music. They headlined ArcTanGent Festival when I went and it poured down throughout their set. It was beautiful. Their best album is F♯ A♯ ∞, it has an apocalyptic feel to it and opens with a grotesque monologue in Dead Flag Blues. I can still feel a bit of the acid lingering in my body from last night. I think listening to this right now is not the best idea.

… car's on fire… no driver… muddied… lonely suicides… dark wind blows.

The words echo.

The music and lyrics are pranging me out a little, I'm going to lie down.

*   *   *

I woke up hours later on the sofa, fully dressed and my headphones still on, spurting out Godspeed You! Black Emperor on repeat. I was covered in sweat.

DAY 127 (MONDAY).

BELIEVE.

Maybe I should make a new religion. One where you worship back pain and I can be the messiah. The chosen one.

A man is sat in front of me on the bus. I want to stab him in the neck. Not for any reason other than he is slightly fat and his neck is red with sunburn apart from on the creases between rolls of fat. How on Earth I've managed to get my phone out to distract myself is a wonder. I'm falling asleep and not quite able to tell what is real and dream. I thought there was a woman sat next to me, but there isn't.

It's just another day of wishing I was dead.

There's an irony to fundraising for a mental health charity. If you have depression there is a good chance that you won't want to ask for donations and will find the entire thing completely pointless. You still do it because you know you should, but the fact that you get so few donations is itself depressing. A reminder that most people you know are cunts and no one really cares. The website you use to fundraise shows you other people's fundraising efforts and that just makes it worse. *Why are some people getting hundreds of thousands of pounds and I'm struggling to get a couple hundred quid?* Some people are just going skydiving as their challenge whereas I am doing something that I'm actually shitting myself about. I fear I'll be dead before it's over. And I'm doing it alone.

Right now I'm waiting outside school. Leopold isn't here so the building is still locked and I can see Monty and Bertha near the door. I'm stood at my smoking spot, far enough away so I don't have to talk to them. I'd like to light a cigarette but want to give my lungs a break after the weekend and for the run next week. I'm tempted to just go home right now. Also I don't have any tobacco. And my back fucking hurts.

You could hang yourself from almost anything. A tree. A road sign. A bridge.

I put Cher, Believe on and it makes me smile. I stick it on my Instagram story, saying I'm listening to it. Distractions.

I'm still fucked off with Audie, but I know it's just that she stirred a feeling that I'm already fucked off with. But I wish it didn't come from her. I'm going to have to take pain killers, my back hurts too much. I feel like crying and smashing things. Like I said the other day, I just want to smash things.

I feel like I want to talk to someone about all this but I know I'll regret it afterwards. I don't like people knowing this stuff. I told Stella some of it on Saturday and really regret that, not that she was listening anyway. That night was a proper shit show.

Take Curlos for example, what would I say to him? It would start awkwardly because I don't intend to ask him to be my best man, even though he's been a solid friend and is the obvious choice.

Would it look like this?

[-:-] DEAD: The other night when we were out I ended up asking someone to be my best man, whilst we were sat touching each other under the table opposite our respective partners.

Maybe I need to explain more?

[-:-] DEAD: So it was kind of a double date vibe, and we ended up sat next to opposite partners. Me and the other girl do have feelings for each other and seem to be acting more on it recently. Acting more like a couple.

But I am now at this point where I am worried as to how much I like her. I know I don't love her, but it's one where I wonder if I do. I don't really even believe in love. So we sat and talked in this bar on Friday night with our partners opposite us, touching each other under the table and she was really keen to be best man. And then I mentioned about how I'll need to get to know her more if she is to be my best man, but she says she's a cunt and I won't like her. I tell her to stop pushing me away because I'm not going away. And then she said that I'm the one that messages her and I'm the one that chases her. And it really fucking got to me, but I brushed it off and said that I enjoy the chase. Which is actually true, but it hit me like a punch on the nose. That's what she thinks of me? I thought we were friends. More than friends. But it revealed a concern I've had for a long time, that she doesn't really have feelings for me.

I'm not sure what the point of sending either of those messages to Curlos would be. So I don't message him. I don't message anyone.

But this highlights the feeling that I have, that it is always me that reaches out to other people. No one ever seems to reach out to me, they are always just replying to me. And that's different. *Am I so unapproachable?*

Ask yourself this: do you love Audie?

No, but I like the feeling of wondering about it, like I'm a child playing pretend. I definitely have some emotional attachment and I enjoy thinking about her and getting attention from her. And to get attention, I give her attention. It's convoluted bullshit.

I genuinely think I'm emotionally fucked at the moment.

OK, so I'm going to try and teach something today. My first two hours are in the isolation room and can decide what to teach whilst in there.

Diana replied to my story to say she listens to that song on repeat everyday. It really made me laugh.

*   *   *

I'm going to teach second year calculus this week to the year 12s. That's my goal before I leave, that the class can differentiate more complicated functions. I've made my notes on the back of the only piece paper I could find – a removal form. It's been completed by Margie and it was issued for a student refusing to hand over a phone. Amusingly she hasn't put the name of the student on it, meaning that the kid will completely get away with it. There is only one other removal form in the tray, this one filled in by Graham, for a student "using foul language". Interestingly it also has the student name box empty, meaning another student will get away with it as if nothing had happened. I'm not sure what the point of the form is if the most important part is missing. Everything else on the form is about recording what, where and when. But without the name there is no accountability. No follow up. No fucking point.

Margie wrote the date as "2" anyway. Two of what? What's the fucking point?

It's the end of the two hours and I've listened to all of the Incubus, Morning View album. My ear hurts a little from it being so loud. In my opinion it was the best album by Incubus, but maybe I would say that as it was the first of their's that I heard. Aziz showed it to me. 11 am maintains a position of one of my favourite songs of all time. I mumble it to myself.

... the credits... the end... missed the best part... please go back.

The words echo.

*   *   *

The lesson was OK. It's difficult when you don't have your heart in it, and it's worse when your back is hurting and you're struggling to not be ridiculously moody. I sat and ate an early lunch in the empty classroom and got fed up with my back. So now I'm sat in the hall after using a workout mat that I found to do some stretches on. It hasn't made anything better, but it hasn't made anything worse and I'm all for trying anything to make it better right now. I was thinking this morning about what I would pack in a bag if I were to run away, and then I remembered about how my back didn't hurt whilst hiking last year. It's odd that.

Students are now going to lunch and I'm still sat in the hall. I think I might just sit here until the end of lunch at 2pm. Earlier I had the thought of being sick this week. I guess I could be, still. Would be nice to not be here and to relax, I feel so strung out. I'm so tired, I've done a few micro sleeps as I sit here. The ones where you do a little dream and wake up with the belief it was real. For a moment I thought a woman was sat next to me. I really thought it.

After lunch, in my next lesson, I just get the kids playing chess. At the end of it, one of them asks if they can stay and play more chess.

"What's your next lesson?" I ask.

"LPD... chess is far better than sex education." *I don't even know what LPD stands for.*

His reply reminds me of the scene in Austin Powers where Austin moves a knight to the other side of the board in his first move. Then the person he is playing against says "make love to me you hairy little man". Funny scene, he must have chosen sex education. But there's nothing about sex education in IQ tests.

DAY 128 (TUESDAY).

A STUDENT I USED TO TEACH.

I woke up in so much pain, but it was mostly in my head. My body was heavy and I struggled to move. About an hour earlier I had gotten up to take painkillers and gone back to bed. Right now it was 5:30am and my alarm had gone off.

There was no chance I was going in. Absolutely zero. I imagined being there at school and all I could think about was leaving. And so I picked up my phone and sent an email. This was the best I could achieve.

```
From: DEAD
To: Margie; Frank

Hi both. I cannot come in today I am really unwell. Can't
didn't hebfunemver to ring.
```

I couldn't even write the email properly.

These last days of wishing I was dead have taken a toll on me. And my thoughts about the 22 mile suicide run and finishing this book are making me anxious.

Fuchsia was laid next to me, it was calming. I laid there for the next three hours until I was so sweaty I had to shower. I have to get up to set work online anyway.

I've gone for a fairly long shower and put on my tartan shorts with white socks pulled up to my calves. Fuchsia says I look nice. I still have some of the makeup on that she put on me last night for fun.

Setting the work on Google Classroom is easy, but I'm nervous that no one will tell the students that it's there. I post a message online to my first class, hoping they might have the sense to look on their phones.

```
DEAD [Posted 08:56]

Hi all,

Apologies, I am too unwell to come in today. Think it could be
from getting the second vaccine at the weekend.

I'd like you to continue looking at the chain rule, checking
your understanding on the questions attached (exercise 9C) for
the first 30 minutes, as we usually would do. Then move on to
the product rule.
```

Use the computers in the breakout area.

Any questions, I'll be on here.

DEAD

It was on Saturday morning that I got the second vaccine, before the 80s night. I've gone down the route of saying the vaccine has knocked me, rather than saying I'm depressed as fuck, and I email Margie to ask her to make sure that the students get started on the work. I only got the first vaccine to get an afternoon off work several months ago.

And then an email from Quinn to all staff comes through.

From: Quinn
To: all staff

Dear all,

Following the sad news this morning I would like to remind all staff that we are very mindful of your well-being and people cope differently when situations arise…

It continued, but it didn't explain anything. *What sad news? What the fuck has happened?* Someone has died. Clearly someone has died.

I email Margie again, this time asking what has happened. She replies shortly and says it's a student I used to teach who has died. *Fuck this, I know this is going to get worse.*

Ten minutes later Quinn emails to let me know what has happened. And it's true, he's taken his own life.

Fuck this shit.

Fuck.

    This.

        Shit.

This is such ridiculous timing. I'm depressed as fuck and my mind is racing with thoughts of suicide.

Even Fuchsia is sad and she didn't know the kid. She just knows how fucked up society is. It was only an hour ago, whilst I was in the shower, that she got an email saying the work she did for free over the last week has been for nothing. They don't want to employ her, but she's no longer lecturing and needs work. She hates how her industry does this, it takes advantage of people.

But then again, most things do.

I feel like it's almost in bad taste, but I share the news to my Instagram story with a link to my JustGiving page again, thanking people who had already supported. It is a suicide prevention charity after all. A few people messaged me, such as Rosie and Becky, and that was nice. Obviously there is one particular person who hasn't messaged. She might not have seen it. She might not care enough to look at what I do.

But then I noticed that she did see it.

And she had posted about going for a run. Well, it might not have been a run, but she was on the Cinder Track, which I can only assume was a run. It was with a caption saying "this week has kicked the shit out of me and it's only Tuesday" with an upside-down smiley face. It gave me some motivation to go for a run myself. Fuchsia was running a bath and I figured I may as well. I might even bump into Audie and can either ignore her or try to move on from the awkwardness I currently feel.

So I went out and ran. I just ran. Didn't see her but didn't care. I even skipped a little while listening to 99 Luft Balloons. Doc once said that the song's about balloons that were released and people thought it was a nuclear attack. I'm not sure I believe him. The run was going so well that I extended it with some hill running and the 199 steps, as grotesque as it is, pushing myself as hard as I could.

When I got in, Fuchsia was still in the bath so I climbed in with her. It wasn't anything sexual, it was just hanging out in the bath together. Afterwards, downstairs, Fuchsia rubbed my back whilst I looked at shoes online. I don't intend to buy any, it was more just interesting to look at all the different styles of Adidas shoes in size 11. I've only bought Adidas shoes for about five years, since damaging my feet doing the marathon in Converse that were too small.

I start to feel a little uncomfortable in the position I'm in so I turn Fuchsia around and lay her over my lap. I'm still on my phone, but pushing my free hand between her legs and sliding it up towards her lower back. And then I give up on my phone, Fuchsia lays on her back and I put my head between her legs. This was all going perfectly well, but my mind kept wandering off to places. It sounded like she was enjoying it, but she said to not press as hard with my tongue. I knew I had been, but I was questioning my method and just kept doing it until she said. Also, it tasted a little different. I changed a little and started using my finger at the same time. She sounded like she was enjoying this too, but my mind was still wandering off. She said not to go as fast. I no longer cared about sex and was just acting on some sort of autopilot.

I laid my head on her thigh and continued with just my finger. But I was completely gone now. So I sat up and then laid down next to her and stared at the ceiling. We didn't really interact after that.

What the fuck are we doing?

DAY 129 (WEDNESDAY).

PUSH THROUGH.

There was a new man on the bus that I'd not seen before when I got on. He was talking to the old fella that is always there, who gets off just up the road near the Aldi. Five minutes later, on the way to Robin Hood's Bay, this new man had turned in his seat and was facing me. We caught eyes and I looked away. He better not fucking talk to me.

I kept looking at shoes on my phone for some reason, researching what the shoes are that I have. I got them from eBay last year, my white Adidas Pro-Models, but I have often wondered if they are fake because the logo peeled off and the insole some reason says "DB". All I've ever thought is David Beckham, and have no fucking idea why it would stand for that. This morning I found out that it does actually stand for David Beckham, as he released an all white version and an all black version of the Pro-Model. It doesn't really make sense to me. And this new guy is chuntering away to himself about something.

The little kid gets on, we are in the outskirts of Scarborough now. The new guy looks about the bus and says:

"Does anyone smoke, I have two spare lighters?"

I shake my head. I can't be arsed to engage with him. *Why doesn't he just keep them?*

The other old fella that looks like a character from On the Buses has just got on. He's a generic old man, dressed all in beige and looks faded like he's still in the 70s. The new guy starts to talk to him but the old fella puts his hand up as if he were stopping traffic, trying to shrug the new guy off. I can't tell what the new guy is saying but the old fella clearly doesn't want to listen. New guy turns to face away and the old fella gets up and goes upstairs. That's how much he doesn't want to be part of the conversation. The new guy then turns around and talks to the little kid. This is what I was worried about happening. I give them a moment to see if it fizzles out. She is just sat there nodding her head as the new guy is motioning to the now empty seat near him and then he points upstairs. The little kid is still nodding. *Fuck, I can't leave her to listen to this maniac.* I get my bag ready and put it on my shoulder to walk to the front of the bus and talk to the new guy myself, saving the kid. And then he turns around. And the kid buries her head into her phone, probably messaging her parents that some maniac was talking to her on the bus. Poor little shit, having to put up with that. Even I don't like to put up with people like this guy. None of the other fucks on the bus gave a shite though, all they care about is themselves. Especially Billy, what the fuck would he do? What a pathetic excuse of a 19-year-old.

As the bus gets closer I start to realise a thought. *What the fuck am I doing here?* I should be at home I feel so bad.

* * *

"I should try and teach you something." I'm covering one of Margie's year 10 maths classes but my heart wasn't in it.

"Can you teach us about how to deal with existential dread?" Said the student nearest to me. We spoke about it for a while as a class. *They know nothing.*

"I've got you down for a group cry sesh, Sir." I laughed at him and gave him a look that says please fucking continue. He seems to be the spokesperson for this class.

"You're a doomer." To which I again laugh and ask him to explain it. I understand what it means, I just want to hear his explanation. Students never realise this, they just think you're stupid.

He explains it. Badly.

A little later in lesson I called that student a dickhead because he was clearly playing a game on his laptop. When I started the class I said as long as it looks and sounds like you are working, then I'm happy. They all seemed shocked a little that I called this student a dickhead, but they don't know the kind of person I am. I apologise to him later though and said I was just in a bit of a grumpy mood. *They've not had a teacher like me before.*

I managed to hide for the rest of the day, giving a pretence of doing work when I have actually done nothing. I literally hid, did a lesson, ate a fake egg sarnie from Sainsbury's this morning, and hid some more. Whilst I hid I watched videos, listened to music and at one point I even wrote some notes for the end of this book. When I started to fall asleep, I went to get coffee from the maths office. There are only two coffee pods left so I stash them in my drawer to ration them for the rest of the week. I doubt Margie will buy any more now. I think I successfully failed all of the Teachers' Standards today.

Eventually, I did get to the end of the day and went home. On the side in the kitchen there was a letter from St Catherine's, the charity that I did the fundraising for last year with the marathon row. *Is this finally some acknowledgement and gratitude for what I did?*

No.

It was just a letter trying to sell me raffle tickets. I got changed and me and Fuchsia went out to the gym. She's really not in a good place today, she was still in bed until 11am and only got up for an interview. She rang me for five minutes before my second lesson to say the interview went well and she sounded really excited. Clearly the excitement didn't last long. It's hard being around someone who's sad and grumpy. The sad part makes you want to make them feel better, whereas the grumpy part just pushes you away. I sponge up some of her emotions and start to feel down myself. I worry that it's me that caused this last night, but I try to push it out of my mind. In the gym it's fairly empty. Fuchsia climbs onto a cycling machine and I say I'm going into the next room to row. She doesn't seem a fan of the idea for some reason. Maybe she doesn't want to be left alone, so I get myself onto the treadmill next to her, starting off a lot slower than my usual pace and then, for the last kilometre, pushing faster than ever before. The result is a mediocre average pace. Fuchsia has already finished on her bike and is sat doing some overhead lifts. I go over and talk to her. She asks how the run was and I say it felt awful. She seems surprised and I remind her that I did do a 10 kilometre run last night and that I still feel tired from it.

"Oh, so that's why you wanted to row."

"Yes."

"Well, that explains that."

We bumbled around a few of the machines together, taking it in turns, doing super sets. I think that's what you call it where instead of a rest between sets you do something else. So we were doing that between the leg machines. Fuchsia got a bit annoyed when she clocked me lowering the weight when I got off. She thought we were doing the same weights and was keeping up with me, but I told her that we started the same and I cranked it up for myself. I didn't know what weight she was doing, I was just trying to save her from realising we were doing different weights as I knew it would bother her. She wanted to go home, she'd had enough gym.

This has been one of those times when you really try to push to get through feeling shit, but this time it just hasn't worked. I'm going to have to try something else.

Since it's such a nice night I take us for an indirect walk back. I thought I saw Al's car outside the gym but didn't see him in there. We walk down into town and decide to get beer and tobacco from Bargain Booze to make a Wednesday night bifta and beer, and sit on the cliff.

This day marked ten years since I became a Master of Physics. It made me think about how I'm not in touch with anyone I went to university with, then Velma replied to my Instagram post saying we had the same supervisor. Small world, I didn't actually know her at university. This morning I had posted a photo of me in my glad rags, stood with my supervisor. Turns out she was the year below me.

DAY 130 (THURSDAY).

NUMBING SPRAY.

I'm remembering when I was at university. There is some sort of nostalgic feeling about this bus ride today, perhaps spurred on by yesterday. *Master of Physics*. So I'm sat here with a feeling of going to university or some sort of educational institute where I'm part of a group of passionate academics. It feels great. I really miss that feeling. My mind turns to studying and wondering if I studied enough, or studied in the wrong way. Looking back it's always easy to see where mistakes were made, but I'd probably do the same again. I used to fixate on concepts I didn't understand and sometimes spend weeks on something that was mentioned in about five minutes of a lecture and not really that important. Consequently I would get behind easily and often, and when it came to exams I occasionally did abysmal. In Liverpool I smashed everything, I really did and came top of the year. But when I moved to York for my second year, it all started to unravel. That was when I started to get depression too. It's not the only reason, but my relationship at the time caused a lot of problems to my mental health. I felt trapped. I stayed in that relationship for another eight years though.

At York, I recall there was one exam where it was asking about the CNO cycle. *Fuck me, I couldn't remember that one.* And then the exam asked what would happen if there was 1% less hydrogen in the universe, or some shit like that. Again I had no idea, but this wasn't for the fact of just not remembering, it was because I had no idea what the question wanted from me. It was just too vague. *I mean, what, we wouldn't have balloons? No, wait that's helium. Hydrogen... Hydrogen...* I cobbled together some bullshit answer saying how life would not exist, which is obviously not the physics styled answer it wanted, but I had no idea what else to say. What a load of fucking shite. In hindsight, I should have written about star formation, synthesis and the likes. But I still maintain it's too vague for a bullshit ten-mark question in a two-hour exam. That works out to be about 15 minutes of an exam that I'm meant to spend on imagining a slightly different universe formation, and then write about it... *Maybe no Stalin? Fuck me, I don't know.* I wish I complained at the time.

Now I think about it, that was probably the start of feeling nihilistic about studying physics. A few years later I was doing an exam for my PhD and after five minutes of reading the question paper, I took the empty answer sheet, wrote my name on it, got up and left. I'd had enough. That was the last exam I did. A few more years later I learnt about feeling nihilistic in general.

The bus is at my stop and Billy is getting off, but I might stay on until the next one and go for a walk. He smelled like detergent again today. He always fucking does.

* * *

There was this email in my inbox this morning.

```
From: Alice
To: Margie; DEAD

Hi DEAD and Margie,
```

I am concerned that the Further Maths and Maths reports are almost identical and that there is no comment in either made on their recent PPE grades. Pudge got an E in Further Maths PPE but his report reads as if he is doing great. See attached.

The following need amending:

1. Comment on exam performance and what they learned from this.

2. Alter reports so they are not repeats by 12 noon today, so that they can be printed.

Regards,
Alice

She also attached a document called "Maths Report", which turned out to just be one of the reports that I had written. The email annoyed me and I vented by writing my reply and then posting it as an Instagram story with a little commentary, rather than actually replying with it.

@DEAD1.414: Yes my reports are identical because they are the same students. You don't need to attach an example report, I know what it says because I fucking wrote it. I'm ringing every parent tonight so the fucking reports are pointless anyway. Amend by 12? Well, I'm teaching all day so I'll use magic, yeh?

Bear in mind that this is the person that observed one of my lessons and said it was shite because I wasn't wearing socks… Also, I'm leaving so they can fuck off.

No one ever does student reports properly anyway. The first time you do them, you spend ages writing bespoke reports for each student, identifying every little thing that will help a student work better. Then you realise it was pointless, no one cares. So every term after that you copy and paste the most relevant student's report from that first time, change the name, change pronouns and bam, job done. Every teacher does it that way, it's the same for UCAS references. Pudge is doing great in Further Maths, but his recent topic tests didn't reflect it, hence the grade. Since all Further Maths students are in ordinary A-Level Maths, there was nothing different I could write for them, they are the same students. When Margie came into the office I told her that if it needs changing, someone else can do it.

In the morning staff briefing, Monty gave me my winnings from a sweepstake we did for the football. I walked to the front of the hall, shook his hand and took the envelope of money. About £30. When I sat back down, I don't know why I said it, but I said:

"I'm going to buy a firework and stick it between my bum cheeks."

* * *

Before CPD, Doc was fannying about trying to fix the door closing mechanism to the maths office. He had a handful of tools from the workshop downstairs and once the mechanism was in bits on his desk and on the floor, it took about five seconds for him to say "yeh, I don't know".

The CPD session was about the student activity happening next Monday and Tuesday. Some electricity company is coming to run a workshop with the students. We've all been put into small groups with the students and it's run as a competition. I love this kind of stuff, but was a bit gutted when it was revealed that Ricky had cherry-picked himself the best team. I didn't really understand the point of that, it may as well not be a competition any more. What the students will have to do is solve a load of problems related to the National Grid, such as where to put power lines and how to design a pylon etc. I asked a lot of questions, mainly because I am looking forward to it, but I think it annoys some of the other teachers as they think it's a waste of time. Bertha was whinging that she has "naughty kids" in her group. Hamlet was one of them. All I was thinking was that my group has the kid in it that recently got excluded for being racist. I'd much rather take one of her "naughty kids" than a racist little fuck. At least we could have a laugh.

On the walk to the bus, on the bus, and at home I rang parents from my mobile, dialling 141 before their number. I'm essentially verbally explaining the reports that got sent this afternoon. After doing about half, I give up. I'll just say no one answered.

The rest of the evening was as follows:

1. We had a smoke.

2. We had sex. Fuchsia used throat numbing spray and went cross-eyed. She looked like she belonged on r/gothsluts and r/ahegaogirls and she said I fucked her "into dementia".

3. We had another smoke.

Two things that happened today that I forgot to mention:

1. In the year 12 Further Maths lesson, I won some second-hand shoes on eBay. White Adidas Stan Smith's. It was an impulse, I don't need them.

2. Diana sent me a screenshot of her phone, showing she is listening to Cher, Believe on full volume. It made me laugh.

DAY 131 (FRIDAY).

ISOLATION TO ISOLATION.

In year 12 Maths we played a game called the Pirate Game. Doc is a massive fan of it and he always plays it at the end of term when he can't be arsed to teach. He sent it to me in an email subjected "Enjoy, me hearty". It's a fairly simple game, kind of like battleships but the squares have either money to collect or an instruction like "steal another player's money". The aim of the game is to have the most money once all squares have been played. It's not real money, everyone just writes down what they have.

The game suited my mood perfectly, I really couldn't be arsed and my routine was already out of whack today. I didn't shower this morning since I had three showers yesterday (morning and before and after sex). And on the bus there was no Billy, I had to press the button for my stop myself, something I've never had to do.

Fuchsia has had a productive phone call with the doctors to discuss about how she always feels down, tired and in stomach pain.

[10:28] Fuchsia: She was a mint doctor, listened to every little symptom I had with zero judgement.

[10:28] DEAD: Cool.

[10:29] Fuchsia: Gonna have some blood tests to rule out early menopause and going in later today for her to examine my tummy.

[10:29] DEAD: Early menopause… never even thought of that. Wouldn't that show in your ovulation tests though?

[10:30] Fuchsia: No, menopause has like three stages and could explain the crying and struggling to cum.

We don't use contraceptives, Fuchsia does ovulation tests and I pull out at certain times of the month. It works.

I think I'd like to message Audie. Just to let her know it's OK and that I've not fallen out with her, it's more that I don't really care. Sometimes I do care, but it's only when I feel really down and I distract myself with other people's feelings. And right now I'm fully aware of my feelings. I am content. So I think I might message and say that I'll drop off her sandals that she left last Friday, after she vomited in the sink and passed out at ours.

I can hear a noise outside the empty classroom I'm sat hiding in. It's going to be break soon and it reminds me that I've barely done duty this entire term. I don't really see the point when there are barely any students in school now. I don't really need to be there wasting my time. Checking on the noise, I see Hamlet sat at a computer in the break-out area.

"The internet isn't working again, Hamlet." It's not been working properly since that student did the DDoS.

"I'll go spit on it," he says. I don't reply, but inside I laugh.

I walked from the classroom past Quinn and she caught eyes with me whilst she was talking to Frank. I could tell she wanted to say something so I slowed down. Turns out that I marked a student present on the register yesterday even though he is COVID positive. He wasn't in, it was just my mistake but the admin staff had a meltdown thinking an infected child was in the building. I laughed a little to myself as I went into the maths office to grab a quick bite of my lunch and to correct the register on my laptop.

Whilst I'm doing both of the above, Doc comes in to talk to me. We sit for about 20 minutes talking about nothing particular and then I suddenly realise that I'm meant to be overseeing isolation. I run over to the room to see if there is anyone in there that needs me to cover them. There's one kid and Frank in there. I tell him that I'm meant to be on duty and he thanks me and says he can wait whilst I go get my laptop. I run off and return with my toys. Frank takes a few minutes to finish what he's writing and then leaves me with Walker. He's an interesting kid this one. As a child he was one of the only white boys in the area of Liverpool he grew up in. He joined gangs for protection and was delivering drugs for his family at the age of eight. Doc has said how Walker has said that he laughs at people when they pull out knives around here because in Liverpool if someone did that it meant you were going to get stabbed. But not here. He still is pushing drugs, apparently for his uncle, and I've often heard other staff saying he's "playing up because his mother didn't let him have any weed over the weekend". It's an unusual one, especially since Doc says he's clever. Whilst we are in isolation he is sat actually doing work, it's a lot more than some students do. I recall that racist kid from a few days ago, he didn't even have a pen in isolation with him.

Fuchsia messages and says she's been offered that job with the office in Spain and starts on Monday. I'm really pleased for her and she follows it up by sending me some of the photos we took the other night whilst having sex.

Quinn comes into the isolation room and asks if she can have a word. I walk to her, just outside the room. My mind immediately goes to me having done something else wrong, but the look on her face is different.

"Were you in close contact with Pudge yesterday?"

Of course, he's in my year 12 Maths and year 12 Further Maths classes and I recall he came in late to the lesson and so stayed late whilst I explained what he missed.

"Yes," I spared her the details.

"He's also had a positive COVID result, you will need to isolate."

She says other words but my head is spinning. I squat down on the floor and hold my head in my hands. Ten days of not leaving the house. Ten days of nothing. And next week is my last week of being a teacher. I can't say goodbye to my students. I can't give a leaving speech. I can't do my run.

Fuck.

DAY UNKNOWN.

WAITING INSIDE.

I've been doing nothing. Nothing, except play guitar and be depressed as fuck.

Supposedly you're not even meant to leave the house, but I have been going out on an evening for walks just because I've been so miserable. I saw some dolphins on the seafront on one of the walks. That was something.

Those people got in touch and offered me that job. I wanted to tell them to fuck off since it has been so long since the interview. Instead, I asked them to remind me what the job even is. I listened, but I didn't care. It makes no difference to me anyway. That being the case, I accepted the job. Figured it was the correct thing to do.

DAY 138 (FRIDAY).

THE LAST DAY.

This is day nine of isolation and I got woken up to my phone vibrating from an email to my personal account. It's Margie reminding me to be in the meeting at 10am, it's the end-of-year staff meeting. I didn't want to attend, but I decided I would. I put on my white shirt and my black skirt, and got my laptop ready. I never did get to wear a skirt to work.

The meeting is online because I'm not the only teacher isolating. It's just generic bullshit garbled by Leopold, and then he acknowledges that I'm leaving, saying I'm the guest in the meeting. I laugh at this since I'm actually getting paid until the end of August. So technically I'm a teacher until the end of August. Margie spoke some nice words, which I followed up with some random bullshit. Something about how I really appreciate some of the people and I'm not going to name them, but they know who they are. It was hard because I really wanted to let SLT fucking have it. And the rest of them. Rip into them all, talk about diversity and their idea of equality. That the education system is fucked and I became a teacher because I wanted to change it and fix it, but it's unfixable. It's a representation of society as an unfixable fuck up, that some of us just don't feel like we fit in. When I quit, Leopold described me as a free spirit. *What kind of free spirit wants to punch a school Principal in the face?* Fuck, it was hard to not say all this.

I did remind them about my run and that they can still donate. I explained I'm going to do it on results day, 10 August. The day before Robin Williams died.

Leopold had a final word to say, he says he's got me a gift and that it's a little bit tongue in cheek. It's a pair of socks.

Jesus Christ, fuck this isolation.

* * *

So I have fucked this isolation. Me and Fuchsia are in Spike's garden with him and Stella. We've taken a fuck load of mushrooms, drank multiple bottles of alcohol including my birthday Dead Man's Finger, smoked several biftas and I set fire to his fence, gate and birdhouse.

In all honesty, things were fairly civilised until I said "the thing is, right" in a West Country accent for no reason. Spike noticed and laughed whilst I was mid-drink. I laughed at him laughing and snorted into my rum. That in turn made him laugh again, and the cycle began. The night proceeded for several hours, the same.

I've never laughed as much in my life.

PART THREE

(AGAIN)

SUMMER HOLIDAYS.

DAY 139 (SATURDAY).

SECRET'S OUT.

I don't know whether to still be numbering these days, but I have done. I woke up on the sofa bed in Spike's attic room with Fuchsia laid next to me. I get up and gather my belongings together. Fuchsia wakes up and tells me she got a bit lairy last night once I passed out, wanting to see Spike's pills. She also says she thinks she told him about what we did with Audie and Al that night. I'm disappointed, but say it's OK and that it doesn't really matter. I know Spike will be pissed off, purely because him and Stella were asleep upstairs at the time when it happened.

My body has a small window of being able to cope, I can tell, so we left rather abruptly. As soon as we got home, the hangover arrived.

* * *

Hours later I woke up again, as I needed to feed Audie's cats. She's away camping this weekend and asked if I could. She did want us to go camping with them, but I didn't want my last day to be at a campsite. I wanted to be on the beach, but isolation kind of blew all those plans out.

Also, it's not the summer holidays if I'm no longer a teacher. Although I am still paid until the end of August, so I kind of still am a teacher and it still is the summer holidays. So I will still call this part of the diary the Summer Holidays.

DAY UNKNOWN.

SOMETHING TO LOOK FORWARD TO.

It's been about a week and I want to get pissed in the day since I've got fuck all to do. Well, I have got things to do, but I don't want to do any of them. I just want to fanny about. Knowing Audie is also free this summer when she doesn't have her kids, I ask if she can help me out.

    [11:17] DEAD: I need your help with something.
    [11:21] Audie: What can I do for you?
    [11:28] DEAD: Day drinking buddy :)

```
[11:28] Audie: That's one of my specialities.

[11:29] DEAD: Excellent!

[11:29] DEAD: Meessage me when you are available.

[11:30] Audie: I will meessage you.

[11:30] DEAD: Gay boy…

[11:30] Audie: How about Thursday?

[11:30] DEAD: Wait, what day is today?

[11:31] Audie: Monday, I think.
```

Three days.

DAY UNKNOWN.

PSYCHOPATH?

I've not long been up and Audie has messaged. It's nothing to do with our last conversation.

```
[09:29] Audie: Hi, I've been updated on some shit and been
thinking. Our friendship group is too toxic and I'm going to
distance myself from it. Thanks for feeding my cats.

[09:29] DEAD: That's sad.

[09:40] DEAD: I think I know what the shit is, but I can't be
sure.

[09:46] DEAD: Audie, does this mean no to Thursday?

[09:49] Audie: Yeh, I can't continue this friendship.

[09:50] Audie: Sorry.

[10:02] DEAD: Well, it's been a pleasure to get to know you
this last year. I'm sorry that I've been up and down with you,
I've been rather childish.

[10:17] DEAD: Do me a favour and block me.
```

I felt like crap and spoke to Fuchsia, it's all new to her. I sit and do fuck all for a few hours.

* * *

Fuchsia spoke to Stella and it is what I thought it was about. Fuchsia did tell Spike the other night. And, since they didn't really break-up, Spike told

Stella, who then spoke to Audie about it. The problem is that Fuchsia said how she didn't really want to do anything with Al. Al and Audie have taken offence to it, and now don't want to be friends with us.

The funny thing is that I've always thought that this friendship group is toxic, but that Audie is the toxic one. I've been OK with it though, because it's just fucking life. What else am I going to do, be a boring fuck? *Jesus Christ.*

I've ditched friend groups multiple times. Mainly because I feel no connection to them and move on. But this time it's different because Fuchsia is involved. Really she has done nothing wrong but expressed that she felt uncomfortable with what happened. And now she has lost friends from that. Ever since that night at the cocktail bar, I've wondered if Audie is a psychopath and now I feel convinced.

I want her to block me because I know I'll get drunk or high and message her.

DAY UNKNOWN.

HIGHS AND LOWS.

I was meant to have gone camping with Curlos this weekend. If I've never explained him, he's my friend from the Royal Society and we go hiking and camping together. We've done over a thousand miles, just the two of us. The Coast to Coast, the North Coast 500, the Two Moors Way and loads of weekenders. Our last get together was when we hiked the Ridgeway last summer. Anyway, we were meant to meet up and go camping, but with what has happened, I don't feel like it. Yesterday I explained the situation to him and he got a train up to stay for the weekend. So right now we are at one of Fuchsia's friend's parents' house. It's Rosie's parents' house and it's a fucking huge mansion near Robin Hood's Bay, I've passed it twice a day on the bus to school. Since her parents are away in one of their other homes, Rosie and Raymond are house-sitting and have invited a few people around. Before we came out I ate some mushrooms, and I've had some wine, and now Raymond's rolled a bifta. He says it's weak but I can smell it's not weak to me.

* * *

I've lost my shit. Time is happening in jumps and I keep wondering what has happened for the last five minutes. I'm listening to conversations but I don't know what people are saying. And then I'm OK and I take part, I crack a joke. Then suddenly Fuchsia is looking at me.

How long have I been sat here? She says someone is talking to me. *Who is? Raymond is playing a song for me?* OK. I see Raymond is on the grand piano playing Zelda's Lullaby. *This is nice.* I go take a photo of him but it's blurry.

Now where am I? I'm stood in the hallway in the dark, wondering which toilet I'm supposed to use. I go back to the dining room and sit down. *Fuck, I still need a piss. Is everyone looking at me? How long am I going to get away with this?*

I explain that I don't know which toilet to use and Rosie says any of them.

"Even the one upstairs in the dark? I like that it has a big mirror." I don't know where these words came from but it sounded like it was my voice.

She says yes.

It's been like this for several hours. *I think it's hours. I really can't be sure.*

Rosie mentions the Cinder Track. *Fuck, I'm supposed to run it in three days time.* I've told the room this. Well, someone in my voice does. We all laugh, but I don't know why.

I'm now stood in the kitchen. This person I've just met called Penelope is in there. Earlier we were talking about her dad, since he was my primary school teacher. I said he was the reason that I could do maths and she was pleased that I became a teacher. You could see it in her face, she really was. But I felt bad for having just quit, like I've let her dad down. He died a few years ago.

"Are you OK?" Penelope is looking at me. *Fuck, how long have I been stood here?*

"Yeh, sorry. What? Sorry, I've not been listening." The words almost vomit from my body at having nearly been caught out high as fuck. *She shared the bifta too, why isn't she high like this? Is this from those mushrooms I ate as well? How fucking strong are they? Wait, how long have I been stood here now?*

"I'm getting my coat." The words fell from my mouth and bounced around the kitchen in Comic Sans whilst I exited the room. I've decided to call it a night, I can't cope. We were meant to be staying in one of the several rooms in this mansion. But I just can't cope. *Have I let people down? At least Becky can give us a lift back to Whitby.*

Later on I feel as though I have come down a bit and I look at my phone only to see I have messaged Audie.

```
[22:52] DEAD: Seriously.

[22:54] DEAD: If you don't want a relationship then I want you
to block me.

[23:22] Audie: A) That's childish and B) There's no reason we
can't still be civil to each other.

[13:37] DEAD: I think it's fucking childish what you are doing
in the first place.

[23:38] DEAD: *have done.
```

Why do I do these things?

DAY UNKNOWN.

CATCHING-UP LATER.

It's time I write what happened that weekend when I said I would catch-up later. At the time I was so fucked I didn't even know what day it was. It was 111, it followed DAY 110.

It was fucked up.

It started with going to Hopper's birthday barbecue. Fuchsia, my sister and me, the designated driver. Since my sister couldn't get a babysitter for her newborn until 5pm, we went a bit later than intended and it was in full swing when we got there. Everyone was either drunk or just stupid. Hopper's other friends were weird, they acted weird and looked fucking weirder. I'm vain, I don't mind that fact. It's almost like I can't help but struggle to talk to someone who looks just fucking weird. Like their eyes are in the wrong place, or their nose is on upside down. I'm sure I could've gotten over it if they weren't talking absolute bollocks and had the intelligence of a fart. Writing this I feel tight but I know that's what I felt at the time. I hid it well, though, and I smiled and talked to people whilst Fuchsia and my sister, like everyone else, got trollied.

One guy gave Hopper a lap dance whilst wearing a cardboard box. Another guy couldn't drink without gesticulating so much that he sprayed his beer everywhere, completely unaware. Then there was the guy who turned up and introduced himself by saying he pissed the bed last night. His partner was the little chubby girl wearing leopard skin tights, doing karaoke into a spoon. One girl was really pretty, the kind that should be on r/gothsluts, but she said nothing and just hung out near her partner who had a flat cap on, a ginger beard and bad teeth. In fact, so many of them had bad teeth. Oddly enough I'd met all of these people online, on Hopper's livestreams, but face to face it was very different. They were very different. For instance, another girl there had ALS, which I didn't know beforehand, and she said she smokes weed to help but had run out. I gave her all of mine. Then there was the girl I knew as just a username with random numbers, who was with some old dude who I presumed was her older partner. Turned out to be her dad. So fucking weird, who brings their dad to a party? And me being a teacher, I learnt everyone's name straight away whereas no one could remember who I was. Especially the guy who was drinking Tesco own brand cider. Not that it matters, but he was called Hopkins. Hopper and Hopkins, like some sort of detective duo. Hopkins was extra weird. He was unusually thin and had a huge trapezoidal-shaped head on a five-foot-eight frame, with pointy and small teeth. It felt surreal and I don't get why it got to be so much. It just did. I'm sure they were all lovely people, I just didn't gel. But I maintain I hid my opinions and I looked fucking awesome, my outfit was banging. Skinny camouflage trousers that I bought from Foot Asylum in Bristol after going to ArcTanGent, an off-white vest from a shop called Sting that used to be on Piccadilly Circus, a denim jacket from a charity shop in Wood Green with sleeves rolled up, and my white Adidas Pro-Models with invisible socks.

Anyway, when it came to home time I had to round up the kids. It took about an hour and I started to get concerned about driving back, sat in the front of the van with two drunks. Well, it was more my sister that concerned me. With her not having drank since getting pregnant a year or so ago, she was getting rather screamy at the barbecue. But in the van she was fine. I put my 80s playlist on and we all sat on the front seat singing along. We dropped her off at hers, went home and I decided it was time for me to catch up and get fucked up too.

So I ate some of the mushrooms, smoked some weed, drank some rum and danced. And then we decided to go to Audie's.

She was having that party near my birthday. A few days before it she had asked if I was going, to which I said no because of Hopper's barbecue. But my own reason was because I didn't really want to see anyone until after my birthday. It was a mix of not wanting to get drunk the same week as getting a tattoo, but also because my birthday was my rebirth and didn't want to see anyone before it. It's odd looking back at it post-birthday, the rebirth didn't really happen in the way I wanted it to and drinking made no difference to getting the tattoo.

The fear of drinking before a tattoo was based on when I got my Zelda tattoo in London. It took five hours to get an intricate moon and triforce design on my spine and I hadn't slept in 36 hours before it. Truthfully that wasn't drink related, that was from forgetting my key and locking myself out before going to a Christmas party. Come 2am I was riding the Piccadilly line back and forth until daylight because Curlos had hooked up with a girl we used to work with. I used to like her, so I didn't bother messaging him, it would have been too weird.

Anyway, halfway to Audie's, on the big bridge, the mushrooms started to kick in. All the lights started to turn into X's that streamed across my vision and the saturation of everything started to pulse. Fuchsia was just feeling sick. I had my Bluetooth speaker in my bag so I grounded us with the sweet sounds of the TopGun soundtrack. It worked a fucking treat and we danced the rest of the way with Danger Zone on repeat. Around the corner from Audie's, Fuchsia decided we should burst in listening to Playing with the Boys really loud. No one knew we were turning up. Fucking mint idea. So we did.

The reaction was unexpected. There was only a couple of people in the living room, one of them being Al. He started screaming and trying to touch us, aggressively grabbing my crotch. I ignored it and we started jumping up and down together, screaming like the primates from the beginning of 2001: A Space Odyssey. I stopped screaming. He didn't. HE just kept screaming. It was then that I realised someone had given him coke. He was fucking demented.

Weeks later I found out that Al had been aggressive with Fuchsia too. Al was a fucking mess most of that night, borderline being a rapist. Thankfully he did calm down and represent some sort of regular human in the early hours. Audie was apparently chuffed we turned up, but I didn't see that because of the screaming me and Al were doing. She said to me that she knew we were going to turn up. I said that's weird because I didn't know we were, but I was happy to see her. Stella and Spike were also there but seemed rather nonchalant at seeing us.

Hours later I hadn't really been drinking, just doing coke and smoking. Spike went for a lie down, which I found unusual, he was being weird. I joined him for about ten minutes, as the mushrooms were sitting a little funny on me and I wanted to check he was OK, but he didn't really talk. Me and Fuchsia had a nice moment where we took a bag of coke and locked ourselves in the bathroom, just chatting. We never get to do that at a party and we laughed, saying that we should just leave with the bag.

We didn't leave. And when Spike and Stella had both gone to bed, the rest of us had sex together in the living room.

And when everyone else had finally gone to bed, Audie and me stayed together and slept on the sofa. It felt nice and natural. A postman knocked on the door at one point. We laughed. And that was that.

And now this is this.

DAY UNKNOWN.

THE LAST, LAST DAY.

I've never read Dracula, but a while ago I read this excerpt from from Mina Murray's journal:

> The little river, the Esk, runs through a deep valley, which broadens out as it comes near the harbour. A great viaduct runs across, with high piers, through which the view seems somehow further away than it really is.

It's dark at this time of morning. 3am was always an amusing time to set off for a run and people kept saying "why not do it later in the day?" The point was always that a run followed by a full day is the challenge. To do something so laborious, just to do a shite job.

Right now I'm stood in the middle of the viaduct, on the small ledge that separates the path from the wall. This ledge is from when the train line closed and the track got excavated slightly, leaving a little ledge either side of the pathway. The weather's dry and a little chilly.

I rest my hand on the wall and look down into the darkness below. In the moonlight, without my glasses on, I can't make out the bottom. I don't even know if the tide is in or out. It could just be sludge down there but I don't hesitate. I unclip my running belt and put it next to my feet. My phone lights up inside as it senses movement. 41:10. It's just something I have to do.

My eyes are squinting against the rushing air that whistles past my ears as my soundtrack. My arms and legs are stretched out like a starfish, parallel with the ground. And in the brief moment before I hit the world, I think of Fuchsia.

Place me in the garden, I am DEAD.

PS

EPILOGUE.

BEING DEAD.

I keep thinking about the end. About suicide. About being dead. And I wish I could tell someone. Tell my friends and let them know this is why I'm being an arsehole. But if I told them, I know they wouldn't react in the way I would want.

I can imagine their faces and it's something I don't want to even risk experiencing. I don't want to hear them say something that they think is going to magically make me OK. But I wouldn't be asking for help, they can't fix me. I just want them to know that I always think about being dead. And I think it because there's no point to being alive.

And I'd just like someone to say "yeh, it's fucking shit isn't it".

I wish I could tell my dad.

I wish I could tell my mum.

That sometimes, like right now, I wish I was dead. And it's because there is no point in existence.

I went on the Calmzone website to see if there was anything that could help my feelings right now, but when I click on the suicidal thoughts section, the mood I'm in just makes it a page of blurry text. I just don't give a shit about these words enough to make my eyes have the patience to focus on them. There is a lot of text and I don't have a great attention span at the best of times.

I did see they have a list of reasons why someone might be feeling suicidal, but my reason isn't there. There isn't a "no fucking point to existence" one. I can imagine the usual recommendations are to take up a hobby like painting or running, but hobbies are just distraction pieces to waste away the time until we naturally decompose. I tried to learn to tattoo and found that I was crap at it. I just wish I was good at something. The Olympics, look at these fucks who are much more capable than you. I started playing darts but had no one to play against because I'm an antisocial fuck when I'm like this. I wrote a book, but my character jumped off a bridge. The same bridge I go over every time I run.

In a few weeks there is a memorial for Aziz to mark ten years. Although I think about him most days, I can't fucking go. I'm such a hypocrite. I think well done, he fucking escaped.

If someone wants to end their life, we shouldn't chastise them for either the thought or the action.

EXISTENCE.

What is the point of my existence? What even is existence?

I seem to have the ability to think and so I will take that as proof that I exist. I have thought and the feeling of free will. Some people may argue that we do not have free will, but within the laws of physics I can do what I want. Some people may say that everything is predetermined and we live in a simulation for example, but it still gives me the appearance that I can do what I want, so I will take that appearance as my free will. Sure, I could not make someone love me, but then again, perhaps I could by learning social tricks like some sort of Leil Lowndes meets Neil Strauss. In fact, she has a book about making people love you. I've never read that one though.

Anyway, what is the point of my existence? I am the kind of person who struggles to get out of bed without knowing why I exist. I think I am too dumb to understand this concept of existentialism. Or is it nihilism? Or even absurdism? I'm really not sure.

Sometimes I feel like I can fool myself into getting out of bed by convincing myself that there is no point to existence and that is hilarious. And so my existence amuses me. Existence is just a comedy that I should go watch unfold.

But then that sinking feeling of lethargy and hopelessness sets in. Sure I said I have free will but what fucking good is it if I am too stupid to use it? Drop me into a barren forest and I will be dead within days, I do not know how to survive. Earlier today I thought of people in medieval times who had far less to entertain their existence with, did they have this problem? Or did the struggle and strife of their lives keep them going? Maybe it was war. And then I thought, I wonder what percent of the population was involved in war 500 years ago. And then I realised I have no fucking idea how to work something like that out.

What am I good at?

I went to university and studied maths and physics and I have been thinking of a maths problem today: a number system with an irrational base. Could such a thing exist? So I looked it up on the internet and had no fucking idea what it was saying. How is Wikipedia mathematically smarter than an A-Level maths teacher with a master's in physics?

I do not know how to start a business. I do not know how to publish a book.

When I was younger, my existence was to understand as much as I could about the universe before I died. I wanted to be the smartest physicist ever in history. And then one day when studying for a PhD in particle physics in Brighton, I broke. I snapped like a cable on a zip line and came hurtling down to the ground. When I landed, physics, in fact all of science, was immoral. The science community were spending millions and millions of pounds on experiments to find things that may or may not exist. Things that will have no effect on ordinary life currently. We may as well have been saying that we were searching for fairies in the garden. My god, it would have made more sense. My PhD was creating a simulation of an experiment to find fairies.

Fairies do not exist, but do I?

NOTES OF WHEN I TOOK ACID.

I'm suddenly having memories of tonight. I'm still fucked. The keyboard is moving on my phone. The buttons are pulsing. I look at Raymond and he is somehow functioning. But I know it's OK because he's a seasoned drug user. He knows how to trip. He's had this before. Me, this level is all new. I can't remember some of the feelings I had tonight. I know I might be forgetting them already, my memory is fucking up. There was a point earlier where I couldn't tell which way was up. And at the gig I forgot how to piss.

Baader-Meinhof.

Frequency illusion.

Red card phenomenon.

I have a feeling I just saw my mind working. It was a spherical pearlescent object and the word I was looking for plopped out of it before I even knew I wanted the word. This is great. I feel like I'm watching my subconscious mind work.

I have a feeling that no one understands, no one has ever been high before. I know I'm being pretentious and hope I wasn't. I'm really fucked and this experience is personal to me because of who I am, where I am, and who I'm with. My ecology.

My nose is hypersensitive.

*   *   *

Oh my god. Existence is fractal! You are never going to learn the purpose of existence because there is always a layer underneath that needs to be given purpose.

I thought of this by watching Star Trek and trying to summarise conversations and then making summaries of that. I kept summarising everything until I had the most basic summary of the episode: the episode started and ended. And therefore the episode has no purpose of its own and so I summarised the next thing above it: the episode was made by people. And you keep summarising until you summarise everything by its most prominent feature and all you are left with is: the universe existed. And then what? You summarise again: there was existence. And then you summarise once more and you get nothing. Because all that came before didn't matter and there is nothing to come after.

Therefore, existence does not exist.

There is no such thing as existence.

You try to look for it but you are looking for something that can never be found.

It can be applied to my life. Summarise my book: I wrote a book. The book changed who I was, so summarise that: I changed emotions. Then summarise that to a higher point, it's like contour lines of a parent peak. And that ultimate summary, the parent peak, is always going to be what the point of existence is. And it could be anything, like "existence is cheese". But the only summary that comes after that is nothing. So that purpose of existence could've been anything because it doesn't actually exist.

Asking the purpose of existence is pointless. There isn't one.

So if there is no such thing as existence, what am I doing?

I am doing what I feel is morally right and I follow some path in life guided by that. So my life is already decided. I have no free will. So I must do what I want. What do I want? *That's the question.*

Every moment is a discovery. That's why people say to greet every new moment, it's all a happy discovery.

Oh, so this is what I'm doing, this is what existence is.

Do everything and accept death.

LIST OF ACRONYMS AND ABBREVIATIONS.

A-Level Advanced Level

AS-Level Advanced Subsidiary Level

ALS Amyotrophic Lateral Sclerosis

AQA Assessment and Qualifications Alliance

ASOS As Seen on Screen

AWOL Absent Without Official Leave

BAS British Antarctic Survey

BDSM Bondage, Discipline, Sadism, Masochism

CAD Computer Aided Design

CBD Cannabidiol

CCF Combined Cadet Force

CD Compact Disc

CMS Content Management System

CNO Carbon Nitrogen Oxygen

COP Close of Play

COVID Corona Virus Disease

CPD Continuing Professional Development

CV Curriculum Vitae

DDoS Distributed Denial of Service

DfE Department for Education

DNA Deoxyribonucleic Acid

DT Detention

EAL English as an Additional Language

ET Extra-Terrestrial

FSM Free School Meals

FYI For Your Information

GCHQ Government Communications Headquarters

GCSE General Certificate of Secondary Education

HMRC Her/His Majesty's Revenue and Customs

HSBC Hong Kong Shanghai Banking Corporation

JD Jack Daniel's

IED Improvised Explosive Device

IP Internet Protocol

IQ Intelligence Quotient

ISS International Space Station

LGBT Lesbian, Gay, Bisexual and Transgender

LPD I actually don't know this one

MA Master of Arts

MC Master of Ceremony

MSN Microsoft Network

NQT Newly Qualified Teacher

OAP Old Age Pensioner

Ofsted Office for Standards in Education, Children's Services and Skills

PA Personal Assistant

PDF Portable Document Format

PGCE Post-Graduate Certificate of Education

PhD Philosophy Doctorate

PLT I actually don't know this one

PPE Pre-Public Exams

PS Postscript

QTS Qualified Teacher Status

RE Regarding

RSPB Royal Society for the Protection of Birds

SEN Special Educational Needs

SLT Senior Leader Team

SOHCAHTOA Sine Opposite Hypotenuse Cosine Adjacent Hypotenuse Tangent Opposite Adjacent

TA Teaching Assistant

TS Teaching Standard

TV Television

UCAS Universities and Colleges Admissions Service

UK United Kingdom

USP Unique Selling Point

URL Uniform Resource Locator

VFX Visual Effects

VHS Video Home System

WEX Work Experience

ZAMM Zen and the Art of Motorcycle Maintenance

LIST OF MUSIC REFERENCES.

1. **Juice WRLD**, Wishing Well – DAY 3

2. **JPEGMAFIA**, Baby I'm Bleeding – DAY 5

3. **Eiffel 65**, Blue - Flume remix – DAY 5

4. **Notorious B.I.G.**, Juicy – DAY 8

5. **Eminem**, Shake That – DAY 10

6. **Depeche Mode**, Policy of Truth – DAY 11

7. **Oingo Boingo**, Stay – DAY 12

8. **Caspian**, Sad Heart of Mine – DAY 13

9. **Deftones**, My Own Summer (Shove It) – DAY UNKNOWN

10. **The Offspring**, I Choose – DAY 43

11. **The Wombats**, Kill the Director – DAY 44

12. **Michael Nyman**, The Morrow – DAY 59

13. **Ben Howard**, Rivers in Your Mouth – DAY 60

14. **Foo Fighters**, Wheels – DAY 62

15. **Antemasque**, Memento Mori – DAY 67

16. **Coldplay**, Viva la Vida – DAY 73

17. **Måneskin**, Zitti e Buoni – DAY 76

18. **Rush**, Tom Sawyer – DAY 78

19. **Arcane Roots**, You Are – DAY 93

20. **Moloko**, Pure Pleasure Seeker – DAY 94

21. **Gossip**, Standing In the Way of Control – DAY 94

22. **Snow Patrol**, Chasing Cars – DAY 102

23. **Hopper Loggins**, Danger Zone – DAY UNKNOWN

24. **Hopper Loggins**, Playing with the Boys – DAY UNKNOWN

25. **The Beatles**, I Want to Hold Your Hand – DAY 118

26. **Boris Brejcha and Laura Korinth**, Gravity – DAY 118

27. **Linkin Park**, Sharp Edges – DAY 121

28. **Cyndi Lauper**, Girls Just Want to Have Fun – DAY 122

29. **Godspeed You! Black Emperor**, The Dead Flag Blues – DAY 126

30. **Cher**, Believe – DAY 127

31. **Incubus**, 11 am – DAY 127

32. **Nena**, 99 Luft Balloons – DAY 128

33. **Koji Kondo**, Zelda's Lullaby – DAY UNKNOWN

TIMETABLE.

WEEK 1/A

MONDAY

Form >> ~~Free~~ (FM10) >> FM11 >> Break >> MA13 >> ~~Study Cover~~ (Isolation) >> Lunch >> FM12 >> MA12.

TUESDAY

Staff Briefing >> Form >> ME >> FM11 >> Break >> ~~Study Cover~~ (Isolation) >> MA12 >> Lunch >> MA13 (and FM10) >> FM12.

WEDNESDAY

Form >> FM12 >> ~~Study Cover~~ (Isolation) >> Break >> ~~Free~~ (FM11 and FM10) >> MA12 >> Lunch >> ~~Study Cover~~ (Isolation) >> MA13.

THURSDAY

Staff Briefing >> Form >> MA13 >> FM12 >> Break >> MA12 >> ME >> Lunch >> CPD >> CPD.

FRIDAY

Assembly >> Free >> MA13 >> Break >> MA12 >> ME >> Lunch >> Enrichment >> Enrichment.

WEEK 2/B

MONDAY

Form >> ~~Study Cover~~ (Isolation) >> ~~Study Cover~~ (Isolation) >>
Break >> FM12 >> MA13 >> Lunch >> ~~Free~~ (FM11 and FM10) >> Free.

TUESDAY

Staff Briefing >> Form >> FM12 >> Free >> Break >> ~~Study Cover~~
(Isolation) >> Free >> Lunch >> MA12 (and FM10) >> MA13.

WEDNESDAY

Form >> ~~Free~~ (FM10) >> ~~Study Cover~~ (Isolation) >> Break >>
~~Study Cover~~ (Isolation) >> FM12 >> Lunch >> ~~Free~~ (FM11) >>
Free.

THURSDAY

Staff Briefing >> Form >> MA12 >> MA12 >> Break >> FM12 >> MA13
>> Lunch >> CPD >> CPD.

FRIDAY

Assembly >> MA12 >> MA13 >> Break >> FM12 >> ~~Free~~ (FM11) >>
Lunch >> Enrichment >> Enrichment.

… thank you.

Printed in Great Britain
by Amazon

57333509R00138